"YOUR REVOLVERS ON THE GROUND. EVERY
DAMN ONE OF 'EM! THE MAN WHO TRIES
ANY TRICKS IS FINISHED!"

Instead of obeying, Boyle gave a broad smile
that thinned his lips over blunt teeth. "Look at
it this way, Lassiter," Boyle drawled. "You got
a six-shooter. You leave one chamber empty...
so the hammer comes down on air instead of a
shell in case it gets fouled up somehow. So that
means you got five shots in that .44 of yours.
There's *six* of us."

"I can count," Lassiter threw back at him

"You can get five of us. But the sixth man will
nail you dead, my friend."

"Which one of you is it gonna be?" Lassiter
asked through his teeth as the men stared,
their viciousness bottled for the moment by
the threat of his gun.

"You want to figure it out, which one it's
gonna be, Lassiter?" Boyle went on. "Or just
start shootin'?"

LOREN ZANE GREY

THE LASSITER LUCK

LEISURE BOOKS NEW YORK CITY

A LEISURE BOOK®

April 2008

Published by special arrangement with Golden West Literary Agency.

Dorchester Publishing Co., Inc.
200 Madison Avenue
New York, NY 10016

ISBN 10: 0-8439-5815-4
ISBN 13: 978-0-8439-5815-7

The name "Leisure Books" and the stylized "L" with design are trademarks of Dorchester Publishing Co., Inc.

Printed in the United States of America.

10 9 8 7 6 5 4 3 2 1

Visit us on the web at www.dorchesterpub.com.

THE LASSITER LUCK

Chapter 1

A sudden spring rainstorm hammering the flatlands only added to the hell of the evening as a
lone rider, his slicker a shiny yellow, moved slowly
across a rise of ground. He rode with his right foot
deeper in the stirrup than the left to ease the burning
of his wound. It felt as if a wire had been plucked from
hot coals and laid across the skin. All because of the
kid who had been trying to kill him—no doubt about
that. He was full grown but with the mentality of a ten-
year-old trying to act like a man.

His name was Rodney Rucklor II. The man he had
shot was known throughout the West simply as Lassiter. Lassiter kicked his horse into a trot, heading
through the rain-swept darkness toward a distant haze
of lights where he had a strong hunch he'd find his at-
tacker.

The pain was beginning to subside, but not Lassiter's anger, which was aimed mainly at himself for
getting talked into such a trap. It had been Len Crenshaw taking his last breath in a doctor's back room up
at Overland that had tightened the spring on the trap.
Lassiter had been summoned by telegraph.

"I knowed the kid's gran'daddy, I worked for his
pa," the gray-bearded old man said hoarsely. "Ham
left everything to his kid."

"Leave the ranch to his son? Sure, Ham would do

that." Lassiter studied the gaunt face of the dying man. "How old is the boy?"

"More'n twenty, I reckon," Crenshaw gasped.

"You calling him kid, I thought he was younger."

"Ham never called him nothin' else. Rodney was raised by his ma's sister, back in Philadelphia." Crenshaw extended five skeletal fingers and gripped Lassiter's thick wrist. Lassiter smelled the man's sweetish breath and saw the grayish cast to the face. Both were indications of the dreaded scourge of the West—cholera. He had ridden practically night and day after receiving the old man's plea.

Crenshaw was saying, "I had my doc write the kid up at Denver. I can't hold a pen so good no more. I said I was sure I could get you to give him a hand with the Fork Creek outfit. Till he gets things squared away."

"I dunno, Len. . . ."

"Do it for me if not for Ham Rucklor's memory. You an' him was mighty close. Do it for one of us, anyhow."

Lassiter was a solidly built man at a hundred and seventy-five pounds, five foot eleven, now hunched in a chair beside the brass bed. His blue eyes could be friendly or as cold as a January midnight, depending on the occasion. His mouth was wide and most times friendly, under a strong nose. Heavy shoulders tapered to a narrow belted waist that supported a holstered .44. The ends of black hair curled from under a flat-crowned sombrero tipped back on his head.

"Len, about this kid, this Rodney the Second . . ."

"Lawyer is Rex Manly," Crenshaw interrupted. "He'll see you get some money out of it, Lassiter. . . ."

Lassiter's blue eyes were saddened at the sight of the man he had looked up to when he was younger, had ridden beside on long trails into danger. A man cut down by the dreaded cholera while on the way home after a visit to his sister. The fat and nervous doctor said he hoped Lassiter hadn't picked up any germs from the old man.

As with most things, Lassiter had no fear; he had to be that way or he would never have survived so long on the rough frontier. He was a fatalist. Each morning when he awakened and drew a deep breath, he would give thanks and say to himself, "Well, I made it through another day."

But he was realist enough to know that at any time a faster gun or swifter knife blade could finish him. He would never have thought in a hundred years that the end might come at the hands of a petulant greenhorn in a lonely campsite.

Len Crenshaw had worked up to the last for the Fork Creek Cattle Company, which Rodney Rucklor had inherited. The Villa Rosa country was no place for a timid soul, which Lassiter had a hunch would describe Ham Rucklor's offspring.

But he learned differently when they finally met down at Villa Rosa. Rodney was a slim, handsome and well-dressed dude, but he was also brash. They were in Rucklor's shabby hotel room.

"Oh, yes, you're Lassiter. Mr. Crenshaw wrote that you would no doubt work for me."

"Len died."

"Oh, a pity." The curly ends of brown hair showed at the edge of a bowler hat. His eyes were steady enough. His suit of dark brown wool was slightly wrinkled from long hours in a stagecoach. He pointed to a portmanteau and a large carpetbag where they had been dumped after being brought from the stagecoach two days earlier. "You may bring my baggage along to the next stagecoach that we'll be taking to the ranch. By the way, when does it leave?"

"For your information, there's no stage line to Fork Creek. It's either the saddle or a wagon."

"Oh. I wasn't told. I've hardly been out of this horrible little room. I expected you to be here when I arrived."

"Seems I wasn't," Lassiter said dryly.

"I understand you knew my father."

"We were good friends."

"Did he ever talk to you about me?"

"He mentioned only once that he had a son."

Rucklor's mouth twitched. "I see," he said without emotion.

Rucklor tilted the bowler hat and mopped his forehead with a fresh linen handkerchief. A late afternoon spring sun boiled into the room from windows that overlooked an alley. An old man herded two burros laden with firewood along the rutted alley. Rucklor took one look at him, raised his chin and turned away.

"I imagine I'll have to buy a horse," Rucklor said.

"It's late," Lassiter pointed out. "Maybe you'd better stay over and we'll get an early start. . . ."

"Stay another night in this dismal place? I prefer not to."

"Suit yourself."

"You may bring my baggage." Rucklor opened the door and started down the hallway at a brisk walk. Lassiter called him back. "Yes, what is it?" Rucklor demanded impatiently.

"Handle your own baggage."

"You're defying me." Rucklor sounded incredulous.

Lassiter gave a short laugh and looked him over. Rucklor stood at six feet, with a long aristocratic-looking face and an obstinate mouth.

"I'll see you reach Fork Creek," Lassiter said, "because I promised Len Crenshaw. Then you're on your own."

"That's fair enough. I imagine I'll find many loyal employees at the ranch."

Lassiter didn't say anything. Crenshaw had told

him that the ranch was being run by the segundo, Lake Burne. "A pure son of a bitch," Crenshaw had said in his gasping voice. "Me an' Ham kept him under our heels. But he's squirmed out from under since Ham went down an' I took sick."

"I was there when Ham was killed," Lassiter had reminded the old foreman. "And I know all about Lake Burne." Crenshaw's mind had been slipping.

Rucklor purchased a saddle horse and pack mule at the livery stable. Lassiter bought a few supplies at the store.

When they were ready to ride, Lassiter eyed the dude in his fancy suit, bowler hat and button shoes. "You want to buy some riding clothes?"

"I wish to look presentable when I face my men for the first time. I'll go as I am," he said, causing Lassiter to shake his head.

They rode out with half the town coming to stare at the dark-faced Lassiter and the elegant-looking easterner. There were many sly smiles.

Just before sundown, Lassiter said they'd make camp.

"I don't see why we can't ride on. I'm anxious to get there."

Ignoring him, Lassiter unsaddled his black horse and hobbled it where there was grass. Lassiter said that Rucklor should do likewise.

Rucklor's lips tightened. "Isn't it your place to do it for me?"

"Out here every man pulls his own weight. Or he damn soon goes under."

Rucklor stubbornly said he'd do the unsaddling later. What he really meant was that he expected Lassiter to eventually do it for him.

Finally, when Lassiter had unloaded the pack mule, Rucklor said, "Sometimes I have the feeling I'm working for you, instead of the other way around."

Without replying, Lassiter got a fire going. Soon bacon and beans were sizzling in a pan.

"It seems you don't talk much," Rucklor said when they were seated on the ground, eating their frugal meal.

"And you don't do much to bring talk out of a man," Lassiter snapped. "All you do is irritate."

"If that is your attitude, I doubt very much if you'll be working for me very long."

"Got a hunch you're right," Lassiter said with a thin smile.

When the meal was over, Rucklor tossed his tin plate aside. Lassiter told him to find some sand and scrub it clean.

"I'm hardly used to doing my own dishes, Mr. Lassiter."

"Then in the morning you can eat off a dirty plate."

While Lassiter cleaned his own plate, Rucklor, grumbling, followed suit.

"I understand my father died a hero's death."

"Where'd you hear that?" Lassiter was mildly surprised.

"Rex Manly, the lawyer, wrote me. But he didn't give many details. Do you know how he died?"

Lassiter nodded.

"Tell me, Mr. Lassiter."

"Better let somebody else do it."

Rucklor was suddenly hostile. "I demand that you tell me!" In the twilight, the gray eyes narrowed. "Or was there something strange about his death?"

"I liked your father. But I can sure see how you take after him."

"Just how do you mean that, Mr. Lassiter?"

"Oh, for Chris' sakes, lay off the mister. I mean that he was ornery and sure passed it on to you."

"Before this discussion gets out of hand, Mr. Lassiter,

I better tell you that I have been instructed in the handling of firearms by one of Philadelphia's best marksmen. He is a captain of police and a close friend of my late aunt's." Rucklor made a move under his coat, then sucked in his breath when Lassiter's .44 seemed to magically appear in his right hand, the hammer eared back.

"Seems your captain friend didn't tell you never to make a move for a gun unless you mean it."

The speed with which Lassiter drew his weapon had obviously shaken the younger man. Finally, Lassiter let down the hammer and returned the gun to its holster.

"You had me at a disadvantage," Rucklor said, once he had gotten himself under control.

"In what way?" Lassiter asked narrowly, not really giving a damn. He was more than fed up with Rodney Rucklor II.

"I'm wearing a coat and you're not."

Lassiter let out a bark of laughter and shook his head. "The way things are going, we might not even last together till I can get you to Fork Creek." There was a strained silence while the small fire sputtered and smoked.

"If I've annoyed you, and apparently I have, I'm sorry. But there's one thing I do wish you'd do. Tell me about my father."

"I'd rather somebody else did it."

"For some reason, are you afraid to speak the truth?" Rucklor was leaning forward, his face taut in the firelight.

Mention of the truth was all Lassiter needed from this upstart. "It's the truth you want?" he demanded.

"The unadulterated facts concerning his death. You're so evasive that I'm beginning to wonder . . ."

"Your pa was moving cattle and he came across this old buffalo. He decided to get him with a rifle. He missed. The buffalo gored his horse and set him afoot. Instead of getting the hell out of there as he should have, your pa tried to bring him down with a pistol shot. He shot off the old bison's ear. The bison charged. End of your pa."

"An entirely different version than the one I've heard," Rucklor said stiffly. "The part about the bison is correct. But my father gave his life to save two of his men who were about to be attacked by that savage beast."

"I knew I should've kept my mouth shut."

"It was a clumsy attempt on your part to malign my father."

"You better hold that tongue in your head. It's flapping like a sheet in the wind."

"I want to know why your version is different from the one my father's own lawyer tells."

"Your father was a plain damn fool. Maybe the lawyer didn't want to let on to you. Now are you satisfied?"

"I am not!" Rucklor jumped up. "On your feet, Lassiter!"

"Oh, for Chris' sakes . . ."

"On your feet!"

"Listen to me, you crazy fool! I told you the truth."

In the early darkness Lassiter studied the strained white features of the young man. Then he got carefully to his knees, making calming motions with his two hands. "Just hold it, Rucklor . . ."

But his voice was drowned out by Rucklor's shout. "On your knees, begging, by God!"

That was too much. Lassiter started to spring to his feet, intending to slam into Rucklor. But as he came up from the ground a wink of orange-red in the early evening told him the ending would be different. With the spiteful crack of a weapon came fire slicing across flesh.

Lassiter swore as a frantic Rucklor bounded into the saddle and spurred madly toward the distant glow of yellow lights.

Already Lassiter's left arm was throbbing and beginning to stiffen. The pain was dull but aggravating as he saddled up. Then he kicked out the fire and rode north, leaving behind Rucklor's gear and the hobbled pack mule.

As he rode in the direction the young man had taken, pain from the wound and his rage were equally raw. His face, heated from anger, felt a cooling drop of rain, then another. Soon it was pouring. As he halted and reached for his slicker, he hoped Rucklor got caught in a swollen creek and called for help. Lassiter would have to debate with himself whether or not to pull him out.

By the time he reached the lighted windows of Simosa's Tavern, the rain had stopped. Several horses were drooping their heads at the rack. But not Rucklor's pinto. Lassiter found it wandering on the far side of the building and brought it back. Rucklor had not even taken time to tie it at the hitch rail.

Lassiter removed his slicker and moved his left arm a few times, bringing stiffness and increased pain.

A glance through a front window showed only five men in the big room, with its empty deal tables and long bar. Lack of customers, he supposed, was because roundups were over and men hired on extra had already drifted. Added to that was a silver boom in Colorado that had drained off most of the young and adventurous males. As he stared through the window, his wound burning like fire, he wondered if his pledge to the late Fork Creek foreman included saving the heir from his own stupidity. Rucklor was facing three known troublemakers.

Lassiter slipped into Simosa's and put his back to the door. The three men at the bar were listening to Rodney Rucklor. Their eyes, those of the predator, were amusedly on the tall young easterner as he spoke in a strident voice. . . .

Chapter 2

. . . and I left a pack mule and all my personal belongings. Some items quite personal, I might add. I'll be willing to pay one of you gentlemen to recover my property for me."

Harve Dolan, his hat tipped back on a thatch of red hair, looked up and down the long bar with mock seriousness. "I don't see no gentlemen."

Then his eyes caught Lassiter standing tall in the doorway. At first Dolan looked startled. Then he grinned with his weak mouth. "Back from the dead you are, eh, Lassiter?"

Rucklor wheeled around and stared, his jaw dropping. Then he snapped it shut. "I don't need you, Lassiter. These gentlemen, I'm sure, are going to assist me. . . ."

"They'll assist you by picking your pockets." Lassiter's boots slid through dirty sawdust that covered the floor. He halted five feet from the bar. John Simosa, a solidly built man in his forties, leaned behind the bar with thick arms folded.

"Fancy britches here claims he shot you," Simosa commented, jerking his head at a staring Rucklor.

"I look shot?" Lassiter asked quietly.

"Claims he got you in the chest," Harve Dolan put in.

"He claims wrong."

Simosa got a wise look in his black eyes. "All right, then, let's see you lift your arms, if you ain't shot."

There were tight grins on the faces of the three on-lookers, one man nudging another.

Lassiter's smile was cold. "Take my word for it," he said and hooked his left thumb in the shell belt. Even that slight movement produced a flash of pain. But he didn't waver and the cold smile remained fixed on his dark face. He hooked his right thumb in his belt.

Down a corridor a redheaded girt put her head out a doorway.

"Hey, Maudie," Dolan shouted a little drunkenly, "we got a dude here with a powerful itch for a female. . . ."

Rucklor's face reddened. "No, no, you misunderstand. . . ."

"Leave him alone." Lassiter's voice rang sharply through the big room.

Quickly assessing the tense drama, the girl ducked back into her room and remained out of sight.

"Get over by the door, Rucklor," Lassiter said.

The Fork Creek heir shifted from one foot to the other, licking his lips. Dolan's reddish brows were raised in mockery. "How much you reckon we could get for a pack mule an' the junk this fella's left behind? Huh, Lassiter?"

"Forget it, Dolan."

"Maybe he's got silk underwear we could sell," Chuck Olan said, his words hissing through a gap in his front teeth.

"Bet he's wearin' silk," Dolan laughed. "Maybe we oughta make sure. Rucklor . . . that is your name, ain't it? The same name as ol' Ham Rucklor, the son of a bitch. You two fellas kin?"

"I already told you that Rodney Rucklor was my father."

"Rodney? Never heard of no Rodney."

"It happens to be my name, also my late father's. . . ." Rucklor was upset.

"Bet you got on silk drawers, sure as hell," Dolan remarked, bringing a titter from the men. Every eye was on Lassiter to see how he was taking it.

"Get over by the door like I said, Rucklor," Lassiter drawled. "These gents are about ready to chew you to bits and spit you out on the floor."

"I doubt if these gentlemen mean me harm," Rucklor responded nervously.

"Why don't you hold him for ransom?" Simosa suggested, his eyes dancing in his moon face.

Dolan guffawed. "Fork Creek Cattle Company wouldn't pay a dime for his hide. They'd be glad to be rid of him." Then Dolan straightened up and eyed Lassiter. "I hear there's some sheriffs would pay fancy money to get their hands on you."

"Yeah? On what charge?"

"Oh, they'd figure somethin' out. They don't like fellas like you buttin' into their business, as I hear you done plenty of times. . . ."

"And those few are either dead now, or run out of office. Yeah, I butted into their crooked games. And the voters took over from there."

"You don't say." Dolan downed a shot of whiskey.

"Rucklor," Lassiter said coldly, "I'm asking you for the last time to get over by the door."

"Tell him to go to hell, Rucklor," Dolan said. "Or is he your nursemaid?"

"Of course not. I can look after myself. Lassiter, I . . . I . . ."

"Suit yourself." Lassiter backed to the door and went out.

Dolan turned to lank Chuck Olan, whose jaws moved on a wad of cut plug. "Go make sure he leaves, Chuck."

Olan stepped out into the darkness and looked around for Lassiter. He was craning his neck when the barrel of Lassiter's gun rapped him smartly behind the ear. Olan dropped facedown on the ground. Lassiter bent and turned the unconscious man over on his back so he wouldn't suffocate from mud clogging his nostrils. He drew Olan's gun and threw it far out into the darkness. It made a dull splash in a mud hole.

Inside Simosa's, Dolan was saying, "Empty your pockets, fancy britches."

Rucklor paled. "You must be joking. . . ."

The red-haired Dolan grabbed him from behind. "Tex, go through his pockets."

"No, no!" Rucklor was screaming. "It isn't right, it isn't legal. . . ."

"Holy Christ, so it ain't legal." Dolan howled with laughter. "Maybe we better strip him down, then go through his pockets. Without him bein' in them clothes, maybe it's legal."

"This fancy suit an' them shoes oughta bring twenty-five round silver dollars." Tex Ander, pale-eyed and with a beard stubble on his long jaws, reached into one of Rucklor's coat pockets.

Rucklor tried desperately to squirm out of Dolan's grasp.

"That shirt's silk sure as hell, so that'll fetch another five." Dolan grinned.

Tex Ander reached around and started to unfasten Rucklor's belt buckle. Rucklor tried to kick him and got a meaty hand laid sharply across the mouth. Rucklor cried out. Dolan turned him loose, laughing. Rucklor reeled, his face white.

At that moment Lassiter stepped back into Simosa's. "Far enough, boys."

With an oath, Dolan whirled and grabbed for his gun. But before he could touch it, Lassiter's .44 hammered a bullet into the floor near the toe of Dolan's left boot. Dolan jumped.

"Guns on the bartop, boys," Lassiter ordered the pair.

"Hey, wait a minute," Dolan protested and looked wildly at the door. "Where the hell's Chuck?"

"I just cut down the odds a little." Another shot came close to the toe of Dolan's other boot. *Do what I said!* Lassiter shouted.

"You're shootin' up my floor," John Simosa complained.

"Be thankful it's not your head."

Grumbling, the two men finally laid their weapons on the bar. Keeping his gun on them, Lassiter ordered them to turn around. With his free hand, he searched for hideouts. He found none.

"Pick up their guns, Rucklor," Lassiter said to the ashen-faced Fork Creek heir.

A trembling Rucklor, holding the captured guns against his midriff, backed to the door with Lassiter.

Outside in the darkness, Lassiter got the men's rifles from saddle scabbards and said, "We'll dump 'em all in the biggest mud hole we can find."

There was a splash as Rucklor followed Lassiter's suggestion. Then they were riding south at a good clip. After the brief rainstorm, the curtain of clouds had parted to reveal a glittering array of stars.

"I . . . I guess I must thank you, Lassiter." Rucklor sounded shaken.

"Maybe you learned something tonight."

"I could have sworn I shot you. . . ."

"You did."

Rucklor turned in the saddle, his mouth hanging open, as he stared at Lassiter's shadowy figure. "Yet you didn't even show it in there."

"I felt it." When they reached the campsite, a half

moon was in the east. "We better get the hell out of here. That bunch will be in a foul mood. But first they'll have to clean their guns." Lassiter laughed ironically.

Fortunately, Lassiter hadn't unrolled the blankets he had purchased. They were still rolled up in a tarp. Quickly they loaded the pack mule and soon were heading west. After a few miles Lassiter then turned north. He thought it wise not to arrive at Fork Creek in darkness. There was no telling what he might find. Lake Burne had been left in charge—a competent man when it came to the cattle business, but no one to let have the upper hand. Lassiter intended to reserve judgment until he looked the situation over and made his recommendations to Rucklor. Whether the young heir wanted to follow them or not was up to him. Already Lassiter had had more than enough of Rodney the Second.

A campground was found on a rise of ground, lined with boulders and thick brush. Out on the flats occasional buffalo wallows were shadowy saucers in the moonlight.

Rucklor seemed chastened. "When I . . . I think how close I came to killing you . . . thank God I missed."

"I'll say amen to that. Get yourself some sleep."

"Lassiter, you're a remarkable man. I . . . I shouldn't have lost my temper with you. I promise not to again."

"Well, I won't be around long enough to find out."

Rucklor was sitting on his blankets. "What do you mean by that?" he asked anxiously.

"I'll see you settled at Fork Creek, then be on my way."

"But I don't want you to leave," Rucklor wailed. "Not now . . ." He gave a deep sigh. "I guess I've been pretty much of a fool. But I was told that the only way to get along out here was to assert myself—and never let anyone get the upper hand."

Lassiter was sitting on the ground. He had pulled off his shirt and was examining the wound as best he could in the darkness.

"Is it bad, Lassiter?"

"Just a scratch." When he had lunged at Rucklor, his arms had been outstretched. The bullet had nicked him under the armpit.

"I . . . I guess I just went all to pieces when you were telling me about my father. I knew he didn't care a hang about me. And when you said he'd only mentioned me one time, I guess the hurt went deep."

"I can understand."

Lassiter got a half-filled whiskey bottle from his saddlebag. After taking a long pull, he splashed some of it on the wound. It stung.

In the morning, Lassiter shot a big jackrabbit. Taking a chance on Dolan and the other two who were hunting for them, he built a small fire.

"Never in the world did I think I'd actually enjoy roast rabbit for breakfast," Rucklor said enthusiastically. "Nothing in a fine restaurant has been cooked to such perfection."

"You're just hungry is all. A cooked boot would have tasted as good."

When they were pushing north once again, Rucklor spoke hopefully of Lassiter staying for a while.

"I promised Len Crenshaw I'd get things squared away for you at Fork Creek. It's the best I can do."

"You're angered because I acted like such a damn fool with my gun."

"Maybe you learned never to pull a gun unless you figure to put a man down. You didn't put me down. I could have blown you outa your shoes."

Rucklor shuddered. "I realize that . . . now. After our . . . er . . . altercation and I reached that Simosa place, I wondered why you hadn't gone on a few miles and stopped there. Instead of camping out."

"It was no place for a greenhorn like you. That's why."

"I can understand that now. Never in my life have I felt so helpless as I did in that place. I thought I could order them about because of my name. It didn't work out that way." Rucklor cleared his throat. "How long will you stay with me?"

"A few days oughta do it."

"Look, I had no idea how things are out here."

Some different than you're used to, Lassiter was thinking.

"I . . . I have a confession," Rucklor faltered.

"Lord, what now?"

"When I stopped off in Denver and I got lonely . . . I . . . I telegraphed Regina. In fact, we exchanged several telegrams."

"Regina?" Lassiter had reined in to study the trail behind them. But he saw no sign of Dolan or the others.

"Regina and her friend Ellen had begged me to let them come West with me. There was this banker in Denver who had known my grandmother. I stayed with his family. He and the others in his circle seemed to respect my name. So I thought . . . well . . . I thought that if I could manage so well in Denver, I could at Fork Creek."

"What's this Regina got to do with it?"

"We're betrothed." Rucklor drew a deep breath. "Regina and Ellen . . . they'll be here the last of the month."

"So, it's marry the girl and live happily ever after," Lassiter said dryly.

"It's why I need you, Lassiter. . . ."

"I'm not marrying her, you are."

"I can see that without you by my side I'll be nothing

but a straw man." Obviously it was a hard fact to admit.

"Sending for the girl before you got your feet on solid ground was a fool stunt," Lassiter pointed out. "Looks like you'll have to make the best of it."

"Then you'll change your mind and stay around?"

"Nope. It's time I moved on." Lassiter pointed to a flock of wild geese in arrow formation across the shimmering sky. "I'm like them. I get itchy feet to see new territory."

Some elk gazed at them from the lip of a distant buffalo wallow, then resumed feeding. In a great stretch of flat country they saw deer nibbling at shoots of spring grass.

"This is beautiful country," Rucklor said. "I had no idea."

"Beautiful, yeah. But always remember it can kill you quicker'n you can blink."

Rucklor shuddered. "Seems I'm learning fast about this great West of yours."

"It's yours also, remember, Rodney."

"Back home, my aunt would never let anyone call me Rod. But it's a name I like. Will you call me Rod?"

"Yeah." It had surprised him to learn that Rodney had also been Ham Rucklor's legal first name. He found himself almost beginning to like young Rucklor, despite getting off to such a bad start. But he wouldn't let himself be swayed to the point of hanging around. Hell, no. . . .

Chapter 3

L ake Burne stood in the shade of cottonwoods and watched two members of his Fork Creek crew hustle a trunk across the yard. They had been moving things from Burne's former quarters to the main house. It was Manly's idea that he should take over the main house once the business with young Rucklor was settled. And settled it must be by now, although he hadn't heard a word from Harve Dolan on the subject.

Two days ago he had seen Rodney Rucklor II arrive by stagecoach. Rex Manly had said Rucklor would probably arrive with a bodyguard. But he was alone— a petulant snob from the looks of him, and someone much easier to handle than Manly had figured. With Manly out of town on business, Burne had taken it upon himself to handle the situation, but in a way so his own hands were clean.

The men were just finishing the moving job when Dolan and four men rode in. Burne, well over six feet tall and weighing a shade under two hundred and twenty pounds, turned his muddy brown eyes on Chuck Olan. Olan's hat was canted because of a crude bandage around his head.

"What happened to him?" Burne demanded when Dolan dismounted.

"Somebody snuck up on him," Dolan said rather sheepishly.

Burne eyed the redhead coldly. "What in hell's that got to do with the business you was supposed to take care of?"

Dolan dug a toe in the dust. "We saw 'em leave town an' figured to get ahead of 'em."

"Who's *them?*"

"Rucklor an' Lassiter."

"*Lassiter!*" Burne towered over Dolan, who wasn't a short man. "That bastard didn't lose any time hornin' in. What happened?"

"We was about to go lookin' for Rucklor when he rode right in on us. We was at Simosa's—"

"Get to the point, Harve."

"Well, he said he'd gunned down Lassiter, so we believed him. Well, we figured to have some fun . . ."

"Go on," Burne snapped when Dolan hesitated.

"Right then Lassiter butted in."

"And took the kid away from you," Burne guessed. "Is that what happened?"

"Reckon it is, Lake." Dolan hung his head. "I figured I needed more men, so I got Arnie Bates an' Bill Tingle." Dolan introduced them. Burne grunted.

"Guess I'll have to move my stuff back," Burne said with thinly disguised anger. "For now, anyhow."

"But not for long," Dolan added with a short laugh.

"The sooner Rucklor's hash is settled . . . and Lassiter's . . . the better. You'll have to figure somethin' else out." Burne was angered that Dolan had flubbed an important job. But he didn't want to show it. For now, at least, he needed Dolan. But the damn young fool had too many women and too much whiskey on the brain to be reliable. He had even spoken to Manly about it, but the lawyer liked Dolan and had wanted to keep him on.

Burne had just finished supervising the removal of his personal effects from the big house back to his original quarters when he saw Lassiter and the dude approaching. Dolan and friends were down at the cook shack getting something to eat. Burne would have to warn them to stay out of sight.

He stepped away from the cottonwood shade and turned to face the new owner and Lassiter. Rucklor still wore the brown suit and bowler hat and the button shoes he'd had on when he got off the stagecoach.

"Howdy, Lassiter," Burne sang out heartily.

Lassiter came riding up, dark and tough-looking as usual. His mouth was a little hard around the edges. And those blue eyes that could bore a hole into a man clear to his backbone were chilling.

Lassiter stepped down. He introduced the soft-looking young man as Rod Rucklor.

Rucklor was still in the saddle, an awed look on his face as he saw the ranch buildings for the first time: the main house on an elevation of ground, surrounded on three sides by leafing trees, two barns and corrals and some sheds farther away and a long narrow bunkhouse with many windows, in thick cottonwoods. The cook shack, which could feed forty men, was tacked on the end. Burne's quarters as segundo were in a lean-to on the west side of the building. A larger lean-to at the main barn had been headquarters for the foreman, Len Crenshaw. Horses in the nearest corral were curious about the new arrivals, sniffing the air to get the scent of the two saddle horses and the pack mule.

Lake Burne's thick legs carried him over to Rucklor, still in the saddle. Burne reached up and seized the younger man by the hand. "Welcome to Fork Seven—or as it's better known, the Fork Creek Cattle Company. Can I give you a hand down, Mr. Rucklor?"

"I can manage." Rucklor dismounted and stood holding the reins as if wondering what to do with them.

"Your poppa was one of my best friends, Mr. Rucklor," Burne said in the unctuous tones used by peddlers of elixirs in medicine shows. Burne slung a heavy arm across Rucklor's shoulders. "Let me show you around, sir."

"I've asked Lassiter to do the showing, if you don't mind," Rucklor said and stepped out from under the arm.

Only a brief lance of anger showed in Burne's eyes. But the affable smile remained intact. "Whatever is your pleasure, sir. Just call on me if there's anything you want."

Rucklor started up the wide veranda steps, an awed look even more pronounced on his aristocratic face. He was seeing for the first time the house where his father had lived for so many years.

Lassiter turned to Burne and said softly, "Lake, your tongue must taste of shoe polish from all the licking around you been doing."

"Was only tryin' to make the kid feel welcome." A belligerent Burne stood with his fists on his hips. "How'd you get into this? I thought you was movin' on."

"Decided to stick around for a spell."

"Rucklor hire you?"

"More or less." Lassiter gave a lazy wave of the hand at the pack mule. "That's Rucklor's stuff in the trunk and the carpetbag. Better get somebody to bring 'em into the house."

"You too proud to heft a little baggage?"

"No. But I just like to have my hands free." Lassiter looked Burne in the eye. "If you know what I mean."

"No need to get hard-nosed just because you an' me have had a run-in a time or two."

"And have somebody put up the pack mule. I'll be busy showing your new boss the layout."

He ran lightly up the porch steps and entered the house.

Lake Burne wheeled and strode along a path through thick cottonwoods toward the bunkhouse. He slammed the door at his back and walked the length of the building to the cook house where Dolan and the other four were drinking coffee. Burne called Dolan to a corner near the big stove. A stockpot for the week's soup was bubbling on a back burner.

"I want you to get Lassiter." His voice shook. "I don't give a damn how you do it, just get him."

"That ain't gonna be easy."

"You scared of that bastard?"

"Hell, no. But last night he outfoxed us pretty neat, he did." Dolan used his fingers to comb his thatch of thick red hair. "I figure the price is gonna be somewhat higher than us just goin' after that stuck-up dude Rucklor."

"Chris' sakes, I told you in town that Manly's good for a thousand dollars. That sounds pretty good to me."

"Split five ways it don't sound like much."

Burne gave him a hard grin and took a hitch at his heavy gunbelt. "You know damn well you'll take the big end of it for yourself," he said in a low voice. "Them others'll just get the leavings."

"Make it two thousand."

"*Two!*"

"Manly's so damn set on him an' you gettin' your hands on this spread that he'll stand still for most anything."

Burne thought about it and finally nodded. "All right. Two thousand it is."

Dolan gave him a sly smile. "Be somethin', now wouldn't it, if we was to get Rucklor at the same time?"

"That's the whole idea."

"But you see, it works this way. Lassiter kills Rucklor.

We see it happen an' we take off after Lassiter. But he puts up a fight an' we have to cut him down. Instead of turnin' him over to the law." Dolan looked pleased. "How's that sound?"

"You didn't do so good last night with your fancy plans. Make sure the new ones work." Burne looked toward the bunkhouse door. "Harve, you better clear out. I don't want Lassiter to run into you here."

"Lassiter here?"

Burne nodded. "He'll be showing the new boss his ranch. Watch your chance an' catch 'em away from the home place here. Camp out if he doesn't do it today. But keep your eyes open."

"New boss, you called him," Dolan said with a wise look. "But not for very long."

Burne clapped him on the shoulder. "Just do a good job."

Chapter 4

Lassiter showed young Rucklor around the large house, with its oversized parlor and kitchen and bedrooms. What most impressed Rod was the library where Ham Rucklor and his friends had played poker. It was a large room, with book-lined walls and deep leather chairs around an oak table. On the walls were the heads of many animals—deer, elk, puma, mountain goat, and even a grizzly. Every one of them, Lassiter told young Rucklor, shot by his father. But there was no bison head. It had been Ham Rucklor's obsession to add one to his collection and that had been his undoing.

Leaving Rucklor to wander by himself, Lassiter walked down to the foreman's quarters. Len Crenshaw had kept the place neat. There was a bed with a brown coverlet, two chairs, a table and desk. A faded strip of carpet added some color. On the table was a daguerreotype of a young woman with a sweet smile. Crenshaw had once told him that she was his wife. She had died years before Lassiter met him.

He went through the desk. All he found of interest was a notation concerning the roundup after Ham's death.

In the yard he found Lake Burne just coming from the bunkhouse.

"How long since roundup?" Lassiter asked the segundo.

"Two, three weeks," Burne replied. He was watching Lassiter closely.

"That was after Crenshaw went to visit his sister up north?" And when Burne nodded, Lassiter said, "You sell the beef?"

Burne hesitated. "Yep, sold some."

"Sold it where?"

"Buyers came here," Burne said after thinking it over.

"Seems I've got to drag every goddamn word out of you, Burne. Who'd you sell to and how much did they pay?"

"I got nothin' to do with that. Manly's runnin' things."

"Not anymore he isn't. Young Rucklor is."

"If you ask me, he won't hang on here long enough to spit."

"I'm gambling that he will."

"The odds ain't in your favor, Lassiter."

"Meaning just what?" Lassiter shoved out his jaw.

"Meaning Manly gets Fork Creek if the kid ain't around to take over," Burne said in angry triumph. "You can yell an' say it ain't fair. But that's how Ham wanted it done."

Lassiter studied Burne's broad, sweated face, wondering how much to believe. "And the money from the cattle sale. What happened to that?"

"I turned it over to Manly."

"How much was it?" Lassiter demanded.

Burne cleared his throat, looking up at frothy clouds. "Don't rightly recollect the exact figure. But it was over sixty thousand dollars."

"Seems like I'll have to have a talk with Rex Manly. He acts like he owns the place."

"Well, according to Ham's will, if young Rucklor ain't around, Manly's next in line for the ranch."

"So you already said. Tell me about it, Burne."

"Ham put it in his will is all I know."

"In other words, Rod Rucklor dead would give Manly the ranch."

"That's about it."

Lassiter gave Burne a hard look. "I bet Manly hopes something happens to Ham's son."

"Oh, no, Manly ain't that kind."

Lassiter's laugh was chilling.

Burne licked his lips and watched a wild canary, yellow against the green of leafing cottonwoods. "Manly is a right nice fella."

Lassiter didn't agree. He remembered Rex Manly as an egotistical dandy with the eye of a viper.

At the house he confronted Rucklor to ask if he knew anything about Manly being next in line for the ranch.

"It was explained to me in a letter from Manly," Rucklor said quickly. "But all I could think of was coming West. I tell you, Lassiter, I was sick of my life back east. It was literally strangling me."

"Did Manly know you were coming out?"

"I wrote him."

"So he expected you."

"Why is Manly so important, Lassiter?"

"Because he takes over if something happens to you."

"Well, yes, but . . ."

"I don't know what in the hell your old man was thinking of when he set this thing up."

"You seem angered. . . ."

"You're the one who should be angered, for Chris' sakes. Tell me, why would your pa do such a stupid thing?"

Rucklor stared down at his tense fingers locked at his belt line. "Truth is, I guess, he never cared much for me."

"Cared so little that he didn't give a damn if you got gunned down?"

Rucklor's gray eyes widened. "Well, I wouldn't go *that* far."

"What else is it but an open invitation to Manly? To see that you don't live long enough to work up a decent sweat."

"You mean . . . you mean my father wanted to see me *dead?*"

"Maybe he wasn't thinking straight when he did it," Lassiter said, trying to smooth the rough edges and spare Rucklor's feelings. "But the fact is, he did it," Lassiter continued. "And turned his own son into a bull's-eye on a target."

Rucklor sat down abruptly in a leather chair and stared dazedly at the floor. "Good God, you mean I'm actually in danger?"

"You might as well face up to it, Rod."

"That means Regina will also be in danger." He beat the heel of one hand against his forehead and said, "How could I have been so foolish?"

"The nearest telegraph station is at Overland—about ninety miles from here. Telegraph Regina to stay home."

"I'm sure she's already on her way. It's been nearly two weeks since I telegraphed her to come."

"Two *weeks?*" Lassiter shook his head. "Just where in the hell have you been all this time?"

"I stayed around Denver for over a week. My grandmother's banker friend took me in a wagon party up to Estes Park. And then after leaving Denver I dawdled. Because I wanted to see the country."

"And tightened the rope around your neck by all that sightseeing."

Rucklor looked startled and lifted a hand to his throat as if already feeling the pressure of a noose. "Looks as if I've cooked my own goose, as the saying goes," he said dismally.

"There's one way out of it." Lassiter told him to go ahead and send the telegram, then go up to Denver. "Put this ranch on the market, get what you can out of it and go back east where you belong."

Rucklor heaved himself to his feet. For the first time, Lassiter noticed a shred of character in the smooth face instead of petulance and fear. "I can make a life for myself out here. It's what I planned—what I've dreamed of."

"Too bad you didn't tell your pa about those grand dreams."

"But I did. I wrote him. I finally realized Aunt Margaret had tried to turn me against him all those years. But he never answered one of my letters."

"Too bad."

"I suppose I should have come out here anyway, whether he wrote or not, and tried to patch things up between us."

"Probably."

"However, it's too late for regrets." He sounded so forlorn that Lassiter almost felt sorry for him.

"But my father must have felt *something* for me," Rucklor said after a minute. "To leave me the ranch. Even with all these deadly loose ends you've mentioned."

Maybe a test, but a damned strange one, Lassiter was thinking. To see if the son was man enough to stand up to Rex Manly and fight for what was his. . . .

Since Ham Rucklor's tragic death, a lot of the old-timers on the crew had been kicked out, Lassiter soon learned. One of few remaining was Joe McCready, a stocky and weathered rider.

"Joe, what do you figure is a rough tally for Fork Creek beef?" Lassiter asked the cowhand. They were alone by a barn. It was nearing sundown with the west shot with reds and pinks.

McCready said that as near as he could figure it, the tally was less than two thousand head.

"I talked to Rucklor just before he was killed," Lassiter said. "He told me then that there was four thousand head, and he figured to sell off some of them this spring."

"About a week after we buried Ham an' you took off, Len Crenshaw got a letter from his sister sayin' she's purty sick. He takes off. Right after that, Burne started roundup. He peddled two thousand head. Buyers came to him with a crew of their own an' drove off with 'em."

"Thanks, Joe." It more or less confirmed what Lake Burne had told him. "There's something else you can do for me, Joe."

Lassiter said he'd get Rucklor's measurements. Then McCready was to go to town and purchase work clothes for the new boss, including boots. "Tomorrow's soon enough."

Lassiter, in a rocker on the veranda, his feet on the railing, was sipping his second drink from a glass that bore the initials of the late owner of Fork Creek. Ham Rucklor had always kept a good stock of fine whiskey, but Lassiter had managed to locate only one bottle. He was frankly surprised there was even that much left, the way Burne had taken over.

Young Rucklor came to the porch and frowned at the glass. "You seem to be doing a lot of drinking."

"This is what's known as letting down. Last evening at Simosa's wasn't exactly a summer picnic."

"I'm certain of that. . . ."

"Things could have gone wrong at any second. And another thing."

"Yes?"

"My left arm's still a little stiff from your bullet that just grazed me instead of punching out my lights."

The finely chiseled features bore a high flush. "I apologize again. I . . ." Rucklor broke off, standing with his fists clenched. "And I realize it's none of my business how much whiskey you consume."

"Forget it. I just got a little irritated for a minute."

"Aunt Margaret hammered the evils of alcohol into me so thoroughly that I react automatically. She always said she didn't want me to acquire a taste for what she called the devil's brew."

"A devil's brew it is. For some."

"A taste my father seemed to have. Did he drink much, Lassiter?"

"He did his share. But I never saw him drunk. He could handle it. Best to find out early if it's poison to you. If it is, leave it alone. End of lecture."

Lassiter shifted his left arm. There was still some pain. After arriving at the ranch, he had cleansed the scraped place on his flesh and applied arnica. He was only thankful it wasn't his right arm that was stiff. Because he had a hunch that before his association with this young aristocrat was over, he'd be forced to demonstrate more than once his ability with a gun.

"I wonder how Regina will like it out here," Rucklor said, his voice betraying anxiety.

"You oughta know what she'll like."

"Regina's led a sheltered life. Sometimes I imagine her as a Dresden doll packed away in silk and to be shown only on special occasions."

"Let's hope your married life will be a little more active than that," Lassiter said with a laugh. Color flooded Rucklor's face.

"It's something we've never discussed—marriage and what it means."

"You know, of course," Lassiter said tentatively, looking up at Rucklor, who fidgeted and seemed embarrassed.

"I . . . I've read about . . . marriage, though."

"But never experienced it . . . firsthand?" Lassiter asked in surprise.

"You mean . . . been with a woman? No. Aunt Margaret always stressed that I was to keep myself pure for Regina. But now I don't know. On my trip I saw things. . . ." He looked bewildered. "Things that frankly surprised me."

"Life is full of surprises," Lassiter commented, realizing that the burden he had assumed, thanks to the late Len Crenshaw, was becoming heavier by the hour.

"That banker friend of my grandmother's in Denver that I looked up," Rucklor said falteringly. "He . . . he had a charming wife and yet he . . . well, he told his wife we were going to a political club meeting. But it wasn't that at all. It was a place where there were . . . young ladies."

"But you kept yourself pure for dear Regina."

"Yes. Yes, I did." His gray eyes narrowed. "Are you by chance making fun of me?"

Lassiter shook his head. "I've kicked around so much in my life that I just look at things differently is all." What else could he say? He had on his hands not only a fragile product of a harridan aunt, but a young man expecting to marry and not even knowing where to hang his hat on the wedding night.

Lassiter drank the last of the whiskey, thinking that

it was criminal to shove a young man out into the world as unprepared for life as this one seemed to be.

"Too bad you didn't live out here with Ham," Lassiter said.

"He always held it against me because I went to live with Aunt Margaret. When my mother died, she offered to give me a life of ease. It appealed to me. I was six years old at the time. Sometimes I wonder if I made a mistake."

The next morning, Rucklor said, "Lassiter, let's take a ride. This place . . . I don't know . . . it seems to be pressing in on me. Because my father lived here, I suppose."

Lassiter said that the pinto Rucklor had purchased in Villa Rosa wasn't much of a horse. At a corral, several of the hands were saddling up. They greeted Lassiter, some guardedly, aware of the enmity between him and Lake Burne.

They looked Rucklor over with critical eyes as Lassiter selected a sturdy roan from the bunch of horses in the corral. When he roped it, his arm gave him some trouble. But he ignored the slight pain.

Soon he and Rucklor were riding out along a creek. It forked some miles below the ranch house. It was because of the fork that the ranch had gotten its name. Fork Creek was the main stream, Lassiter explained. "Far as I know, nobody ever got around to naming the branch."

Rucklor sat in his saddle, taking it all in. South from the headquarters buildings, the stream at first had flowed through cottonwoods, but at the fork the country was open, one branch flowing eastward, the main one turning west. It was a pleasant spring day with only a few gauzy clouds floating against the intense blue of the sky. A carpet of small yellow flowers splashed color across the flatlands.

Lassiter pointed to the north where the Santa Marias were a towering barrier. Lower slopes were green with aspen and spruce and pine. But above were peaks of sun-splashed granite, craggy and formidable. A few still wore winter crowns of white.

"Your line goes clear to the foot of the mountains," Lassiter explained. "More than a hundred thousand acres."

Rucklor whistled softly. "By Philadelphia standards, it's an empire." He removed the bowler hat and wiped his forehead with a linen handkerchief. "I wonder if Regina will be as impressed as I am."

"If she likes open country, she'll love it. If she doesn't, well . . ." Lassiter didn't finish.

"It's so . . . lonely, I guess. Denver was so alive— much more so than Philadelphia."

"You can always sell out," Lassiter said tentatively.

"But that would admit defeat. No, I can't just quit. Lassiter, I can make it if you'll help me."

Lassiter didn't say anything; he just sat watching a breeze rustle the miles of grass. He could envision his situation here as walking right into the heart of a giant spiderweb. He grimaced. It just couldn't become a long-term project, he told himself. He'd stay just long enough for Rucklor to get his feet on the ground, then move on. But even though he tried to impress it upon his consciousness, the decision was already beginning to crumble.

They were riding again, heading south. At times they encountered bunches of cattle. Lassiter pointed to the Fork Seven cattle brand. "Remember it, Rod. The brand belongs to you. Fight for it if you have to."

"Oh, dear Lord, I hope it won't come to that."

Lassiter looked at him. "Your pa once had to fight a damned bloody range war to hold onto this place."

After about five miles, Rucklor saw some low hills to the west that offered partial shade. He suggested they ride that way. They were a mile into the hills when Lassiter felt the first cold twitching at the nape of his neck. At once he felt uneasy.

Quickly he reined in and squinted along their back trail. The grim set of his mouth caught Rucklor's attention. "What's the matter?" he asked in alarm.

"Thought I heard something."

"An animal, perhaps," Rucklor said hopefully.

"An animal with somebody riding it." Lassiter sat with his dark head tilted, straining to hear every sound. An eagle soared overhead, its great spread of wings beating lazily against the warm air.

Rucklor had been talking about the day following his visit with Despars, the banker, to the establishment where there were young ladies. He continued, to ease the tense moment. "I had a sudden urge for Regina. Of course, I had consumed much wine and I'm not used to it. I fairly raced to the telegraph office and dispatched my first wire."

The sound reached Lassiter again, clearly this time, the faint chinking of a shod hoof glancing off rock. Lassiter inclined his head toward a nearby hill that was higher than the rest and with a summit covered with fewer trees than most of them. At the crown of the hill was a circle of large boulders.

In a low voice, Lassiter asked Rucklor if he saw it. Rucklor, looking puzzled, nodded his head.

"Head for the hill," Lassiter hissed. "Fast as you can go!"

"But, why?"

"Don't ask questions! Just do as I tell you!" Lassiter was losing patience, because Rucklor seemed frozen and bewildered. Leaning over in the saddle, Lassiter used the ends of his reins to give Rucklor's roan a sharp slap on the rump.

Immediately the animal lunged into a dead run. The bowler hat went flying.

Lassiter's black horse at a gallop shied away from the rolling hat, nearly throwing him.

Someone behind them yelled in a startled voice, "They're gettin' away!"

A rifle opened up. Lassiter's back muscles tensed. Another gun crashed behind them. Spurts of dirt pockmarked the ground just ahead of Rucklor's speeding mount.

Already Rucklor's horse was crowding through a breach in the big rocks. Lassiter pounded in right behind him. As a bullet ricocheted off a granite slab, Lassiter was on the ground, his rifle in hand.

Wheeling about, he pumped three quick shots downslope and into a group of riders charging toward the base of the hill. He recognized Harve Dolan's fiery red hair, the lanky Tex Ander. Chuck Olan with his skull bandaged threw up his hands and uttered a bellow of pain. One of Lassiter's shots flipped him backward off the rump of the speeding horse. A second man was down, heavyset and with a black beard. He was writhing in the dirt.

Dolan spun his horse desperately. He and Ander and a third man started back for sheltering trees. Lassiter fired again, his bullet taking down a horse instead of its rider. Tex Ander, on all fours, scooted into some pines.

Lassiter quickly reloaded. "That'll keep 'em cooled down for a spell."

He turned. His jaw dropped. Rucklor lay on the ground on his back, still clutching the reins of his roan. A bubbling redness was soaking into the collar and right sleeve of his brown coat.

"Good God, what next?" Lassiter breathed.

Shifting the hot rifle to his left hand, Lassiter loped over to where Rucklor lay so frighteningly still. Then he detected a faint movement of the chest. He bent over the man, seeing that his face was drained of color. His lips trembled.

"Pain," Rucklor gasped. "It . . . it's awful . . ."

Before Lassiter could reply, there was a sudden clatter of rocks at the far side of the hill. Somebody climbing afoot, from the sounds of it, probably making more noise than he counted on as loose rocks tumbled downslope under his boots.

A bullet ricocheted off the trunk of a stunted cedar and struck a pinecone on the ground, sending it into the air.

As Lassiter started to straighten up, Rucklor, in his panic, got hold of the front of Lassiter's shirt and hung on. "Don't leave me!" he cried.

Suddenly pulled off balance, Lassiter nearly fell on his face. But by stiffening his legs, he quickly recovered—his left fist grabbing Rucklor's, tearing the cloth. Two buttons popped and went rolling across the dusty ground.

Lassiter whirled in time to see a face at a wedge of rocks—a wide, toothy grin below a thick mustache that covered the edges of the mouth. As Lassiter sprinted away, a shot whipped past the side of his face. He fired, seeing a spurt of rock dust. The man blinked, then leveled the long barrel of a revolver that gleamed in the sunlight. Lassiter recognized the face—Arnie Bates, rustler, gunman, probably wanting to make sure of getting the money he and the others had been promised for a job of murder.

Bates snapped off another shot, but Lassiter was angling swiftly to the left, to draw fire away from the prostrate Rucklor. A cry came from Rucklor. It turned

Lassiter cold, thinking the man had been hit again. But the cry diminished to a whimper of pain.

"You want somebody, Bates, aim at me!" Lassiter taunted as he ran.

"You're dead, Lassiter," Bates shouted and fired twice. But Lassiter changed pace in his wild run, throwing Bates off. Bullets ripped through the stunted cedars and one of them thunked into the bole of a spindly pine.

Lassiter, at a hard run, stumbled over a rock. A stab of pain shot up his leg as he came down on a knee. It brought a shout of triumph from Bates. But Lassiter was flinging himself on his left side, sparking more pain from the pressure of the flesh wound at the armpit. In the fall he had dropped his rifle, but came up with the .44. He snapped off a shot from a sitting position. Bates appeared to jerk his head violently backward. Lassiter was ready to fire again, then realized it was unnecessary. Blood poured down the man's face, soaking his mustache. Bates suddenly dropped from sight.

Warily, Lassiter trotted over. On tiptoe he peered through the notch in the rocks. Bates lay facedown, the back of his skull reddened and pulpy where the bullet had made its exit.

Breathing hard, Lassiter shifted his gaze to the thick stand of trees fifty yards away, where he had last seen Dolan and Tex Ander. Nothing moved.

Slowly he walked back and stood looking down at Rucklor, who was biting his lips in pain.

Young Rucklor needed help, and fast. One thing for sure, John Simosa's tavern was much closer than headquarters at Fork Creek. He looked into the dazzling sky and saw that the sun was directly overhead. They had been some hours in the saddle.

Already vultures were gathering to hover over the

dead. There wasn't even time to pile rocks over the bodies to keep the predators away.

He had to gamble that Dolan and friend weren't lurking nearby to shoot him out of the saddle. . . .

Chapter 5

Somehow he got Rucklor into the saddle, with him groaning and gasping from the pain. Then, with every nerve on edge, he rode with him from the hilltop fortress. Instead of heading west where Dolan might be waiting for them in the cover of trees, he headed east.

Once on level ground, he steadied a moaning Rucklor in the saddle. Rucklor's eyes were squeezed shut and his color was no better.

All I need now is for him to die on me, Lassiter thought grimly.

Even though the fortress hill was between him and the spot where Dolan had last been seen, Lassiter glanced over his shoulder every few yards. Thankfully there was no sign of pursuers. Evidently he had either given them the slip by his maneuver or they had lost the stomach for continuing the battle.

One thing was coming to mind as he rode. Yesterday he had glimpsed a redhead talking to Lake Burne near the bunkhouse. But they were in the shadows of cottonwoods and he really couldn't see the redhead too clearly. Besides, the man had his back turned. But now that he thought back on it, the man had had Dolan's build. By damn, it *had* been Dolan!

Finally, Simosa's long building with its barn and corral was in the hazy distance. Because of their slow pace, it seemed to take them forever to close the gap. Clouds had moved in and the air grew crisp. All that was needed now was a downpour, Lassiter reflected sourly. Rucklor sagged badly and it was all Lassiter could do to hold him in place.

At least he had one break. No horses were at the rack in front of Simosa's. Still a little early in the day for customers, he supposed. The bulk of Simosa's business was at night, from travelers who used the rutted north-south road that ran past the lonely place.

It wasn't easy to get Rucklor out of the saddle. When Rucklor started to sink to his knees, Lassiter straightened him up and walked him through the doors and across the sawdust-strewn floor.

Simosa's blocky figure dominated one end of the empty place. He looked up, pretending surprise. But Lassiter knew damn well they had been spotted through a window.

One of Simosa's hands, Lassiter noticed, was below the level of the bartop, the other resting on a newspaper he had been reading.

"Let me warn you, John." Lassiter's voice echoed in the barnlike place. "If you've got your hand on a gun, I'll take you with me."

He gave Rucklor a slight shove and stepped aside so Simosa could see the .44 in his hand.

Simosa got the message and carefully placed both hands on the bar. Only then did Lassiter walk a wobbly Rucklor over to a chair at a deal table and set him down.

"A *bloody* fancy britches," Simosa said with a hard laugh as he got a closer look at Rucklor.

"He's been hit. He needs help. I want bandages and arnica. And a cot where he can lie down."

"He can use my room." It was a young girl's voice.

Lassiter turned his head and saw her, slender with

high-piled blond hair held by a green comb, wearing a light green wrapper. She stood in a doorway holding a large feather duster. Evidently she had been cleaning her room.

"All right," Lassiter agreed. "But I'll have one eye on you." He looked around at the squat Simosa. "You walk ahead of us, John."

"Don't see why . . ."

"Why? Because I don't want you at my back. That's why."

"Tough, Lassiter," Simosa grunted, but came gingerly around the end of the bar.

With Simosa leading the way, Lassiter walked a staggering Rucklor into the room. It was small, with a table and chair, a lamp and a few books. A bright curtain hid the closet. She had thrown an old coverlet over the bed because of the blood. Rucklor flopped down on it and looked dazedly up at the girl. She smiled. He seemed mystified by her presence.

Lassiter got Rucklor out of his coat and threw it on a chair seat. When he started to unbutton Rucklor's shirt, the girl moved closer and did it for him. Her long, deft fingers undid the buttons.

Rucklor groaned a protest. "But you shouldn't be doing that, miss," he said haltingly. "See a man's naked chest. . . ."

"Oh, I'm quite used to it." She gave a small, bitter laugh. Lassiter guessed her to be twenty, perhaps less, with a nice smile and warm blue eyes.

She glanced a little apprehensively at Simosa, who stood with lips pursed, looking at Rucklor stretched out on the bed. She was removing the bloodied shirt.

"John, I'll need bandages and the rest of it," she said to Simosa.

"I'll get it, Blanche." Simosa turned for the door, but Lassiter stepped in to block him.

"You tell me where the stuff is, Blanche," Lassiter said. He then frisked Simosa to make sure he wasn't wearing a weapon under his shirt. He left the room. What Blanche needed was on a shelf at the far end of the bar.

A thin swamper with a graying beard and watery eyes was just setting down a box of cuspidors he'd evidently emptied and polished. As Lassiter stepped behind the bar, the man picked up a broom to start sweeping up last night's cigarette butts.

"You ain't s'posed to be back there," he said in a reedy voice. "John won't like it none."

"John knows about it." Lassiter kept one eye on the man while moving behind the lengthy bar. At the far end he found arnica and laudanum and a roll of clean cloth covered by a towel. An establishment prepared for violence, so it seemed.

Lassiter also found a double-barreled sawed-off shotgun on the same shelf. Quickly he unloaded the weapon, dropped the two shells into his pocket and snapped the shotgun shut. After replacing it on the shelf, he returned to the room.

With John Simosa looking on, Blanche was bathing Rucklor's wound. Water in a pan beside the bed was pale red. "The bullet's still in him," she said to Lassiter, sounding a little anxious. "I can feel it."

"It'll have to come out."

"I can do it," she said firmly.

Lassiter studied her; she seemed sincere, her eyes filled with concern, the red lips slightly parted. "It can be tricky," he pointed out.

She looked him in the eye. "I've done it before."

"Well, it's got to come out. So go ahead."

She lit a lamp on a narrow table and removed the chimney. Then from a drawer she got a small knife and began to heat the blade over the open flame to sterilize it.

Lassiter looked at Simosa. "John, have you got a wagon?"

Simosa gave him a surly look. "In the barn. Why?"

"I want you to order your swamper to hitch up a team."

"Yeah, I understand." Simosa seemed anxious to obey.

"You need any help, Blanche?" Lassiter asked from the doorway; Simosa was hurrying across the barroom.

"I can manage," the girl said as she tested the knife.

Then Lassiter started walking rapidly after Simosa. "What's your hurry, John?"

But Simosa didn't reply. He was rushing along behind his bar. Upon reaching the far end, he came up with the shotgun. His lips were stretched thin in the round dark face.

"You're through givin' me orders, Lassiter," he said, his voice shaking with anger. He jerked his head at the swamper who stood, broom in hand, staring. "Fred, get behind him. Get his gun."

"Hold on a minute, Fred," Lassiter said calmly. Removing the two shotgun shells from the pocket of his torn shirt, he held them up for Simosa to see. Simosa's face seemed to collapse.

"You bastard," he breathed. Sweat suddenly popped out on his forehead. He shoved the shotgun down the bar shelf away from him as if the weapon was suddenly contaminated.

"I'll be needing that wagon," Lassiter said. "I'll see you get it back and the team. Fred, how about you hitching it up for me? Tie our two saddlers to the tailgate."

Fred licked his lips and darted a glance at Simosa, who nodded his head. "Yeah, go ahead, Fred," he said angrily.

When Fred shuffled out to the barn, Lassiter herded Simosa back to Blanche's room. She had gotten the bullet out. It lay on the table beside the pan of reddish water, a distorted lump of lead. A few inches to the left and it could have been fatal.

Rucklor seemed out of it from the laudanum she had given him.

"He'll need somebody to look after him," Blanche said softly, and Lassiter felt he knew what she was getting at.

"Well, I dunno about that. What'll Simosa say?"

She gave a bitter laugh and started to reply. But at that moment Rucklor groaned. She hurried over to the bed.

Lassiter decided to let Rucklor rest for half an hour or so. The wagon was ready, the team tied to the corral fence. As Fred continued his chores, he eyed Lassiter warily whenever the latter put his head into the barroom.

Business picked up in the afternoon. Customers drifted in and out as the time passed. Lassiter had shoved the shotgun far down in a barrel of trash near the rear door.

A perspiring Simosa was busy setting out bottles and glasses and collecting money. Lassiter stayed at the bar where he could keep one eye on Simosa and one on Blanche's doorway. Talk in the bar was mostly of a new silver strike in the Rockies.

Most of the drinkers were in work clothes, but one of them was a drummer with a wagon loaded with junk. The redheaded girl Lassiter had seen briefly during the business with Dolan the night before bought some lace and bright ribbons from the stranger. As she walked past Blanche's doorway with the drummer, she looked inside.

"You playin' nursemaid?" she asked with a laugh.

"Just a bird with a broken wing, Maudie," Blanche said.

Maudie shrugged, and walked on. A door down the hall opened and closed.

When the place emptied, Lassiter took Simosa back to the room with him. Rucklor had been expertly bandaged, Lassiter noted with approval. Although Rucklor's color was only slightly improved, he no longer had the chalky look.

"You ready to move, Rod?" Lassiter asked, leaning down.

"I'd like Blanche to come along." Evidently he and Blanche had been talking. "She knows quite a bit about nursing. She can be a help to me, Lassiter."

Lassiter flicked a glance at Blanche, who stood on the far side of the bed, her fingers locked demurely under her breasts. "You sure, Blanche?" he asked narrowly.

"I'm tired of this place, Lassiter," she said. "I'm in a trap here. It seems John has always got his hand in my pocketbook."

"Ain't so," flared Simosa.

Blanche shook her head. "I can never seem to get ahead. I want to go live with my sister in Arizona. She's always asking me. She has kids and I can help her."

Lassiter was surprised at the emotion apparent in Blanche's voice. But in her profession she had probably learned to be a very good actress.

He made Simosa get some blankets, then help him walk Rucklor out to the wagon, where he stretched out on a pile of blankets in the bed.

"Damn you, Lassiter," Simosa hissed when Blanche came out of the building. "You not only steal my shotgun, but take my best girl."

"You'll find your shotgun . . . eventually. But about Blanche? That's up to her."

They wedged Blanche's small trunk in beside Ruck-lor. She was wearing a coat and bonnet. Before climbing to the wagon seat, she turned and exchanged waves with Maudie, who stood in the doorway.

Suddenly, Lassiter whipped up the team into a run, the two saddlers pounding along behind. Blanche protested. "The jolting will do his wound no good."

"Can't help it," he responded, shouting above the roar of hoofbeats, the clatter of the wagon. "I want to put some distance between us and Simosa."

But after a hundred yards or so, he slowed the team and began to let down. But the relaxation was only temporary; there were still the long miles to Fork Creek. Anything could happen on the way. In the hours that Rucklor had been at Simosa's, Lassiter had been thinking things over. It was apparent that someone had paid Harve Dolan to kill them both. A man like Dolan didn't pass the time with murder on his mind unless money was involved. Two names were fixed in Lassiter's mind as the suppliers of cash, Lake Burne and Rex Manly.

On the long drive, Blanche's body would occasionally slump against his arm when they hit a rut on the rough road. Even though he was weary after the gunfight and the long day, her subtle perfume revived him somewhat and started the hairs twitching at the back of his neck. Although there seemed to be a sweetness about her, he knew from experience it could very well be false.

They met only a three-wagon freight outfit southbound. But here the countryside was as flat as a platter and Lassiter pulled off to let them pass. Some of the teamsters looked at Blanche in surprise, then waved. Blanche lifted her firm chin and ignored them. When one of the swampers, bearded and with a shirt sticking

to his heavy torso, cupped his hands to yell something, he got a closer look at the dark-faced man with
the piercing blue eyes at her side and changed his
mind.

"Friends of yours?" Lassiter asked dryly when they
were rolling again.

"Friends? Hardly."

Then he noticed that the knuckles of the hands
clenched in her lap were bone white. "I'm sorry,
Blanche."

She only shrugged off his apology.

At last they left the main road where it veered more
west than north and swung onto wheeltracks. They
were on Fork Creek range.

It was nearly dark when they came clattering into the
ranch yard. As Lassiter pulled up in front of the house,
Lake Burne came hurrying up from his quarters.

"How come the wagon?" he asked. Then he saw
Rucklor lying on the pile of blankets.

Coldly, Lassiter told him about Rucklor's wound.

"Sure sorry to hear the boss got shot up," Burne
said, then fixed his attention on Blanche, who was
climbing out of the wagon. "What's *she* doin' here?"

Lassiter ignored the question. "Help me get the boss
inside."

When Rucklor was stretched out on the bed in his
late father's old room, Blanche removed her coat and
hat. "I'll try and scrape up the fixings to make some
broth for Mr. Rucklor."

Her heels rapped on wooden floors as she went off
to hunt for the kitchen.

"Sure a shame about the boss," Burne said with a
sad shake of his large head. "Wonder who could've
done it?"

"I've got an idea," Lassiter said, looking him in the

eye. "Have the crew in the bunkhouse after supper. I've got some things to tell 'em about their new boss."

"Hell, I can do the tellin'. Just let me know what—"

"I'll do it myself," Lassiter said abruptly.

"Well, sure, but . . ." Burne's heavy frame stiffened.

After Burne had closed the front door, none too gently, Lassiter stepped into the kitchen. "You all right, Blanche?"

"Fine." She was slicing beef that she had found in a cooler. Her sleeves were pushed up on rounded forearms. A fire that she had made in the stove was beginning to catch. Leaning over, she adjusted the damper on the tin chimney.

"You seem cheerful," he pointed out.

"I am. Getting away from Simosa was a blessing."

Lassiter asked how she had happened to be there in the first place.

It took her a few moments to respond. Then she met his eyes. "I was raised in a family of five older boys. My mother was dead. When I was twelve the oldest boy started in on me. Then, when he got married, the next one took over. And so on. Finally I got sick of it and ran away. I felt I might as well get paid for what they were forcing on me."

The supper Blanche cooked was tasty. She spiced up the leftover meat with dried onions. Fried potatoes rounded out the meal. Lassiter complimented her.

"Oh, I learned to cook when I was quite young. My brothers saw to that." A shred of anger touched her voice. After taking a sip of coffee, her mood changed and she smiled. "If I can help someone like Mr. Rucklor, it will make up for a lot."

Rucklor was asleep in the bedroom from the laudanum, and she had spoon-fed him the broth.

Lassiter went down to the bunkhouse. The men had finished eating and were talking in low tones. But they broke off when he entered to stand in the doorway. He saw at a glance that Lake Burne wasn't among those present.

"Somebody tried to kill your new boss today," Lassiter said coldly. "And me along with him."

Men exchanged glances. Some of them, Lassiter noticed, grew edgy under his gaze. He nodded to a lean, brown-faced cowhand. "Go fetch Lake Burne."

The man hurried out. This was followed by a nervous clearing of throats and shifting of bodies. Presently, Burne swaggered in.

"Why didn't you come for me yourself?" Burne asked, trying to smile. "Hell, I forgot all about you wantin' me here. You oughta know you're always welcome at my diggings."

"Welcome like a diamondback rattler," Lassiter countered.

"Wasn't no cause to say that." Burne looked offended. "I aim to get along with you."

"Too late for that, Burne. You're fired!"

Jaws dropped and there was instant tension in the long bunkhouse, with its bunks, the big table for card games and the cast-iron stove for heat. Tendons stood out on Burne's thick neck.

"What'd you mean by that, Lassiter?" he growled.

"Just what I said. You're through on Fork Creek!"

"You got no reason—"

"You set Harve Dolan on us today."

"Now, you got not one sliver of proof that I done a thing like that." Burne started waving his large hands for emphasis, the right coming dangerously close to the butt of a holstered revolver. Lassiter stiffened. Just in case, he wrapped his fingers around the grips of his .44.

Noticing this, the men ducked away from the possible line of fire, some throwing themselves across the bunks. There was still enough daylight left so that Lassiter could see mingled rage and humiliation in Burne's muddy brown eyes.

But Burne had sense enough to stop waving his arms about. But he did shove his jaw out and say, "Lassiter, you're trying to cut yourself too big a slice of cake. You're what is known as outnumbered." He gave the men a broad wink.

Lassiter faced the crew. "I'm gambling that men who were loyal to Ham Rucklor will be likewise to the son." Several of the men spoke up, affirming it. He counted twelve in this group, now bunched toward the rear of the building.

Three of the crew had sauntered up to stand by Burne, their grins cocky. They had evidently expected others to join them. But as they saw the changing tide, their confidence started oozing away.

Lassiter settled the matter for them. "You three go with Burne."

"Now, wait, I ain't done a damn thing," a heavy-shouldered man named Amos Tyne said angrily.

"You and your two friends here sided with Burne when you figured he had the upper hand." Lassiter spoke calmly, but his nerves were twitching. In the confines of the bunkhouse, tensions could explode into violence at any moment. And he didn't know for sure how many of the twelve he could really count on. Not yet, anyway.

For a few moments, Burne spluttered and threatened, then with a sour expression on his broad face, accepted the ultimatum.

Burne and the three cowhands were a sullen quartet that rode south toward Villa Rosa in the early darkness.

Lassiter singled out bearded Joe McCready. "Joe, if any of you boys see one of 'em back on Fork Creek range, you know what to do."

Some of them nodded their heads that they understood. Others just sat, thinking about the grim turn of events. From the looks on the faces of the older ones, including McCready's, it would seem they did not look forward to the possibility of a range war.

Too many of them remembered a previous bloodletting that involved Fork Creek and a powerful neighbor.

Chapter 6

That Lassiter would become involved in his plans had never occurred to Rex Manly. Therefore, it took him a few minutes to digest what Lake Burne was trying to tell him.

"He kicked me off the place," Burne finished.

They were in Manly's office on the second floor of the Manly Building. He had just returned from a business trip to Beeler and fully expected that by his return the matter of Rodney Rucklor II would have been settled. Manly was tall and lean, with rather narrow but aristocratic features. His brows were a darker shade of brown than his hair. Hazel eyes locked on Burne's sweated face.

"You let him kick you off? *One man?*" Manly bit off the end of a cigar and spat it into a cuspidor beside his desk. His hand shook as he lit a match.

"I could've had the crew behind me," Burne said quickly. "But I didn't think it was smart to put 'em to the test right then. So I backed down."

Manly waved aside a cloud of blue smoke from his cigar and said, "So you backed down. Jesus Christ, do you think Lassiter is just running a bluff or what?"

Burne gave a hard laugh and went into detail about Lassiter's role at Fork Creek.

Manly thought about it. "Apparently he's appointed himself young Rucklor's guardian. Knowing Lassiter's rep, I'd think he'd have something better to do."

"He and the kid's pa were friends, don't forget."

"Nobody was ever much of a friend of Ham Rucklor's. He'd never let anybody under that tough hide of his. Not even his own son. About the closest he ever came was Len Crenshaw."

"At least I didn't have to worry about that old bastard," Burne said. "He conveniently died on me."

"Seems that Crenshaw is the one who talked Lassiter into giving the kid a hand," Manly said.

"Where'd you hear that?"

"At the Saber. This morning Doc Straffer was talking about it. A doctor friend of his up at Overland wrote him. It seems the good doctor had one ear to the door when Crenshaw was talking to Lassiter, trying to convince him. And apparently he did."

"Well, we've got an ace in the hole when she shows up," Burne said with a wise smile.

"She? You know I hate riddles. Who're you talking about?"

Burne, flushing at the lawyer's harsh tone, told of the night young Rucklor had run off from Lassiter and ended up at Simosa's. There Rucklor had done some talking that Harve Dolan had passed along. The interesting part of it concerned Regina Balmoral, whom Rucklor had telegraphed to join him at Fork Creek. "They're betrothed," Burne continued.

"More complications, it seems."

"Dolan claims he kept braggin' how beautiful she was. The way I look at it is this, Rex. We get our hands on the gal an' that'll be the end of it. Give Rucklor a few dollars an' send him back to Philadelphia."

"Well and good, but that doesn't settle Lassiter."

"Nobody's gonna get in a lather if you kill him."

"*I* kill him?" Manly asked narrowly. He was sitting on the edge of his desk, immaculate in a freshly ironed gray suit. His eyes were bright. Some said he could look at a man and make him think he was ripping off skin and bone to get a close look inside his skull. Manly was thinking about what Burne had said. Of course, he could take Lassiter in a gunfight, all because of a trick he had learned that gave him a decided edge. He stared at the hulking former Fork Creek segundo, and said softly, "Gunwork is what I pay you for, Lake. Seems like so far you've botched it with Lassiter."

"There'll be another day." Burne flushed at the memory of Dolan's failure. Five men against two. One of the two a known gunhand, but the other a rank tenderfoot. He told Manly about it, sounding disgusted.

"I figured the odds were good," Burne continued. "We might lose a man or two, but Lassiter an' Rucklor should've been down."

"Either Lassiter has all the luck in the world or Dolan got careless."

"Tell the truth, I never thought Dolan was very heavy with brains," Burne put in.

"He's a good man," Manly defended. "Lassiter probably put on too much pressure. How soon do you think Rucklor's sweetheart will arrive?"

"Anytime at all, so Dolan claims Rucklor was sayin'."

Manly pursed his lips. "Next southbound is due the day after tomorrow. She could be on it, if Dolan's information is correct."

"I'll bank on it. Maybe he's got so he can't shoot a gun worth a damn, but he don't lie."

"Let's hope you're right. As for the shooting part of it, I'm inclined to reluctantly agree. Lassiter should be six feet under by now. Did he have anything else to say before he threw you off the ranch?"

Burne's chair creaked as he shifted his bulk in anger. "Damn it, Rex, he never threw me off. I just figured it wasn't the time to make a stand."

"You didn't answer my question."

Burne got up and walked to a window. He stared down into the single block that made up the business district of Villa Rosa. "He brought up the money we got for them cows we sold."

"Seems to me," Manly said with a chill in his voice, "that's a damn important matter. Why didn't you mention it sooner?"

"Just never got around to it."

"Or are you scared white that you might have to give up your share?"

Burne looked around, his eyes filled with warning. "I'll tell you one thing, Rex. Nobody's gonna take my share of that money."

Manly drew on his cigar and threw it into the spittoon where it made a brief sizzling sound. Selling off the Fork Creek cattle and pocketing the money had been a rash move, he had to admit. But in the first place he had never thought Rodney Rucklor II would come West. Ham Rucklor, when he made out his will, had hinted that his son was wealthy in his own right. The late aunt who raised him had been a woman of means, so he had claimed. As a consequence, Manly thought that in painting a dismal picture of ranch finances, young Rucklor would be willing to unload it. But instead of accepting Manly's low figure for the property, he had written that he was taking the steam car on the new transcontinental rail line.

"What I can't figure out is why a rich dude like young Rucklor wants to give up an easy life in order to run a cow ranch, which you say he told Dolan he intends to do."

"So Dolan claims." Burne's lips twisted. "I never figured to be saddled with a tenderfoot like Rucklor. He's not only damp behind the ears, he's drippin' wet."

"Seems like you're not saddled with him after all, Lake," Manly couldn't help but say. "Lassiter cut you off from the ranch."

"Will you quit bringin' that up?" Burne protested. "I'll handle Lassiter. But I figured we oughta have a talk before I made a move."

"You already made a move. By sending Dolan after Lassiter and the kid." Manly sounded disgusted.

"Well, dammit, I figured that would be the end of it."

"One thing we don't want, Lake, is for Sheriff Worden to ride down this way and come knocking at our door."

"You've got him in your pocket," Burne shot back. "At least that's what you're always claimin'."

"So I have. And he remains up there in Beeler and leaves us alone. Only because I've the good sense not to overstep."

"Well, we ain't overstepped. . . ."

"As long as young Rucklor insisted on coming West, he could have turned up dead in any number of ways."

"It was what I was gettin' set for, Rex."

"He's inexperienced and could easily have had a mean horse roll on him. Or a wagon team run away with him and crash into a tree. You were right there to see that one of those things happened out at Fork Creek. But you're not there now, are you, Lake?"

"Close enough. If you still want it done."

Manly noted the angry lights in Burne's eyes, the tight set of his mouth. Had he perhaps been pushing too hard with his sarcasm, Manly wondered. He did need Lake Burne. Mainly because in the Villa Rosa country at present there seemed to be a dearth of reliable men. He decided to ease up a little and then try to figure something out on his own.

"I like your idea about Rucklor's betrothed," Manly

said to smooth things over. "We could always blame her kidnapping on some fictitious outlaw gang. There'll be pursuit, of course, but in desperation the outlaws kill the girl."

"Yeah, that sounds good."

"We'll have to see that there are two or three dead strangers lying about to satisfy the sheriff. And that'll be the end of it."

"That'll get you the ranch?"

"Rodney will be along with you," Manly said with a cold smile, "when you're pursuing the kidnappers. He'll be an unfortunate casualty, of course."

"But what about Lassiter?"

"It's your job to see that he's taken care of before the young lady arrives."

"I feel better about things, Rex. I'd halfway made up my mind to take my share of the money an' quit the country."

Manly almost laughed and had to look quickly down at a green rug on the office floor so Burne couldn't read the amusement in his eyes. Then Manly let his gaze drift to a heavy safe next to the rolltop desk. His eyes shifted to a spot on the floor under the desk. A strongbox under the rug held Burne's share of the cattle money. If Burne decided to press the matter, it didn't take particular marksmanship to center his broad back with a bullet or two. Because Manly considered the cattle money his, every nickel of it—especially after the way Burne had botched things up so far.

They shook hands before parting, Manly with a warm smile. "I'll be expecting some good news about Lassiter."

"You'll have it, Rex. Now that I know how things stand."

Burne clattered down a long flight of outside stairs,

swearing under his breath. There was no doubt that Manly blamed him for Dolan's failure. And for not letting the blood flow out at Fork Creek when Lassiter ordered him to leave. Memory of that humiliation in front of the crew was burned into his brain. He had always disliked Lassiter, but now the feeling was cold hatred.

Chapter 7

The only saloon in Villa Rosa was a barnlike place known as the Saber, run by a former buffalo hunter and cavalryman named Kiley Boyle. He was a huge man with small eyes and a mean mouth. A well-defined saber scar ran diagonally across the top of his bald head. What fringe hair still remained was shaved monthly. With his thick arms and shoulders, plus an irascible nature, one didn't have to wonder what the plaque hanging in back of the bar was. It proclaimed him to have been the champion of his regiment not only in wrestling but in bare-knuckle fighting.

A run-in with a major had ended his army career. As a supply sergeant, Boyle had come to Villa Rosa with well-filled pockets. He decided to make a niche for himself on the "Buffalo," as the wild stretch of country between Villa Rosa and the county seat up at Beeler had been known for years.

It was a slow afternoon. Rex Manly sat at a deal table, a glass and his private bottle within reach. The lawyer was frowning at some papers and seemed deep in thought.

Boyle's scarred face brightened when he saw the lean figure of Lassiter approaching the saloon. One man he liked in what he called the "miserable doorstep to hell" was Lassiter. He admired the danger that Lassiter always seemed to have, his luck in getting out of tight corners that would doom the average man.

"Lassiter!" Boyle yelled when the man with the piercing blue eyes entered the saloon.

It caused Manly to jerk up his head. He turned in his chair to stare at Lassiter, tall and dark and formidable-looking in the doorway. Lassiter nodded at Boyle in acknowledgment of the greeting, then veered toward Manly's table.

"Your office was locked. The fella in the saddleshop said he saw you come over this way."

"Just taking a breather. Here, have a chair." Manly put on a broad smile. "Kiley, can we have a clean glass here? Lassiter is joining me."

Lassiter remained standing. "We've got some business to talk over."

The chill in Lassiter's voice caused the two other drinkers in the place to look around in surprise.

"We can talk over our business here," Manly said.

"Up to you." Lassiter told Kiley Boyle to never mind about the fresh glass. He sat down at the table. "I want to know about you selling off two thousand head of Fork Creek cattle."

"Simple explanation," Manly said smoothly. "I felt the ranch would soon need money for operating expenses. And at the time I didn't know whether Ham Rucklor's son was coming out here or not. It's all perfectly legal."

"Is it?"

Manly stiffened in his chair. "Sir, are you impugning my character?"

"That money belongs to Rod Rucklor."

"Of course it does. Have I said otherwise?"

"I'll take the money to him."

"Just a minute, Lassiter. It's Rucklor's place to

demand the proceeds from the cattle sale. Certainly not yours."

Lassiter's smile could freeze the backbone of most men, but didn't seem to faze the lawyer. As they locked eyes, Lassiter told him about Rucklor's wound. "He's not able to come in and demand his money in person. So I'm doing it for him."

"Wounded? Oh, I am sorry to hear that. How did it happen?"

Lassiter only looked at him. "Can we get the money? Then I'll be on my way."

"I'd say that would be a simple solution . . . if I had my hands on the money."

"Where is it?"

"The cattle buyers haven't sent a bank draft as yet. . . ."

"You turned over two thousand head of beef and got no money?"

"The late Ham Rucklor had done business with them for some years. They are very reliable."

"Who are they?"

Manly said they were Benton and Reed from Kansas.

"I don't remember Ham dealing with an outfit by that name."

"Well, he did. Too bad you can't ask Len Crenshaw, but the poor man has gone to his maker, so I understand. However, you can take the matter up with the segundo, Lake Burne. He can certainly verify it."

"I fired Burne."

Manly looked surprised. "It seems you've moved into Fork Creek rather abruptly."

"You've got something in writing from these cattle buyers? A paper saying they're going to pay on such and such a date. I'd like to see it."

Down the bar the two drinkers forgot their whiskey, to pay full attention to the dark-faced man and the smooth-talking lawyer.

"Unfortunately, the paper you refer to is in the bank vault up at Beeler," Manly said firmly.

"Why up there?"

"A simple explanation. We have no bank here and I keep all my important papers at Beeler."

"A two-day trip."

"Better than running the risk of thieves."

Lassiter's smile was hard. "You've got a slick tongue. I'll say that for you, Manly."

"I do resent your demeaning me in front of Kiley Boyle, the owner of this saloon, and the two gentlemen drinking in his establishment. Now, if you will excuse me!" Manly jumped to his feet and, carrying bottle and glass, strode to the bar. The very picture of indignation.

"Mr. Boyle, I ask you," Manly said in the tone of an injured man, "have you ever heard of anyone insulted as I have been today?"

Boyle leaned his heavy arms on the lip of his bar and muttered, "Hell, I ain't heard one damn thing that was said in here, Manly." Boyle's small eyes were fixed on Manly's flushed face.

"I see," Manly said. He finished his whiskey in one gulp and strode out of the saloon.

Lassiter stood at the bar and had a drink. Boyle said softly, "Watch out for that one, Lassiter. He's got scorpion blood."

"He better be careful or I'll drain every drop of it."

Boyle laughed, then grew serious. "There's somethin' I've been wantin' to talk to you about, Lassiter. . . ."

"Tell me later, Kiley. Gotta go." Lassiter tossed a coin on the bar and went toward the general store where the big Fork Creek wagon was being loaded with supplies.

Fifteen minutes later Manly slipped back into the Saber, this time by the rear door. He got Boyle aside.

"Why the hell didn't you play along with me today with Lassiter?" he demanded in a low voice. Business had picked up and over a dozen customers were now lined up at the bar. The place buzzed with discussions of politics and women. There was some laughter.

Boyle said nothing to Manly's question. But he wore a half smile and looked the lawyer in the eye.

"I understand," Manly said after a few moments. "It's a matter of money."

Boyle shrugged his heavy shoulders but still said nothing.

Manly drew several gold coins from his pocket, selected five double eagles, then leaned across the bar to press them into one of Boyle's oversized hands. There was no expression on Boyle's face as his thick fingers closed on the coins.

Boyle made no response. It was beginning to irritate Manly, but he curbed his annoyance and forced a smile.

"Next time Lassiter comes in, pick a fight with him. Break his back. You've done such a thing before. I remember hearing about that private you fought with up at Fort Leeman."

"Oh, that." It was Boyle's only comment. He lumbered down the bar to wait on three new customers. The saloonman's manner turned Manly's irritation to raw anger. But still he held it in.

Manly gave Boyle a nod, then left by the rear door. He walked along back streets to Doc Straffer's house and office. The lean doctor was not busy and agreed to a low-stakes poker game to pass the time as they often did. Today the session would give Manly's nerves time to unravel and let Lassiter get out of town. Or it just might be the day when Kiley Boyle would decide to earn his money. Surely Boyle wouldn't ignore that hundred dollars. There was no denying he was a strange man, tough as they come but independent. But big as he was, he could still be vulnerable to a well-placed gunshot, Manly was thinking, in case he planned a double cross.

Doc Straffer dealt the cards, saying, "Rex, you act as if you're listening for something."

"I am, Ned." Manly grinned. "The first shouts to announce that a fight is in progress."

Straffer frowned. "Who'd be fighting, may I ask?"

"You never can tell, Doc." Manly laughed and picked up his cards. It was his ability with cards that had earned him a chair at Ham Rucklor's poker table out at Fork Creek. Manly on occasion even allowed Ham to win a big pot. Ham actually called him a friend.

At the Saber, Boyle flagged down his barkeep, who had dropped in for a drink, and got him to take over. Boyle wanted to catch Lassiter before he got out of town. Now was the time to make some money out of Fork Creek Cattle Company. And it was up to him to point out to Lassiter just how easily it could be done.

Lassiter had come to town with two of the Fork Creek hands in order to haul supplies back to the ranch. They had been allowed to get dangerously low. He intended to restock the larder at the main house and the cook shack for the men.

The wagon was loaded and the two cowhands were climbing to the high seat. Lassiter was just about to mount his black horse.

"Can I see you a minute, Lassiter?" Boyle walked over to a corner of the store building and waited.

Lassiter joined him, saying, "What's on your mind, Kiley?"

After looking over each of his large shoulders to see

if anyone was within earshot, Boyle said, "Got a market for beef. Top dollar an' no questions asked."

Lassiter stiffened, having an idea where the conversation was going to lead. He eyed the bulging muscles, the oxlike jaw. Boyle's small eyes were bright with anticipation.

"I didn't know you were in the cattle business," Lassiter said coolly.

"I'm not. *We* are." Boyle smiled, his teeth shining; they suddenly reminded Lassiter of a row of tombstones. One thing he didn't need at present was to make an enemy of this Hercules. Before Lassiter could think of what to say, Boyle was expounding on his plan. "I got a buyer. We got cows . . . partner. Plenty of 'em out at Fork Creek."

Lassiter thought quickly. "A herd's just been sold off."

"That I know, amigo. But there's fifteen hundred head that's tallied . . ."

"So I heard, but—"

"An' I know for sure there's another thousand head that Lake Burne pushed into Devil's Canyon. That's twenty-five hundred head. We'll split damn near a hundred thousand dollars. How's that sound to you?"

"Can't do it, Kiley," Lassiter said with a straight face.

"Why the hell not?" Boyle's eyes darkened suddenly.

"I'm working for Rod Rucklor."

"What difference does that make?"

"I don't draw his money and steal from him at the same time."

Boyle stepped back, his fists on his hips. "You got religion all of a sudden?" he demanded harshly.

"No, but I'm no thief."

"Meanin' I am, I s'pose."

"Look, Boyle. I'm working for Rod Rucklor of the Fork Creek Cattle Company. So forget your loco ideas."

"A loco idea, is it?" Boyle rumbled. "A chance to make a killin'. An' it looks like you're too yellow."

"Don't call me yellow," Lassiter said coldly. "It's one thing I won't stand for."

Boyle roared an oath, then started for him. But he halted abruptly as if coming up against a brick wall. He was staring down at the barrel of Lassiter's .44 trained on his wide midriff.

"One thing I don't aim to do in this lifetime or the next, if there is one, and that's tangle with you, Boyle. There's no reason to let that wild temper of yours get out of hand. Now, back off or I'll put a hole in you big enough to kneel in."

"I was kinda proud knowin' you, Lassiter. 'Cause I'd heard so much about you. Heard that you'd do most anything for a dollar."

"You heard wrong."

"Reckon one of these days soon I'll earn that hundred dollars."

Lassiter didn't know what he was talking about. As Boyle wheeled and stalked off toward his saloon up the block, Lassiter was reminded of an enraged bear.

The two ranch hands on the wagon seat had witnessed the exchange but had not heard what was said because of the distance. Both of them looked surprised when Lassiter came back for his horse.

"I never in my life seen a gun pulled faster than you did, Lassiter," said one of them in an awed voice.

From the saddle, Lassiter looked toward the squat building that housed the Saber Saloon. He wondered what the owner had meant about earning a hundred dollars. He had enough complications already in his stay at Fork Creek without making an enemy of Kiley Boyle. But it seemed that he had.

Shaking his head, he started for the ranch, the big wagon lumbering behind. All the way he rode with his rifle across his thigh, in case Harve Dolan or Lake Burne or both of them decided to finish what was already started. . . .

Chapter 8

When Lassiter got back to the ranch, Blanche was reading to Rucklor. Her young patient managed a smile. There was still a wan look about him and he had definitely lost some weight. While looking up at Lassiter, standing beside the bed, he reached over and clasped Blanche by the hand.

"She's pulling me through this horrible period of my life," he said seriously. "Without her, I don't know what I'd do."

"Do you feel up to writing a letter?" Lassiter asked. "A short one."

"My left hand will have to do. I'm ambidextrous to a point." He gave a short laugh. "Who's the letter to?"

"The bank up at Beeler. It's where that lawyer Manly says there is an agreement from a cattle company about payment for Fork Creek cows. And you might ask if the payment has already been made."

"I don't think I quite follow you."

Lassiter explained in detail. When he had finished, Rucklor's gray eyes searched Lassiter's face.

"It seems you believe that Manly is lying."

"I don't figure to jump to conclusions. Wait'll we see what the bank says."

He glanced at Blanche. She sat in a chair beside the bed, an open book in her lap. It was *Territorial Law* by William "Bat" Masterson. Ham, it seemed, had done some heavy reading at times. Blanche was gazing rapturously at Rucklor. The way she was carrying on got under Lassiter's hide. So he decided to jar that look off her face by mentioning Rucklor's betrothed.

"When do you think your Regina will get here?" he asked.

It caused Blanche to jerk around in the chair and stare at Lassiter. Then she turned her attention to Rucklor, who seemed uneasy. "I . . . I don't really know, Lassiter. Anytime, I guess."

When Lassiter brought up the fact that Rucklor had telegraphed the girl to come West, Blanche left the room.

"Why in the world did you have to bring up Regina right in front of her?" Rucklor hissed.

"I've got a hunch she's building dream castles in her head. I figured it's time to level 'em. Before she wastes her time . . . for nothing."

Two days later, Rucklor finished the letter Lassiter had asked him to write. Rucklor squirmed in the big bed. Without meeting Lassiter's eyes, he said, "I think fondly of Blanche."

A glance at the love-sick eyes caused Lassiter to give a silent groan. "You only think you care for her."

Rucklor struggled to reach a higher position on the pillows at his back. The effort caused him to wince with pain. "You don't understand, Lassiter," he whispered.

"What don't I understand?"

"She . . . she's the first girl I've ever . . . ever *known*." Rucklor seemed in agony. "I . . . I can't come right out and say what we've been to each other, but I'm sure you can guess." His smooth young features were fiery red.

"Yeah, I can guess." Lassiter sounded disgusted. Why had he let Blanche talk him into allowing her to come along in the first place? He went over and quietly closed the bedroom door, then came back and sat on the edge of the bed.

"Look at it this way, Rod," he said, keeping his voice down. "You've been initiated. A little later in life than most hombres out here, but . . ." A faint smile creased the corners of Lassiter's wide mouth. "It must've taken some doing, you with your arm in a sling."

"Blanche did it all. She was wonderful, Lassiter. Just wonderful."

"I can sure see she made an impression."

"She's sweet and good and I love her. Now I've said it, and I mean every word." Mingled desperation and defiance were apparent in Rucklor's voice and eyes.

"Listen to me, Rod."

"I want her, and I intend to have her." Rucklor's jaw set stubbornly, which was about the only trait of the late father Lassiter saw in the son. "There have been few things in my life that have been denied me. I won't be denied the love and affection of that young lady."

"Oh, Christ," Lassiter sighed. "You really do have a bad case of it."

"If you mean love, yes I have."

"I guess in the back of my mind, I did think she might show you the joys of life when you got to feeling better. But I never figured you'd fall in love with her."

"Well, I have."

Lassiter leaned close. "Do you have any idea what she did at Simosa's?" Lassiter asked, hoping to shock him. "She—"

"It makes no difference," the younger man interrupted sharply.

"How she made her living? Don't you even *care?*"

"I tell you it makes not one damn bit of difference." Rucklor seemed verging on tears. "Now, shut up about her, if you please."

"What'll you do about your Regina?"

"Send her back."

"You make it sound easy," Lassiter said with a shake of his head.

"I'll tell her it was a terrible mistake and . . ." Rucklor lifted his good hand to his eyes; they glistened in the sunlight. His voice trembled and grew sharp and once again he was the spoiled rich young man from Philadelphia. "Lassiter, you've been trying to run my life. If you don't like what I'm doing, you can get out!"

"I'll be damned. The tiger has teeth."

"I . . . I mean it. I . . ."

"You tried to shoot a hole in me one night only because I was trying to talk sense to you. Then I saved you from that bunch at Simosa's. And then I came close to getting my head shot off when Dolan and the same outfit jumped us. All because of you, my friend. All because of you."

Lassiter walked out, slamming the door. He found Blanche in the kitchen and knew from the look on her face that she had overheard at least a part of it.

He came up behind her, staring at the blond hairs curling at the nape of her neck. She wore her hair up, held in place by a large green comb. Her small ears were delicate. "Well, you did a good job of it," he said softly.

She looked around. Her blue eyes were wet. "Don't be so . . . so despicable."

"I'm surprised you even know what the word means."

"Naturally, you'd say that, being the kind of man you are." She wiped her eyes on an apron worn over a yellow dress. It was tight at the bodice. Her breasts were delicately shaped against the yellow satin. They were within reach and Lassiter was tempted to teach Rod Rucklor a lesson that such women couldn't be trusted.

But she stood there looking so pitiful, tears running down her cheeks, the slim shoulders shaking from her sobs, that he was touched in spite of himself.

"Yes, I know what despicable means and many other words." Her voice was hoarse; tears ran into a corner of her lovely mouth. "I know what you think of me, but I've had some book learning, as it's so quaintly put."

"Among other things," he heard himself say, "it seems you're a pretty fair actress. You can cry on cue."

"I don't care what you say about me. But Rod was lonely and hurting and I . . . Is it the end of your world because I was nice to him?"

Her blazing wet eyes touched a nerve end. "I guess you'll do better at this house then you did at the one run by Simosa," Lassiter said. "Here you'll likely end up with a ranch. If there's any of it left, that is."

"Damn you, Lassiter." She angrily wiped at her eyes. "Rod told me that he'd never had a woman and was scared to try. So I showed him." Her chin came up defiantly. "You didn't have to bring up Regina. He told me the whole story himself two days ago."

They heard a groan and turned to see Rucklor stumbling from the bedroom. His face was haggard. A nightshirt flapped around his long legs. He was barefoot.

"Lassiter, I . . . thank God you haven't gone," he mumbled. "I've been lying there thinking. I apologize. I shouldn't have talked to you as I did."

Blanche sprang into action. "And you shouldn't be out of bed." When he started to sag, she cried, "Lassiter, *help me!*"

Lassiter grabbed him just before his knees buckled. Between the two of them, they got him back to bed.

Blanche was sitting beside the bed, holding Rucklor's hand in both of hers, a brave smile on her lips. Lassiter tiptoed out of the room.

The next morning Lassiter received bad news. Joe McCready got him aside just after breakfast, a hangdog look on his bearded face.

"What's the trouble, Joe?" Lassiter asked narrowly. Some days before, McCready had brought back clothing for Rucklor from town. When Lassiter held up the jeans for the boss's inspection, Rucklor had said, "They look big enough for me and also a friend."

"If you bought them smaller," Lassiter pointed out, "the first time they were washed they'd shrink so much you'd think you had blue canvas for skin." Even Blanche had laughed.

Now McCready was saying, "Lassiter, I reckon I'll be pushin' on."

"Joe, you leaving?"

"Got a brother up north that's feelin' poorly. I reckon I'll go visit him."

Lassiter noticed that McCready failed to meet his eyes. They were standing in the yard under cotton woods. Sunlight made a patchwork of shadows on the dusty ground. "What's the real reason, Joe?" Lassiter asked firmly.

McCready drew a deep breath. "Got a feelin' in my bones that holy hell is gonna bust loose out here one of these days soon. I'm plumb too old to stand up to gunfire."

"Old? Hell, you're a young man," Lassiter said with an encouraging smile.

"I'm forty-six."

Lassiter tried to argue McCready out of quitting, but the man's mind was made up.

"If I could get my time, Lassiter, I'd be obliged."

Young Rucklor had to dig deep in the cash he had brought with him in order to pay McCready off.

From the way some of the other ranch hands had looked, those within earshot, Lassiter had a sinking feeling that McCready wouldn't be the only one to bow out of the potential bloodbath.

Without saying anything to Rucklor, Lassiter left for Villa Rosa early the following morning. He arrived shortly before noon. Today he intended to stay away from the Saber to give Boyle a chance to cool off. Today he wanted no chance confrontation with the man.

He was just coming around behind the Manly Building when the lawyer came skipping lightly down the outside stairs. He was about halfway down when he spotted Lassiter on the bottom step. Manly came to an abrupt halt, his hazel eyes narrowing. Today he wore his well-cut gray suit, with the creases sharply in place. His white shirt had been freshly laundered and he wore a string tie. His hat was narrow-brimmed.

"Back up," Lassiter said, starting up the stairs. "I want a few words with you in your office."

"I'm sorry but I have an important appointment . . ."

"Yeah, with *me*."

"I refuse to stand for this."

"Maybe you'll stand for *this*."

Manly wet his lips when he found himself staring at the black muzzle of a .44. He backed up the stairs and unlocked his office door. As he stepped into the office, Lassiter reached under the man's coat and relieved him of a weapon.

Manly ground his teeth. "Get to your business, if you will," he said in icy tones, "because I'm in a hurry."

"I need ten thousand dollars. Operating money for Fork Creek."

"Are you insane?" Manly started to laugh, but it froze in his throat when Lassiter tapped his Adam's apple with the gun.

"Ten thousand dollars of the money owed Rodney Rucklor from the sale of his cattle. Now open that safe!"

Sweat popped out on Manly's forehead as he glanced involuntarily at the squat safe next to his roll-top desk.

"Manly, I'll count to five. If by the time I reach five you haven't opened that safe, you'll walk with a cane for the rest of your life." Lassiter aimed his weapon at Manly's right kneecap and began to count. At the count of two, Manly whirled and began twisting the dial on the safe.

When the door swung open, Lassiter pushed him aside, just in case the lawyer had a gun hidden among the papers and gold coins.

"You can see for yourself that I don't have ten thousand dollars. I keep most of my funds up at the bank in Beeler."

Lassiter shoved Manly's gun into his waistband and backed toward the office door and locked it on the inside. "Put it all out on your desk. Count what you have."

A sweating Manly did as he was told. When the count was finished, there was a little over six thousand dollars.

"I'll take five, Manly. You can have the rest for now—to run on."

Manly's hands shook as he counted out the money, dumped the coins into a leather sack and handed it to Lassiter.

"I hope you're satisfied, Lassiter," the lawyer said in a voice tight with rage. "Now, if you don't mind, get out of my sight."

Lassiter gave him a hard smile. "You're riding out to Fork Creek with me."

"I'm *what?*"

"Just to be sure you don't sic somebody on me and try to get the five thousand back. Yes, you're going with me all the way. And let me tell you something, my friend. If you try and pull any smart tricks, you'll be walking with two canes instead of one. Either that or you'll be dead!"

They walked together to the livery barn, Lassiter leading his mount. There an ashen-faced Manly ordered the hostler to saddle his horse. Soon they were riding out of town, the lawyer and Lassiter. Several people turned to stare, but no one interfered.

Once they were out of town, Manly turned in the saddle and glared at Lassiter. His lips worked and his eyes were bright with rage. "You've really done it today, Lassiter. I'll nail you for this dirty business."

"You figured to try and nail me anyway, Manly. So I haven't lost a damn thing. Now, shut up and keep riding."

It was nearly dark when they reached the ranch. Lassiter allowed Manly to water his horse, then sent him on the long ride back to Villa Rosa. Manly had asked for the return of his gun. Lassiter searched the man's saddlebags for spare cartridges, but found none. He unloaded the weapon and handed it back to Manly.

"It's inhuman to send a man out in such country without a loaded gun," Manly had protested.

"Also inhuman for Harve Dolan to try and murder young Rucklor, as well as me. Think about it while you're riding home."

Rod Rucklor's face brightened when he saw the sack of gold coins. Lassiter noticed that Blanche's blue eyes seemed interested. He wondered if she'd try to steal the money. If she did, he vowed, she wouldn't get far.

Then he wondered if he might be jumping to conclusions. But all the same, he'd keep an eye on her.

Manly was one of the fortunate few who had been blessed with quick eyes and hands. Early in life he acquired an expertise with guns and soon realized he was what was known as a phenomenal gunfighter. It was in St. Louis, soon after he finished college, that he had his baptism by gunfire. A gambler on a riverboat insulted a lady of Manly's acquaintance. Harsh words were exchanged. Manly's friends begged him to back off before the charges and countercharges reached the point of no return, for the gambler was known as a dead shot and incredibly fast on the draw. Manly refused to back down.

His gun was out of its holster a shade quicker than the gambler's.

He was reading law in his uncle's office at the time, but killing the gambler forced him to leave St. Louis. San Francisco was his next goal. During the trip, he came up against braggarts and killers. Two more men went down before his gun. In San Francisco he read law in a prominent office. Then the call to mining camps of the West proved irresistible. There he acquired a reputation not only as a lawyer, but as a deadly killer.

Soon he was forced to move on. By then, he was thirty years old, and if he was ever to make his stake, it had to be soon. In Villa Rosa he became acquainted with Ham Rucklor.

One day when Rucklor complained about having a bad heart, Manly stressed the importance of leaving a will. After learning of the breach between father and the son he hadn't seen since the boy was about six, Manly cleverly made a place for himself in the will as alternate beneficiary. He was working on ways to get rid of Ham Rucklor when the job was done for him by an a accommodating bison.

In assuring himself longevity in the deadly business of gunfighting, Manly remembered a trick he had first heard of in a mining camp. With the simple device of a swivel holster, a certain aging notorious gunman had been able to maim or kill opponents long past his prime. The trick gave a man the edge of time it takes to blink twice. But a sufficient edge.

After the incident of the five thousand dollars with Lassiter, Manly began to practice. Just in case those he paid to take care of such things faltered and he and Lassiter faced each other in a showdown.

For three days he practiced in a gully outside of Villa Rosa. Lake Burne brought out a wagonload of empty bottles picked up behind the Saber. Manly would line them up, two at a time, widely spaced, then start to walk away. At Burne's count of three he would spin and fire twice, the gun not leaving its holster. All he did was tilt the holster and fire out the end, thus saving the fraction of a second it took an opponent to draw and fire. Each bottle he visualized as the dark face of Lassiter.

On the first day he would shatter one bottle, but miss the second. However, by the time he had practiced for three days, his timing was so good that he could spin and shatter five widely spaced bottles.

Lake Burne was amazed that a lawyer had such deadly accuracy, such impossible speed.

Burne admired Manly's custom-made holster. It was cut low, slightly below the trigger guard, so there was no bind of leather to interfere. It was open at the end.

"Keep your mouth shut about what you've seen out here, Lake," Manly warned on the final day of practice. "No use letting Lassiter get wind of my little secret."

"Lassiter's as good as dead."

"My secret is only in the form of insurance," Manly snapped. "I expect you and Dolan to work something out so I don't have to dirty my hands."

"We'll figure somethin', Rex," Burne said hastily.

Another ace in the deck was the hundred dollars Manly had given Kiley Boyle.

"The bastard better earn it," Manly said, more to himself than Burne.

"Earn what?" Burne asked in surprise.

"Never mind."

They went into the Saber for a drink.

Manly tried to get the eye of Kiley Boyle, but the big man ignored him after setting out the bottle and glasses. He walked down to the far end of the bar. Manly felt his cheeks begin to heat up. . . .

Chapter 9

One day a puzzled young Rucklor asked Lassiter if he knew where his late father had acquired the nickname "Ham." Lassiter smilingly related the story the elder Rucklor had told him. "When your pa first came West, he tangled with a javelina."

"What's a javelina?"

"A wild pig. He was trying to spear it and the bastard turned on him—came close to killing him. From then on, he had a powerful liking for ham. Because he said he always felt he was eating that pig's relatives. The name stuck."

"I guess he . . . he always hated the name Rodney."

"Now we'll never know, will we?"

Later that day while moving cattle, Lassiter got to thinking about Rodney Ham Rucklor. When he was killed and word got out that his son, Rodney Rucklor II, would inherit Fork Creek, it was the first time anyone in the Villa Rosa country knew his first name had been Rodney. Everyone was amazed that a hard-bitten cowhand like Rucklor would be saddled with such a name.

On the day of Ham Rucklor's death, Lassiter had been at the ranch on a visit. He, the rancher and Len Crenshaw had been riding out from town, where they'd done some drinking, when they ran into the magnificent old bull.

"One of the last of 'em!" Rucklor had exclaimed. "I've always wanted a head for my library. An' I thought I was too late for a good one. Thought they'd all been killed off. But there he is, starin' me right in the face." Ham Rucklor had been a big, heavy-muscled man with fierce gray eyes and a laughing mouth. Rucklor reined in, removed his hat and let his brow cool in the breeze. He stared moodily at the buffalo fifty yards away on a sweep of gray-green land that stretched to distant mountains. "I used to dream of my kid ridin' with me on a day like this," he said suddenly.

Lassiter stared at him in surprise. "Your kid? A *son?*"

Rucklor gave a bitter laugh and put on his hat.

"First time I ever knew you had a son," Lassiter said.

As if to get away from possible questions, Rucklor rode toward the buffalo that was grazing on spring grass.

Len Crenshaw fell in beside Lassiter. "For some reason, Ham don't like to talk about his kid," the old foreman said. "I was with him five years before I even knew he was a pa."

"The kid ever come to visit?"

"Ham would never let him."

"Be damned," Lassiter muttered with a shake of his head. He spurred up even with Rucklor, who was drawing his rifle from a saddle boot. Lassiter had always been against killing game only for a trophy, and Rucklor knew it.

"Let the old fella stay alive, Ham," Lassiter urged.

"No. This is my chance an' I'm takin' it."

"What's a buffalo head on your library wall gonna do for you? In a year it'll be a home for moths."

"This is too good to pass up, Lassiter. This one must've got away from the herd. An' he's just for me. You boys stay back. I figure to nail that bastard."

Before anyone could stop him, Ham Rucklor spurred toward the huge bull. It had the traditionally poor eyesight but heard the pound of his horse. Raising the magnificent head that the rancher coveted, it let out a bellow of warning.

Rucklor looked back at Lassiter, his white teeth shining in the craggy face. He waved the rifle overhead in a gesture of defiance, then drove in the spurs. As the sorrel lurched into a hard run, Rucklor began firing. Too much whiskey in him caused the first two shots to miss. Then Lassiter saw a spurt of fur where the third bullet struck a heavy shoulder.

It brought an angry roar from the great bison. Rucklor was leaning over in the saddle as if ready for a lengthy run before downing the animal. Usually a bison would give ground instead of facing its intended executioner. But not this one. Stung by the bullet that had done little more than cut a bloody furrow through its thick fur and hide, it lowered its head.

"Look out, Ham!" Lassiter yelled through cupped hands.

Rucklor desperately tried to rein aside, but a horn smashed through the breastbone of the sorrel. A toss of the head on its mighty neck lifted horse and rider aloft and sent them crashing.

Drawing his rifle, Lassiter started to spur in, but Rucklor, picking himself up from the ground, waved him back.

"I want this one for myself!" he yelled. He had lost his rifle and hat; long graying hair hung on both sides of his sweated face.

The bull had retreated for some yards and was again pawing the ground. Sunlight touched the bloodied horn. Rucklor danced lightly around the dead horse and advanced. He drew his revolver.

"Better keep back, Lassiter," Crenshaw advised in a

worried voice. "If you butt in, they'll hear the boss yellin' all the way to town."

"The crazy damn fool, facing up to that bull afoot. . . ."

The crack of Rucklor's revolver sounded across the flats. The bison's left ear disappeared. Everything that followed was almost too fast for the human eye to follow. As the ear disintegrated, the bull put its head down and lumbered, incredibly swift, straight at the rancher. Before Rucklor could fire again, he was lifted high into the air on a horn, his arms and legs kicking. When he was smashed to the ground, he didn't move.

The bull pivoted and started away with the speed of a runaway wagon. Len Crenshaw's rifle brought him down in a great rolling heap of brownish fur.

Lassiter wondered what good killing the bull had done. Rucklor was dead, the horn tip having taken him in the left side of the chest. Probably right through the heart.

At Ham's funeral, Len Crenshaw in a shiny black suit reminded Lassiter of an aging scarecrow. He didn't realize how vulnerable Crenshaw was to disease until a telegram caught up with him. Crenshaw had put it bluntly: he was dying and Ham Rucklor's son was coming out to take over. Lassiter was needed.

Chapter 10

The slender body of Regina Balmoral rocked to the sway of the stagecoach that hammered its way behind a four-horse team down a long straight stretch of terrible road. How she longed for the comforts of Philadelphia, and more recently, even those of Denver. Rodney had suggested she stop off and rest up with the family of his late grandmother's friend. Malcom Despars had been delighted to take her and her traveling companion Ellen into his home.

They had intended staying only two days, but Ellen became infatuated with a young mining man, Bob Leemart, and didn't want to leave. But after a week, Regina gave her friend an ultimatum: either continue the journey with her to Rodney's ranch or stay behind in Denver. Ellen chose the latter, but begged Regina to stay with her; she was certain Bob would soon ask for her hand in marriage. But Regina had stiffly announced that she would go to Rodney, even though Ellen had pointed out that it would be dangerous to continue the journey alone.

Since leaving Denver, the trip had been a horror. In a settlement two men had tried to take her by the arms and escort her to a dance hall. She twisted away. A big man hopped down from a freight wagon and knocked her tormentors to the ground. A crowd gathered; Regina was mortified.

Later, in another small town, she got in an argument with a man who insisted on paying for her meal at a grubby cafe. And after more harsh words, the man was thrown outside.

Then the owner glared at Regina. "A good-lookin' female like you oughta know better'n to be traipsin' around the country alone. Nothin' but trouble." He stalked away.

Since then, she'd had little to eat. She was famished. When the stagecoach finally rattled into a dismal-looking little town that she learned was her destination, her heart sank like a stone.

As usual on the day when the stage arrived, town loafers and curious townspeople were on hand to see who might be arriving in Villa Rosa. Not many passengers stopped; most continued on to the county seat. But today a well-dressed young woman stepped apprehensively onto the dusty street. Her dark blue traveling coat hung open to reveal a satin dress of lighter hue. Two strands of pearls encircled her slender neck. She carried a reticule and stood looking around with a small frown above her large violet eyes.

"Does anyone happen to know if Rodney Rucklor is in town today?" she asked. It was an effort to keep her voice steady, for she was most upset at not seeing Rodney's face in the circle of onlookers.

Before anyone could reply, a tall dark man stepped forward, removed his flat-crowned hat and introduced himself as Lassiter. "I guess you're Regina Balmoral."

"I am." Her chin was in the air. "Are you a friend of Rodney's?" She was looking him over from his steady blue eyes to his dark pants and dusty boots. A look of revulsion touched her eyes when they settled on the gun belted at his narrow waist.

"You look tired," he said softly. "Let me get you some coffee and we can talk."

He suddenly grabbed her by the arms and pulled her away from the rear wheel of the coach, as the driver shouted and the four-horse team lunged into their collars. She came to a stumbling halt in his arms, her face white as she stared at what she could see of the departing stagecoach through a mantle of dust.

"Thank you," she said shakily. "I guess I didn't watch where I was standing." She adjusted the blue bonnet that had come loose when he pulled her so abruptly.

"I work for the Fork Creek Cattle Company, which your friend Rodney Rucklor owns." As of this moment, he almost added. He pointed at a trunk and carpetbag that had been deposited at the edge of the boardwalk. "Are these yours?"

She nodded. "Is there a porter?" She looked around. He gave her a faint smile.

"Not here, ma'am. I'll be your porter."

Boosting the small trunk to one of his shoulders, picking up the carpetbag, he said, "Follow me." But she didn't budge.

"Why isn't Rodney here to meet me?" she asked and looked a little fearfully at the staring faces. Some onlookers appeared sorry that she had been cast down in such an unlikely spot as Villa Rosa. Others were amused to see a stuck-up lady obviously afraid of the new surroundings.

"I'll tell you about it," Lassiter said impatiently. He noticed that Kiley Boyle had emerged from the Saber up the street to stand with his thick arms folded, staring in his direction. "I think maybe we'd better forget the coffee and get you out to Fork Creek."

"I want more than coffee. I'm famished."

She walked resolutely past three doors to Ruby's Cafe. It was a small place with stools at a short counter and several tables. At the moment there were no customers. A fat woman wearing a greasy apron over a gray dress was clearing dirty dishes off the counter.

Regina sat down at a table near the door. "May I have some ham and eggs? And potatoes," she added.

"Sure thing," the plump Ruby grunted. "Are you headin' out to Simosa's?"

Lassiter came in with the trunk balanced on his broad shoulder, the carpetbag swinging from a long arm. "That's a hell of a thing to ask her, Ruby. Can't you tell she's a lady?"

Ruby mumbled something and asked what Lassiter wanted to order. He told her, "Coffee." Then he walked to a table next to the kitchen wall, put down the trunk and the carpetbag and beckoned to Regina. "Let's sit at this table."

"I don't see what's the matter with this one."

He stood holding out a chair for her, his blue eyes somehow frightening. She sat down and he took the chair opposite hers, his back to the wall.

"Are you afraid somebody will sneak up behind you?" she chided and attempted to smile. But it wavered and the worried look returned to her attractive face.

"Just a habit of mine," he said, trying to think just how to go about explaining the situation. Lassiter had argued half the night, it seemed like, with Rucklor, insisting it was his responsibility to meet his betrothed. But Rucklor claimed he wasn't up to the long round trip and Blanche agreed. In the morning, Rucklor had written a note in a shaky hand that he asked Lassiter to deliver to the girl.

"Maybe she won't even want to come out here, and will just get on the next stage and go home," Rucklor had said with hope in his eyes.

Lassiter had held back an oath, and shoved the note in his pocket without reading it. He had half a mind to tear it up. Now that he was facing her in Ruby's steamy little cafe, sitting at a table covered with stained oil-cloth, he was finding himself short of words. Maybe it would be better to just tell all and hope she wouldn't fly into hysterics. If that happened, then what would he do?

"You never did tell me why Rodney didn't meet the stage," she said in a voice that betrayed her weariness. And she did look exhausted with dark circles under her fine eyes, the corners of her rather full mouth drooping. Aromas of frying ham and eggs caused her to sniff the air appreciatively.

"Rodney had a good excuse for not coming, Miss Balmoral. He—"

"Whatever it was, it certainly could have been postponed under the circumstances," she broke in. Then she put a hand to her eyes. A lock of blue-black hair had crept from beneath her bonnet to lie against the curve of a cheek. Lassiter resisted an urge to tuck it behind her ear.

"Rod has grown up considerably since you saw him last," he said, beginning the grim news he must hand to this obviously distraught young woman.

"Not grown up enough to assume the responsibility of meeting his betrothed, however."

Ruby brought coffee, staring at Regina as if she might be from another world. She set down the platter of ham and eggs.

Regina wrinkled her aristocratic nose at the grease, then started to eat as if she hadn't tasted food in a week.

Lassiter watched her for a minute, then asked, "Didn't the stage make meal stops?"

"There were . . . difficulties. So I didn't even bother to get out."

He thought that was strange, but didn't say anything.

Taking a deep breath, he fished out the note Rod had written from his pocket and held it in his hand. It was good that she didn't seem to notice. Let her eat first, he told himself.

Between mouthfuls of food, she spoke, of the telegrams she and Rod Rucklor had exchanged between Denver and Philadelphia. "He was so enthusiastic at taking over for his late father out here that I caught some of the fever." She briefly described her visit to Denver and the defection of her friend Ellen. "I suppose I shouldn't have tried to come on without my traveling companion. Mr. Despars, who was a friend of Rodney's late grandmother, warned me against trying it."

When she had cleaned the platter and shoved it aside, he was relieved to note a faint smile. But her words stabbed him. "Now, tell me about Rodney. I sense it's bad news."

It caught him by surprise. She gripped her coffee cup as if afraid it might fly away. "Why would you think it's bad news?" he heard himself say. But it *was* bad news. Damn Rodney Rucklor II.

"I could tell from the look on your face, Mr. Lassiter."

"Forget the mister part of it."

"What is your first name, if I may be so bold as to ask?"

"Just Lassiter."

"You mean that's your name? All of it?" And when he nodded, she said, "How odd. And something else seems odd." Her voice cracked, but she swept bravely on. "Rodney not meeting me. And you . . . you acting so strange."

"These are strange times." He kept one eye on the front window in case one of his sworn enemies appeared. He was wasting time sitting here. It was dangerous. He had brought two men in with him in case of trouble. He had to either get her out to Fork Creek or on the next stagecoach to Philadelphia. There was an eastbound stage later in the week. He drew another deep breath, almost handed her the note, but instead told her of Rod's wound.

Her eyes instantly filled with tears. "Rodney . . . wounded? Oh, my God. Why didn't you tell me sooner?"

"There's more to it than that," he said uneasily. "This is the hard part, I'm afraid."

"Worse than being shot?"

Abruptly he handed her the note. She sat staring at the square of folded paper as if it were something alive and with sharp teeth. Her hands trembled as she unfolded it, read the few lines swiftly, then let it fall to the table. She sat staring out the window, with shock in her eyes.

For the first time, Lassiter saw what Rucklor had set down in his shaky handwriting.

Dear Regina: I feel it's best to be blunt. I have found someone else. I'm terribly sorry. Lassiter has money for your passage back home. Forgive me, if you will.

It was signed. Lassiter ground his teeth at Rucklor's insensitivity. How could he have been so goddamn heartless? he asked himself.

"Well," Regina said after a moment, turning to a grim Lassiter. "It seems I've been kicked in the face. Just who is this girl he seems to have found?"

He bluntly explained about Blanche and her relationship with Rucklor. When he had finished, she began to laugh. But when he saw the tears, he sat up straighter in his chair and clasped one of her shapely hands. Was hysteria just over the edge?

She seemed startled by the touch of his fingers.

"Look," he said quickly, "I've got the money to send you back to Philadelphia. . . ."

"Never there. Never!" Her voice was strong again.

"Or maybe to Denver. And forget about Rod." He paused, withdrawing his hand so she could use a tiny lace handkerchief on her eyes. "Either that," he added, "or you can *fight* for him."

She lowered the handkerchief and stared at him with wet eyes. "Fight against a woman like this Blanche? I wouldn't even know how to start. Tell me, is Blanche pretty?"

Lassiter nodded. "She hasn't been . . . well, been in the business long enough for it to show on her."

"Rodney turning to a woman like that. I can hardly believe it."

"Don't run Blanche down. I feel sorry for her more than anything. Blanche was there when he needed her. She's been good to him."

"Quite obviously." She gave a small laugh.

"Good to him and good for him." He looked her in the eye. "She turned him into a man."

Regina thought about it for a moment, then her pretty mouth twisted into a bitter smile. "One thing Rodney and I promised, that we would come to each other pure in mind and body." She laughed again. "Of course, I'm expected to be, it goes without saying. But Rodney . . . I certainly didn't expect him to stray."

"No man should take a wife when he's as ignorant about marriage as a babe."

"And just why not, Lassiter?"

"Because a man who's dipped his toes in the water, so to speak, will be more likely to appreciate a wife. Instead of staring at every pretty ankle that comes along."

She sagged back in the chair, her cloak open to

reveal the pale blue satin gently rounded by firm breasts.

"Stay and fight for him," Lassiter urged. "Show him you'll make a better wife than Blanche."

"And just how do I go about doing that?" She sounded slightly amused, but the strain was still evident. "By sharing my charms with him? As this Blanche has obviously done?"

It shocked him slightly that this well-bred young woman from Philadelphia would speak so boldly. And yet he couldn't help but admire her. Under the brutal blow of Rucklor's treachery, she was bearing up quite well.

"I've had very little sleep for two nights," she said wearily. "My mind's in a muddle. I really don't know what I want to do."

"Can you ride a horse?"

"I've ridden since I was five."

"All right, then, we'll head for Fork Creek and—"

She sat up straighter, her chin lifted, the eyes reddened from tears fixed on his face. "I haven't made up my mind . . . about anything, Lassiter. When does the next stage come through this horrible little town that I can take to Denver?"

He told her it only came through three times a week and that the next one wouldn't be in for two days.

"It seems I'm doomed to stay in this place, doesn't it? At least for two more days while I make up my mind."

"Ride out to Fork Creek and begin your fight."

"I don't think you understand, Lassiter. I've been deeply hurt and humiliated."

"That I can understand, but—"

"I won't recover in a hurry. I assume there's a hotel in this town."

"Sure there is, but I think you oughta come out to the—"

"At present I don't want to see Rodney Rucklor. I don't even wish to hear his name."

That irritated him. "You've had your cap set for a rich young husband. So why in the hell—excuse the cussing—but why don't you grab him?"

"You said rich? You're talking about Rodney?"

"You're an exasperating female. Who else would I be talking about?"

"Rodney rich?" Her peal of laughter was shrill. "If inheriting a cattle ranch makes him rich, then I suppose he is. But that makes no difference to me."

"I heard his aunt left him a lot of money."

"Her estate was in such a mess that Rodney came out of it with very little. His Aunt Margaret was a tippler. She smelled of brandy half the time. Rodney always swore it was medicine."

"Then you're the rich one," Lassiter said with a hard smile.

"Oh, yes. Very. My family never fully recovered from the Civil War. I'm far from destitute, but not rich."

"You two young people have got a chance to make something of your lives. So why in the hell don't you do it? And this time I don't apologize for the cussing."

"Give me two days to think about it, Lassiter. All I wish to do at the moment is go to bed and make up for sleep I lost on that horrid trip from Denver." She yawned, covering her lips with long fingers.

"Look, I'm going to be busy tomorrow. . . ."

"Busy being nursemaid to dear Rodney, I presume." Her smile wavered.

"No. There's a thousand head of Fork Creek beef penned up in a canyon. They've been there too long. Tomorrow I've got a big job to do . . . at Devil's Canyon."

"Rodney might get his hands dirty," she said bitterly.

"He won't be along. He'll stay home. It would give you and Rod a chance to get reacquainted."

"What about Blanche?" she asked, giving him a wise smile.

"I'll see that she comes along with me. Even if I have to tie her to the saddle."

Regina sighed and looked at him for a long moment, then shook her head. "I still want those two days to sort out my feelings in the matter of Rodney Rucklor."

"Your mind's made up?"

"Definitely." She was digging into her reticule and came up with two silver dollars. "For my meal," she said when he gave her a hard look.

But he took the dollars, dropped them back in the reticule and said, "Your meal's on the Fork Creek Cattle Company. Also your hotel room. Ruby?"

"Yeah." Ruby came out of her kitchen and waddled over to the table. Lassiter paid her for the meal.

"You run along, Lassiter," Regina said. "I'm going to sit here and drink another cup of coffee." She smiled up into Ruby's plump, sweated face. "May I?"

"Course you can, honey." She lumbered back to the coffeepot.

"I'll carry your stuff over to the hotel and get you a room," Lassiter said, standing up. "You're a very stubborn young woman. But I suppose you know that."

He was back in ten minutes to lay a key to her hotel room on the table. "Will you do me a favor?" Lassiter asked.

"Depends."

"Take your meals in your room."

"Why?"

"Because Rod Rucklor has enemies."

"And you think they might try and get at him through me?" She gave a small smile.

"Yeah, it's just what I mean. I wish you'd change

your mind and come out to Fork Creek and face up to him."

"You're very persistent, but I refuse to change my mind."

He gave up in exasperation and made arrangements with Ruby to send her meals over to room twelve at the hotel. Then he stepped back to the table where Ruby had placed a fresh cup of hot coffee.

"Stay in your room as much as you can," he advised the stubborn Regina. "And don't talk to anybody."

"What I'll be doing mostly is sleeping."

"One way or another, I'll be back the day after to-morrow. It oughta be enough time to make up your mind." He gave the lovely but tired young woman a two-fingered salute to the hat brim, then walked out.

Chapter 11

Regina sipped her fresh cup of coffee while thinking about Lassiter. When he had touched her hand, it had sent a shock through her like a miniature bolt of lightning. And those blue eyes—compassionate at times, but she had seen them turn to cold steel when he was angered or annoyed.

Never had she felt so alone as she did in the greasy little cafe. After she had come all this way to see Rodney, he had been so callous as to send her a brutal note telling of his change in affections. Turning her down, a Philadelphia Balmoral, for a woman of the streets. *My-God!*

What she would give if there were only a Denver-bound stage within the hour. She would be on it and gone. By now, Ellen was probably betrothed. Her young man had been entranced by her beauty. Regina would attend the wedding, then see what life held for her. Ellen would have made friends by now and it was no secret that there were many eligible bachelors in Denver and a definite shortage of attractive females, which had been pointed out to her by a smiling Mr. Despars. Even though he had been a great friend of Rodney's grandmother, he had suggested she stay in Denver and let Rodney flounder by himself on his late father's cattle ranch.

Ruby pulled off her apron and said, "Dearie, I've got

an errand to run. If anybody comes in, tell 'em I'll be back in a jiffy." Ruby hurried out the back. A door slammed.

Regina was thinking about Rodney. At times, when he wasn't petulant, he could be sweet. She was well aware that his bad traits were mainly due to his late Aunt Margaret, who had so mismanaged her affairs due to her secret imbibing. But Rodney had defended her even when she had squandered most of her inheritance from Rodney's late mother's side of the family. She had browbeaten poor Rodney something dreadful. And now he had turned to jelly at the first pair of flashing eyes encountered in the West.

Ruby returned, out of breath and looking anxious. Rolls of fat under the gray dress moved at each step. She put on her apron and asked Regina if anyone had been in. Regina shook her head.

When Regina picked up her room key as if to leave, Ruby gave her a strained smile. "Hold still, dearie. You deserve a big piece of my apple cake for watchin' the place." She came hurrying over with a large slab of cake. "Folks won't be comin' in much now till supper time, so you just sit as long as you want."

"But after the ham and eggs, I just don't know about the cake." Regina eyed it dubiously.

"Eat. It'll give you muscle to fight off the dudes out here." Ruby's laughter was hollow.

Ruby retreated behind the counter, saw Regina pick up a fork and cut into the cake and breathed a sigh of relief. She hurried out the rear door and looked up and down the alley. She had given one of the boys lagging pennies behind the Perkins Store a half-dollar to fetch Rex Manly and to tell him it was important. She named three places where he might be found: his office, the Saber or at Doc Straffer's for afternoon poker.

She refilled Regina's coffee cup. The cake was gone,

only a few crumbs on the plate. The poor gal was hungry, no doubt about that. Ruby cut her a second piece of the cake, which Regina politely refused.

"Ruby," a man whispered from the kitchen.

"'Scuse me, dearie. It's likely the fella who brings me vegetables from his truck garden."

In the kitchen, Rex Manly waited, a look of irritation on his handsome face. Often he paid Ruby for information picked up from customers. That day, on a hunch, she had stood behind the thin partition with one ear cocked.

"What's so damned important?" he whispered.

Ruby put a finger to her lips, then drew him over to the alley door where she told him about Lassiter and the girl and the things that had been said.

When she finished, Manly gave her a broad smile. "Ruby, you're a genius," he said in a low voice. After telling her quickly what he intended to do, he hurried out the alley door.

Regina was just picking up her reticule, preparing to leave when a smiling, well-dressed man entered. He was probably in his early thirties. "Hello, Ruby," he sang out. His lively hazel eyes saw Regina at the table. "And I'll just bet anything that you're the Miss Balmoral we've all been expecting."

"Well, yes . . ."

"This here's Rex Manly," Ruby gushed. "A lawyer. A mighty important man in these parts."

"How do you do, Mr. Manly," she said demurely as she straightened her bonnet.

After several minutes of lively conversation, Regina went for a walk with him. He showed her the town, which was still a dumpy little place in her eyes, but he did bring up some interesting history. There was a building pockmarked with bullet holes from a time when Indian raiders swept through to try and dislodge the white man from their lands. He told her of the days when buffalo were so thick on the flatlands they became a great moving shadow, seemingly to infinity. His way of telling stories made them sound fascinating.

"In the morning I'll take you out to see Rodney Rucklor," he said as they were walking toward the hotel. "That'll bring a smile to that lovely face."

"I'm not so sure Rodney wants to see me."

Manly's brows arched as he halted on the walk and stared at her in surprise. "Why in the world would you say such a thing?"

"That man Lassiter . . . he painted a rather bleak picture. . . ."

"I wouldn't put stock in what a man like Lassiter says."

"Why shouldn't I?"

"In the first place, he lives by his wits. He's a known gunman, suspected of numerous crimes."

"Are you serious?"

"My dear, his reputation is as black as the inside of a coal scuttle. Just what did that man tell you, anyway?" Manly's soothing voice was most welcome after all the tensions she had experienced: the horrible trip from Denver, then Rodney's cruel note. She told Manly what Lassiter had said about the girl from Simosa's.

"Her kind are not allowed in Villa Rosa. We have children here and decent, God-fearing families. They have to stay out at Simosa's."

"Lassiter said Blanche nursed Rodney when he was wounded. And . . . and he's fallen in love with her, so Lassiter claims."

"Lassiter had no business saying a thing like that." Manly shook his head in disbelief.

"You don't think it's true?"

"Of course not."

"But Rodney wrote a note . . . brutally frank, I might add."

"Undoubtedly a forgery."

"I . . . I never thought of that. Although the hand-writing did seem strange, as I think back on it."

"I have an idea." They were walking again. "Ruby is my cousin, and a generous soul indeed. She'll cook us a fine supper out at my place and—"

"I'm afraid that's out of the question."

"I have to go out of town on business tonight and she'd stay there with you. A fine young lady like you certainly doesn't want to spend the night in a moldy room at that decrepit Regency House."

Although she kept shaking her head no, his persua-siveness finally won the point. Ruby had a gray-bearded man take over the running of her cafe and followed them out of town in a spring wagon. Regina and Manly rode in a buggy with yellow wheels, a fine black stallion in the shafts. Sitting close to him, she was aware of the odors of bay rum and talc on his cheeks.

It would be nice to sleep in a decent bed after nights in a jolting stagecoach. And the promised fine supper wouldn't be so bad either. She was, for the first time since her arrival, in a lighthearted mood. But then as the buggy whirred over the smooth road, she pushed aside the sound of Manly's voice and thought about Lassiter. Remembering his strong, dark face, the in-tense blue eyes, the warm smile. It was a shame that exteriors were so misleading.

". . . and definitely Lassiter is a complete scoundrel," Manly was saying.

Strangely enough, she found herself almost spring-ing to Lassiter's defense. But if what Rex Manly said was true, then Lassiter had lied, and could very well be the despicable person Manly claimed he was.

They began to climb along a curving drive through thick stands of elm and spruce. At last, a two-story house came into view. "I built it for my bride, but unfortunately . . ." He sighed deeply.

"Did something happen to her?"

"She was killed by a mean horse that she was warned not to ride."

"Oh, how awful."

"Well, here we are." He hopped out and tied the reins to the diminutive cast-iron figure of a slim boy.

He helped her from the buggy, then she stood looking up at the house. Rather crudely built, she thought, of heavy planks that evidently had never felt a drop of paint.

Ruby was already waddling up the three front steps and unlocking the heavy door. On one side of the house a wide veranda gave a good view of the town a mile or so away.

The house was rather frightening, she found, with oversized furniture that reminded her of sketches she had seen of pieces from Spain and Mexico. There was a fireplace of matched stones and leather sofas and several deep chairs. Although it was early afternoon, the house seemed rather dreary—almost overwhelming. Regina hugged herself and suddenly wished she hadn't accepted his invitation.

Another disturbing factor was Ruby, who seemed nervous and wore a tense smile whenever she came into the parlor.

"Now that I've seen your very nice house, Mr. Manly, I think I'd like to return to town."

He chuckled. "A long walk, my dear."

"I'm not afraid to walk."

"You're jesting, of course." He took her by an arm and sat her down on one of the sofas. "You're to wait right in this house until I bring your young man out from the ranch."

"He could see me at the hotel."

Manly stood in front of her, looking down like a schoolmaster at a stubborn pupil. "I'm afraid I must speak bluntly. That man Lassiter, whom you met briefly, is in with a gang who are trying to steal young Rodney Rucklor's inheritance."

"Is that the truth?"

"Absolutely. You must trust me. Now, I'm going to ask you to write Rodney a note, just to let him know you're alive and well. And waiting for him. Two or three lines will suffice." Turning his head, he shouted, "Ruby, we need pen, inkwell and paper."

A smiling Manly placed a writing board on Regina's lap before she could protest. Ruby, with a hideous grimace that was supposed to be a smile, brought the requested items.

When Ruby waddled from the room, Manly stood with his hands clasped behind his back. "I'll dictate what you should write," he said, his eyes on the ceiling of burnished wood. "Dear Rodney," he dictated, "I hope you will come for me soon. Love. Then sign your name."

"Why should I write when you're going to fetch him? Or so you said."

"Because Lassiter has planted lies in his head. I feel he should know that you want him desperately. That's a good word. End the note by saying, 'I need you desperately.'"

Regina wrote mechanically, signed her name, then sat looking at what she had written. It was just crossing her mind to tear it up, when Manly whipped it off the board, waved it in the air a few times to dry the ink, then folded and placed it into his coat pocket.

Something in his hazel eyes was suddenly frightening. She leaped to her feet, unthinking in her panic. The writing board and inkwell went flying onto a strip of green carpet as she dashed for the front door. But Manly caught her easily. An arm slung around her waist and pulled her against him with such force it jarred the breath from her body.

"Let me go, if you please!" she cried. *"Ruby!"*

But Ruby failed to appear.

Desperately, Regina tried to free herself of his embrace, but his fingers were locked at her back. Her heart pounded in her chest like a small panicked animal.

"You are quite beautiful." His voice changed and she recognized it. The masculine tone was familiar from her young girlhood; memories of a male voice heated with passion.

"I hadn't really noticed you all that much in town," Manly continued in a husky voice, "in the press of business."

"Whatever might be your business is beginning to cause me concern, Mr. Manly!" Again she tried to free herself, but he was too strong. Her eyes darted frantically.

"Stop squirming and listen to me." Manly spoke through clenched teeth. "Rodney Rucklor will never make it in the West. He's a weak kid and doesn't belong here. You're lucky to be rid of him."

She drew back her head as far as she could and stared into his eyes. The deceit and treachery she read there turned her stomach hollow. Why had she been such a fool as to come out here with him?

"Ruby!" she screamed again, but there was still no sign of her.

Manly said, "Listen to me carefully. I have money. Soon I'll have even more. I can show you a good life here, Regina."

She decided that in her panic, losing her temper and shouting would avail her nothing. So she decided to be clever until some way could be found to extricate herself from this horrible quagmire.

"But I hardly know you, Mr. Manly."

"I want you to put Rodney Rucklor from your mind."

"And then what do I do?"

"Stay here with me. I can give you a good life."

"You mean . . . marriage?"

"I've already got a wife."

"I thought you said she was dead."

"That was another one."

He lies as easily as pouring water into a glass, she thought. When she licked her dry lips, he seemed fascinated by the tip of her tongue.

"Marriage could come later," he said. "I'll get that woman to give me a divorce." He tightened his hold on her. Suddenly the talc and bay rum smell of him was revolting. Her legs felt weak.

"You're hurting my back. Turn me loose and let me think about it."

After studying her a moment, he unlaced his fingers and dropped his arms. She stepped back, thankful to get away from him. She glanced at the front door. Then, hoping to distract him, she said, "I'm so sorry I spilled ink on your rug." She looked toward it.

He looked around, gesturing to indicate it was unimportant. But his eyes swung back to her much too quickly, before she could move. He was saying, "I'm about to pull off the biggest coup of my life. And when it's done I'll want a beautiful woman at my side."

"And you believe I'm that woman?" She tilted her head, forcing what she hoped was a provocative smile. Her heart pounded so that she was sure he could hear it.

And the smile wavered as her lips started to tremble. But she forced them tightly together.

"I didn't think about it at first," he admitted. "But the more I'm around you . . ." He broke off hoarsely, his eyes taking on that strange glint again as they traced over her curves revealed by her traveling dress with the tight bodice.

She edged toward the door and halted. "Could I please have a glass of water?"

"Certainly. I'll have Ruby . . ." He smiled. "No, I'll pump one up for you myself. Then we'll have sherry. Go sit down, my dear." He gestured at the sofa, turned his back and started out a door that she assumed led to the kitchen.

The moment he was out of the room, she bounded to the door, flung it open and began a wild run down the steps to the buggy. But as her fingers tore frantically at the tied reins, the horse sidestepping, snorting, Manly yelled at her from the doorway.

Dear God, there wasn't time to free the horse. She fled down the curving driveway, hoping to lose herself in the trees and then somehow make her way to town. Above the pounding of her heart she could hear his footsteps, his labored breathing as he sped after her.

"Hold it!" he yelled, but she kept going.

Her skirts were lifted for the wild run. Silent prayers that her flying feet would not inadvertently become tangled with them ran through her head.

During the pounding run, his groping fingers touched the nape of her neck. She cringed as he extended his reach. He snatched at her hair, bringing her to a halt. Combs popped from her hair and fell to the driveway. Her bonnet slipped off and her hair tumbled loosely about her face. A kick at his shins brought an oath, but loosened the hold on her hair. She whirled and started to run. But he got a hand hooked at the back of her dress. There was a sound of ripping cloth.

Again he crushed her in an embrace. His chest, from the labored breathing, heaved against her breasts. Managing to free a hand, she tore her nails across his cheek. Bright rivulets of blood poured from the ripped flesh. He let out a yelp of pain, then slapped her viciously.

Lights danced in her head. The next thing she knew he had slung her over a hip, both her wrists gripped in his right hand. His left arm hooked her to his body. Her feet dangled and the long black hair became a screen before her eyes.

Back at the house, he yelled at Ruby to find some rope. And when Ruby hurried, panting, into the room with a length of it, he quickly bound Regina's wrists. Then he roped her ankles and left her gasping on the sofa while he wiped his perspiring face on a handkerchief. He glared at her. The torn dress, parted midway down the back, fell over her bare shoulders like the wings of a weary bird.

"You bitch!" he screamed at her as he pressed the handkerchief to his bleeding cheek. "You were going to have it easy here. But *now!*" His voice was savage. "Now you're going where it's tough. Watch her, Ruby. And I mean *watch* her! I'll be back soon."

Sounds of the buggy being driven at a fast pace down the driveway reached the house. "I didn't know it was gonna be like this," Ruby said, her plump face wreathed in worry.

"Where is he going, Ruby?" Regina asked tensely.

"I reckon to get the boys. They ain't far."

Regina licked her lips. "Get a knife and cut these ropes."

"I'd be scared to do that." Ruby told her to bend over, then pinned up the torn dress. "That'll hold, for now." Ruby stood looking down at Regina and saw the large tears begin to slide down her cheeks. "He had everything goin' fine for him. But he's like all men, I reckon. Get 'em around a sweet-smellin' female like you, and their brains go into their britches. An' all their plans blow like dust in a high wind."

Regina squeezed her eyes shut to hold back the welled-up tears. What a horrible nightmare this place was turning out to be.

Again she pleaded with Ruby to free her, but the woman kept shaking her head so hard that her jowls trembled.

Manly returned with some men. She could see them together in the entry hall. There was a redhead she heard referred to as Dolan. And a larger man was Lake something or other. The lank man with the nasty smile was Tex. She didn't catch the names of the other three. But they were all tough-looking men.

"We've got to get an early start in the morning," Manly was telling them. "Ruby said she overheard Lassiter say that he's going to move that herd we've had penned up in Devil's Canyon. While he's gone it'll give us a chance to finish the rest of our business at Fork Creek."

"How do you know Rucklor won't go with him?" Dolan asked.

"Lassiter said he won't. Likely he's still suffering from that bullet you boys pumped into him."

Overhearing all this made Regina feel more miserable than frightened—at least for the moment. Oh, Lassiter, she said to herself, why did I doubt you?

Ending their discussion, the men entered the parlor, Manly with a black scowl on his face. The eyes of the others were drawn to the sight of Regina rigid on the sofa, her wrists bound in front, ankles roped. They exchanged glances and Dolan smiled and rubbed his hands together.

Regina felt nauseated as an ugly word skipped coldly through her mind. Rape!

But Manly caught their looks from a corner of his eye and said, "She's not to be touched. I'll deal with her later."

His eyes were ugly as he fingered the four lacerations on his cheek. Abruptly he jerked Regina to her feet. Her bare flesh and camisole showed through gaps in the torn dress that Ruby had pinned up. A clock in a corner of the room began to strike the hour.

"Where're you takin' her?" Tex Ander wanted to know.

"Buffaloville."

"Out there?" Lake Burne looked at Manly in surprise.

"Where she'll be safe till negotiations are concluded. After we leave her, we'll get within sight of the ranch building. When we see Lassiter leave, then we'll move in. Ruby, you better bring along some food."

Regina's ankles were freed, but not her wrists. She was forced into a spring wagon. Ruby did the driving. Manly was mounted as were the other men. They rode in silence through some forested hills and onto miles of prairie that stretched like a green carpet in the sunlight.

After what seemed like hours in the jolting wagon, they reached a long, narrow building that appeared to be deserted. Tall weeds reached the windowsills. There were the remains of a corral and some sheds.

Holding her by an arm, none too gently, Manly walked her into the building. Everywhere was thick dust and cobwebs that seemed to cover bunks and chairs and a table. Windows were mere slits that let in very little sunlight. She was shoved into a chair.

"In the buffalo days, hunters used this place," Manly said, glaring down at her. "You better pray that none of them are still hunting and remember this place. You'll wish you were safe in my arms, I can tell you that."

She had an intense urge to spit in his face, but her mouth was too dry.

He handed Ruby a shotgun. "I don't want her touched," he warned the woman. Then he looked significantly at Dolan and Ander, who were to be left behind as guards. "You heard what I just said?"

"You can trust us, Rex," Dolan drawled.

"Manly is the name," the lawyer snapped. "You make a wrong move and you'll earn a face full of buckshot. Come on, Lake, let's move out."

Through one of the narrow, dusty windows, Regina saw Manly and Burne and the three other men ride away.

Hours dragged. Ruby fired up a stove and cooked the meat and potatoes she had brought along. She had dusted the table and chairs and lighted a lamp with a cracked chimney. The two guards carried their food outside.

"I can't very well eat with my wrists tied like this," Regina complained to Ruby and waited hopefully. But Ruby didn't even reply. Fortunately, she had little appetite.

She managed a little sleep on one of the sagging bunks. Whenever she opened her eyes, Ruby was still awake, sitting at the table with a shotgun across her ample lap.

Regina despaired of ever getting free. Or even staying

alive. But she had a feeling Manly would see that she lived—at least temporarily. Never would she forget the look in his eyes when she had fought him back at the house. The look said that she was his property, to do with as he liked . . .

Chapter 12

It was early evening by the time Lassiter got back to Fork Creek. Lamplight shone in the bunkhouse windows, but the big house was dark and the front door locked. He banged on the door, shouting, "Rod, open up!"

Finally, Blanche opened it.

"What're you and Rod doing? Hiding in the dark?" Lassiter demanded.

She walked into the parlor, saying, "He was taking a nap." She lit a lamp. "Rod can't button his shirt for himself. So I have to help him. It's why I took so long answering the door."

Lassiter shook his head, wondering about the lies people tell.

Blanche went into the kitchen, her hips swinging provocatively in the lamplight. A leftover from Simosa's, was the sour thought running through his mind.

Rod came bounding into the parlor where Lassiter was sitting, his feet on a small table. "You yelled loud enough to wake the dead," Rucklor said with a wavering smile. "I . . . I was napping."

Lassiter stared up at the young face, seeing the faint flush of embarrassment. "Regina arrived," he said bluntly.

His face seemed to collapse. "She did?"

"Don't look so surprised. After all, you sent for her."

"I . . . I know. I know. Did you tell her? Did you give her my note?"

"She knows everything."

He stiffened. "Sometimes I think you dislike me intensely."

"There are times when I come close to it," Lassiter admitted.

"Can I trust you to tell me everything about Regina?"

"Why in the hell can't you trust me?" Lassiter was in a testy mood after the long round trip to town and the verbal battle with Regina.

"Well, I just don't know. You tried your best to turn me against Blanche."

"I was only trying to get you to face facts, for Chris' sakes."

"I really didn't expect you to come back here. I thought you might just keep on going."

"I halfway had a mind to. But then I saw Regina."

Rucklor slumped to the far end of the sofa where Lassiter was slouched. He stared at the big stone fireplace with its mounds of ashes from last winter's fires—fires that had warmed the cold hands of the elder Rucklor. It was all too grim a reminder of the impermanence of life.

Lassiter got up, poured himself a drink and sat down again. He hadn't offered one to Rod. Rod could get his own, although he was against whiskey and most sins, Lassiter supposed, except those performed with Blanche. The idea made him laugh, which made Rod twist around on the sofa to look at him.

"What in the world is so amusing?"

"It's the trap you've baited for yourself."

"Is . . . is Regina resigned to going back to Philadelphia?"

"No."

Flickering light from the lamp on a small table revealed beads of perspiration dotting the high forehead of the Fork Creek heir. "What in the world is she going to *do?*"

"I'm trying to talk her into staying. And fighting for you."

"I wish you'd have kept out of it, Lassiter."

"Who begged me to meet her stage? Who the hell gave me a son-of-a-bitching note to hand to that poor girl? The kind of a note the axman gives to the gal who's got her neck on the block. 'Sorry, but I've got to take off your head.' "

"You make me sound like a . . . a despot." He put his good hand to his eyes. "What in the world will I do if she decides to stay?"

"Stiffen your backbone, for one thing. Stop feeling sorry for yourself. You're the one that made this mess, you know."

"Oh, my God, how I know." Rucklor stared at the faded Indian rug that covered half the parlor floor.

Lassiter took a long drink from his glass. The whiskey slid warmly down his throat and spread a minor fire as it pooled in his stomach. "The way things have turned out, you want to know how I feel about it all?"

"Tell me, Lassiter."

"Take Regina to Denver. She won't go back to Philadelphia. Once you get to Denver, put Fork Creek up for sale. Get what you can out of it. And consider yourself lucky."

"But this is my home, my ranch. Blanche says—"

"The hell with what Blanche says. You're not cut out to be a cattleman."

"And my father was, I suppose you're thinking."

"Now you're reading minds," Lassiter said with a hard grin.

Rucklor's lips trembled. "Well, I'm as good a man as he ever was! I'll show you!"

"Calm down, Rod, and face up to something. Regina's not the type to put up with life on a lonely ranch. And neither are you."

"Blanche was raised on a ranch, she's used to it."

"If you've got an ounce of brains, you'll forget Blanche. Give her a few dollars and send her on her way."

Blanche, who evidently had been listening at the parlor door, came blazing into the room. "I'll go on my way, if that's what Rod wants!" she screamed at Lassiter. "But he doesn't have to give me one dollar, let alone a few!"

Then, flinging an arm across her eyes, she ran to the back part of the house, her heels clicking against the plank floor. A door slammed.

"She's improving," Lassiter said, and finished his drink.

"Improving in what way?" Rucklor demanded suspiciously.

"As an actress."

"You're implying that she only pretends her feelings for me. She loves me. She told me. And I . . ." Rucklor clenched his fists, an agonized look in his gray eyes. "I . . . I believe I'm really in love with her."

Lassiter got up and placed a hand on his shoulder. "My first was when I was fourteen. She was twenty. I was crazy in love with her. It happens to most of us, Rod. You'll get over it and make a fine life for yourself in Denver with Regina."

"You were just a kid. And I'm twenty-three years old!"

"I got an earlier start than you did, is all," Lassiter said dryly. "I'll eat at the cook shack. I want to see the boys, anyway. I'm leaving early. Got to move those cows out of Devil's Canyon. If they're still there, that is."

"Let's hope they are."

"We should have done it before this. Lord knows what shape those poor critters are in by now."

Later that evening, Blanche faced Lassiter in the Fork Creek yard. It was after supper. She wore a coat because a stiff breeze had come up. Loose ends of blond hair blew across her face. Directly overhead, the Big Dipper gleamed like diamonds strewn on black velvet.

"I could steal a horse," she said tensely, "but I'm not a thief. So I'm asking you to loan me one. I'll see that you get it back."

Lassiter looked at her shadowed face, with its hollows, and the shining eyes and parted lips as she waited expectantly. "Where are you going?" he asked. "Back to Simosa's?"

Tears welled up in her eyes. "What else can I do? I've got to eat and have a roof over my head. And I'm not bright enough to teach school."

"You are bright, Blanche." He put a hand on her shoulder, feeling its softness. "You're too smart to go back to Simosa's. Will you take a hundred dollars?" Then, thinking of all she had done for Rucklor, he said, "No, make it two hundred."

She wiped her eyes and thought about his offer for a few moments. Then she said, "All right, I'll take it. Only because I've earned it." Her voice shook. "Damn it, I've *earned* it!"

He took her to his quarters, which had formerly belonged to Len Crenshaw. She followed him, a little reluctantly, as if not quite sure of his intentions. After lighting a lamp, he pulled his money sack from under the mattress. He counted out ten double eagles and pressed them into her hands.

"I can't help it if you're not good for Rod," he said quietly and closed her fingers over the gold coins. "It sure isn't your fault."

Because the sack was now considerably lighter, he stuffed it into a hip pocket.

Blanche said, "I saw a chance that day to get away from John Simosa. So I took it. I suppose I shouldn't have."

"With the two hundred dollars you won't even have to think about going back there. You can go and stay with your sister in Arizona and help take care of her kids."

"I never had a sister. I just made that up."

"You're pretty good, Blanche. You had me believing it. But one thing, you did a lot for Rod. His wound and . . ." He didn't finish it, but she knew what he meant.

"All I've done is destroy what he had with his Regina." Her voice broke. "He thinks he's in love with me."

"So that means you don't love him. And that's good. Regina's broken heart is about all we can take around here." An encouraging smile froze when he saw the stricken look on her pretty face.

"But I do love him. Very much . . ." Then she fled out into the darkness. He could hear the sounds of her running footsteps all the way to the house.

In the morning, Blanche sent word by Rucklor inviting Lassiter to eat breakfast with them up at the house. Lassiter supposed it was Blanche's way of showing her appreciation for the money and the loan of the horse.

She smiled wanly inside the house. Her eyes were red as if she'd been crying. This morning Rucklor didn't wear his arm in a sling, but it was still bandaged. Lassiter congratulated him on the progress.

"I couldn't sleep last night," Rucklor said, looking miserable. "Thinking of poor Regina in that horrible little hotel."

Lassiter darted a glance at Blanche across the table, but her eyes were on her plate. This morning she wore her riding clothes. He wondered if she'd told Rucklor that she was going away. Probably, because Rucklor seemed upset.

"A cheap hotel is no place for a lady," Rucklor said as he cut into a thick slice of bacon.

Blanche jumped up from the table, muttered something about a headache and left the room.

"I've upset her, talking about Regina," Rod said, sounding despondent. "Blanche is going to leave. She told me."

"Maybe it's all for the best," Lassiter said carefully. Lassiter wondered if he could put a little more heft in his money sack by getting Rucklor to give him back the two hundred dollars out of the five thousand taken from Manly. He was about qarc. Blanche will probably be gone by then."

"I don't want her gone, dammit. You talk to her, Lassiter," he pleaded. "You're more used to women than I am. You can make her stay."

"Talk about changeable."

"What do you mean by that?"

"Here you were in love with Regina. And all of a sudden . . ."

"I don't really know if I was ever in love with her,"

Rod interrupted. "But I am in love with Blanche. This I know. Please talk to her, Lassiter."

"Go and see Regina. For Chris' sakes, you owe the girl that much."

"But I'm in love with Blanche!"

"She's no good for you."

The front door opened and Blanche entered the house, walked stiffly past the kitchen where they were eating, and on to one of the bedrooms.

Rucklor staggered back to his own room and flung himself down on the bed and stared at the ceiling. Lassiter followed him and sat on a cedar chest that had belonged to Ham Rucklor.

"Listen to me, Rod . . ."

"I asked you to talk to her and you obviously refuse."

Lassiter took a deep breath and stared across the room at a daguerreotype of Ham Rucklor on top of a bureau. It showed Ham with a rifle and the body of the big mountain lion whose head was one of those decorating the wall of the library. Ham, what a goddamn mess you made of everything, he said silently.

He guessed it was a time to keep his mouth shut. While he was away, moving cattle out of Devil's Canyon, Rucklor could have one last time with Blanche. Then she would be gone and Regina would come into his life once again.

It's all for the best, he wanted to tell Rucklor, who was stretched out on the bed, looking pale, with a forearm across his eyes.

"I'll leave a couple of the boys behind, just in case," Lassiter said. "I'll see you when I get back."

Rucklor failed to respond.

Blanche was cleaning up in the kitchen. "You being

here has really stirred up the old hornet's nest," Lassiter said to her back.

She turned and looked at him. No longer did she seem depressed. Apparently she had bathed her eyes. They were clear blue, her gaze direct. "I did some good around here," she said firmly.

"The wound. Yes, you did. I've told you that."

"He really could have lost that arm. It happens more often than not. So my being here wasn't a complete waste. I'll send Fred back with your horse."

"Fred?"

"The swamper at Simosa's."

He gave a sigh of exasperation, then got hold of himself. He said gently, "Don't go back there. Take the two hundred dollars I gave you—"

"You'll find it in your quarters. In a drawer under a spare shirt."

"But it was a gift. Why in hell didn't you keep it?"

"I got to thinking it over. I shouldn't take money from someone who thinks the worst of me, as you apparently do."

"Blanche, I . . ." He didn't know what to say. What Blanche had said about nursing Rucklor was all too true. All those days she had given him her undivided attention and it was just possible that without it he might have lost his arm.

"I want you to take the money."

She turned her back and stood staring out the window.

He could see through the window that what was left of the crew was in the yard, waiting for him.

"All I can do at this point is to wish you luck, Blanche. I've got cattle to move."

She didn't look around.

While he had been in town meeting Regina, two

more men had quit on him. That whittled the crew down to six. He left Barnes and Quimby behind in case there was trouble, and rode out with the four that remained.

A long, hot ride lay ahead of them. Two of the men with him had helped Lake Burne move the herd into Devil's Canyon. They said that a brush fence had been thrown across the narrow end of the canyon. The other end was steep and littered with too much shale for cattle to make a safe exit. But no doubt many of them would try and end up with broken legs. If still alive, they would have to be shot.

He only hoped that the cows hadn't been stolen. If they had been, he'd have to hire more men and track down the rustlers. With all the complications, including Blanche and Regina, and a stubborn Rod Rucklor, the future of the Fork Creek Cattle Company seemed none too bright.

To make matters worse, he sensed that Rucklor was getting apprehensive about what might lie ahead. The other day when Lassiter had brought home the money from Manly, he mentioned that they were in for the fight of their lives.

"Isn't there a town marshal to whom we can appeal?" Rucklor asked.

Lassiter had shaken his head. "No town marshal. And the sheriff is over eighty miles away. The nearest deputy is forty or more."

"Why is this part of the country so . . . so *uncivilized*?"

"It's paradise compared to what it was when your pa came here. There were killings by the dozen. And the place was overrun with buffalo hunters. Nobody tougher than them."

"I almost wish I'd stayed in Philadelphia."

"Amen," Lassiter felt like saying but kept his mouth shut.

Lassiter set a leisurely pace; they had all day to make the round trip to Devil's Canyon. He hoped that when he got back at least one part of the problem would be solved. That Blanche would be gone.

Chapter 13

Hearing voices in the yard, Rod Rucklor assumed that for one reason or another, Lassiter and the slim crew had returned. When he peered out the window, what he saw caused his mouth to drop open.

A slim, angry-looking man was pointing a gun at Barnes and Quimby, who stood with their hands in the air. As Rucklor stared, his breath coming short, he saw another man relieve the Fork Creek hands of their guns.

"Get out!" the angry-looking man shouted. "Don't come back!"

They seemed eager to comply, vaulted into their saddles and spurred south in the general direction of Villa Rosa.

The sight of the men down in the yard weakened Rucklor's knees and he lurched against Blanche, who had come to stand at his side. They might be the men who had shot him and tried to murder him.

The only one he recognized was Lake Burne, the big segundo, who had been here the day of his arrival.

"Who are the others?" he asked Blanche hoarsely.

"Rex Manly's one of them. The lawyer. The other three . . . I think they used to work here."

"Go get my gun," he whispered. "I'll keep an eye on them."

"No, Rod." Blanche was terrified. "You know nothing of guns. You'll just get yourself killed."

"I've got to protect you."

She looked at him in surprise.

"I love you, Blanche," he said fervently. "If I never really knew it before, I do now in this moment of danger."

Her face crumpled and she impulsively squeezed his arm. They had been arguing ever since Lassiter left over whether she was going to leave or stay. Rucklor demanded that she stay. But she knew she shouldn't.

"Go get it, Blanche. Please. I need the gun."

Finally she agreed.

Through the window, Rucklor could see Rex Manly, dapper in a light blue shirt, corduroy breeches and stylish boots, as he approached the porch steps. The other four men stayed below.

Manly was knocking on the door when Blanche hurried up to press a small revolver into Rucklor's hand.

"Just be careful," she whispered.

"Now, leave me, Blanche. Stay in another room. I don't want him to see you."

When he was alone, he shoved the pistol into his waistband, then opened the door to Manly's persistent knocking. "Yes?" Rucklor said, trying to make his voice cold and hoping his nervousness didn't show to the well-dressed lawyer with the piercing hazel eyes.

Manly looked past him and into the house. "Are you alone?"

"Very much so."

Manly studied him a moment, then removed a folded paper from his pocket. With a flourish, he unfolded it so Rucklor could read the few lines.

As he scanned it, Rucklor's face lost color. When he

reached out for it, Manly shook his head and returned the paper to his pocket.

"You can see that it was written by Regina Balmoral. And it has her signature."

Rucklor frowned. "What does it mean?"

"It means that she's in good hands . . . for the present."

"I . . . I don't understand." Rucklor's heart was pumping furiously.

"I'm making you an offer of five thousand dollars for this ranch—"

"Are you insane?" Rucklor interrupted indignantly.

"Not at all." Manly looked him in the eye. "I could take the ranch by other means, which you wouldn't like. After all, I am mentioned in your father's will as his beneficiary in case you fail to survive."

"A foul trick my father played on me."

"No doubt. But beside the point at present."

Manly's men were bunched at the foot of the veranda steps, intent on Rod Rucklor in the doorway and Manly on the wide porch.

"I have with me a bank draft for five thousand dollars, which I will turn over to you once you sign a paper giving up all claim to the Fork Creek Cattle Company. Now, come along, if you will. We have quite a ride ahead of us."

"What in the world does Regina have to do with all this?" Rucklor asked in a strained voice. "That note you say she wrote—"

"You accept my proposition," Manly cut in, "and the young lady is free to leave with you."

"And if I refuse?" Rucklor asked tentatively.

"It would be an unfortunate decision. Particularly for the young lady."

"Unfortunate in what way?" Rucklor's voice had a reedy sound from mounting pressure.

"She won't be free to go."

Rucklor's gray eyes suddenly widened. "You've kidnapped her!"

"I like the word 'detained' better than 'kidnapped.' Which is true for the present. But if you decide to turn your back on me, then I'm afraid I can no longer be responsible for her safety."

"You're threatening her. And me!"

"Only stating a fact."

Rucklor's shoulders slumped. Why wasn't Lassiter here to advise him? Why had he gone to move some damned cattle? Of all the unimportant things to do at such a vital time as this, with poor Regina obviously in danger. Blame for her predicament lay heavily on his shoulders. After all, he was the one who had sent for her in a burst of enthusiasm one day in Denver, rushing like an exuberant fool to the telegraph office.

"May I have time to think your proposition over?" he asked hopefully.

"No, I need an answer now," Manly snapped and touched four deep scratches on his left check.

"There's a law against kidnapping."

"You're telling *me* about the law?" Manly's brows raised in mock surprise. "Me, a member of the legal profession."

"A disgrace to it."

"A matter of viewpoint," he said with a hard smile. "Now, come along. . . ."

"Why . . . why do you need *this* ranch?"

"I intend it to be a nucleus in my plans for expansion." He put his hazel eyes on a distraught Rucklor. "It's too damn bad you didn't stay east and accept my generous offer of six thousand dollars. By rejecting it and coming out West, you've put yourself to considerable expense and lowered my price by a thousand dollars. Not only that, but endangered the well-being of your betrothed, Miss Regina."

"It's a dastardly thing you've done, sir," Rucklor said stiffly.

"I'm losing patience with you, Rucklor."

Rucklor made a wild grab for the gun in his waistband, but Manly was quicker. He yanked it free and stepped back with it. His eyes were vicious. "If you refuse my offer, there's another way of doing this."

Rucklor found himself staring into the muzzle of his own gun. "I suppose you mean to kill me."

"I'd automatically inherit this ranch. And dead men tell no tales. Nor dead girls."

"How . . . how cold-blooded you are."

"No doubt. Now, come along with me. Once Regina's safely in your arms, you sign the quit-claim deed. You collect the bank draft. And both of you can be on the stage that comes through town tomorrow afternoon. Then this whole series of events will be but a memory."

"A bitter one."

"We'll be at Buffaloville before you know it. And then you'll be on your way east with your Regina."

Rucklor got his hat from the rack by the door and went out, his steps dragging. His arm was hurting. It took a few minutes while a horse was saddled for him, then they were riding out. He hugged his bad arm and looked back at the big house he could barely see through the cottonwoods. There was no sign of Blanche at any of the windows. Never had he felt more despondent.

Blanche watched from a window, and when Rod and the others were out of sight, she raced to a corral. It took three tries before she could rope out a pinto. Grabbing the first saddle at hand, she worked feverishly, praying silently that somewhere up in the vast north country she'd find Lassiter and tell him what was happening.

She had only a vague idea of the location of Devil's Canyon, but was determined to find it.

Chapter 14

Some miles from the ranch, Lassiter reined in his horse and looked behind him. They had been climbing steadily, and from this brushy, higher country he had a good view of the flatlands below. In the hazy distance he could see dark blotches that he knew were the trees in the Fork Creek ranch yard. About the only other thing he could make out was a dust cloud, faint from this distance but definitely moving toward the ranch. The dust was made by fewer than a dozen riders, but just how many he had no way of telling because of the miles. Sight of the dust cloud turned him cold. His heart was beating furiously.

Rod and Blanche were alone with only Barnes and Quimby as guards. It wasn't much protection, he conceded. His men had drifted on ahead, but when he failed to catch up, they turned their horses and trotted back.

"What's up, Lassiter?" asked Tod Ruggers nervously. He was a red-faced man with maplike splotches of small veins on his cheeks and nose.

His friend Clyde Appley reined in beside him and pointed a bony finger. "Dust!" he cried.

"Yeah," Lassiter grunted. "Boys, I figure we better go back." He never should have tried it, he well knew. But he had got to worrying about the cattle in the canyon and had decided to gamble.

"Likely it's Barnes an' Quimby ridin' around that's stirrin' up the dust," Willie Cosgrove put in.

Lassiter shook his head. "Too much dust for that," he said grimly. "My hunch is that it might be that bastard Manly."

"If it is, I don't want no part of it," Ruggers blurted.

"Me neither!" Appley cried, his Adam's apple in a scrawny neck jumping like a frog on a string.

"Manly's cozy with the sheriff," Ruggers said hoarsely, "an' we'd be hang bait sure as hell if somebody on their side gets killed."

Lassiter felt disgusted. He looked at the other two, Cosgrove, tall and thin as a post, and the squat Luke Borford. "How about you boys?" he asked in a hard voice.

They exchanged glances. "We'll stick," said Cosgrove.

"Thanks." Lassiter turned to Ruggers and Appley. At first he tried persuasion, then as anger mounted and he saw the dust cloud by now right at the ranch yard, he attacked them verbally, but neither man would budge.

"We'll just keep on headin' north," Ruggers said. "We been talkin' about it before this."

"What about your gear?"

"We can buy more. Better'n goin' back an' maybe gettin' a bullet where your front teeth used to be."

"It ain't ever gonna work out for you, Lassiter," Appley put in, a worried look on his narrow face. "I could've told you right off. Once Ham got killed . . ."

"Come on!" Lassiter shouted at the other two, and they were off, their horses at a hard run down the long and dusty slant.

The defection of Appley and Ruggers was not too surprising, but nevertheless, Lassiter was disappointed. Morale at the ranch had been disintegrating since their new boss had turned out to be a rank tenderfoot. Even so, Lassiter had tried his best to keep the men reasonably contented until he would be able to hire a full crew. But it just hadn't worked out.

Suddenly he saw a slim figure on a pinto some distance to his left, frantically waving arms and yelling to get his attention. He thought it was Blanche, but couldn't be sure. The distance was too great to hear what she was trying to shout.

Lassiter yelled at Cosgrove and Borford and the two men slowed and turned left to follow him.

With her pinto standing with head down, dripping sweat and foam, a stricken Blanche told Lassiter what had happened.

"It's Manly," she gasped, breathing hard. "He . . . he's got Rod." Tears danced in her blue eyes, and cut through the dust on her cheeks.

"He's likely heading back to town," Lassiter said thinly.

She shook her head. "No. Buffaloville."

"Buffaloville? What's that?"

"It's a big old building west of Simosa's."

As she told him the rest of what she had overheard, including the part about Regina, Lassiter suddenly remembered the place. One time when he stopped by the ranch, he and Ham Rucklor had tracked horse thieves over that way. What was Manly planning, anyhow? Lassiter wondered. Take young Rucklor into the wilds and murder him? But why go so far? Why not do it anyplace between Fork Creek and town? Unless that was where Manly was holding Regina. That had to be it.

What desolation for a lady like Regina. A brokendown old building formerly used as a hangout for buffalo hunters in the days when great herds roamed the grassy flatlands.

"I'm so worried about Rod." Blanche seemed on the verge of hysteria.

Lassiter touched her arm. "We'll find him."

Then he and his two men were spurring away, leaving Blanche with her weary horse.

At the ranch yard, Lassiter soon picked up the fresh tracks of horses and began following them south and west of the ranch. During the few minutes spent in picking up the tracks at the home place, it had crossed his mind that Cosgrove and Borford might decide to pull out as the other two had done and others before them. But when he rode on, following the tracks of Manly and company, the two riders were still with him. He gave both men grim but encouraging smiles and pressed on.

If what Blanche said was true—and he had no reason to doubt her—Rex Manly should be shot for kidnapping a defenseless girl like Regina. But as Lassiter thought about it during the fast ride, he decided a bullet would be too easy a death for the bastard. Better to have him suffer the hundred cuts, a punishment some Indians reserved for a mortal enemy who had been a despoiler of women.

There were tracks of six horses, which meant a mount for Rucklor. It was obvious to Lassiter that eventually he would have to face five men. Five against three. All he had was Cosgrove, a loose-jointed, bony man with a missing front tooth, and Borford, overweight and slow-moving. He didn't know either man too well and had no idea how they'd fare in a gunfight.

That he would soon have to put them to the test was evident.

From the spacing of the hoofprints it seemed that Manly was traveling at a leisurely pace. No doubt because of Rod Rucklor's bad arm, which would suffer from a jolting, fast ride.

From time to time Lassiter reined in to study the terrain ahead, but the country was brushy and undulating, with vision restricted to less than a mile. His eyes searched the lower edge of the dome of sky for telltale smudges of dust. But he saw nothing against the layers of boiling black clouds that were rolling in. All he needed now was rain to wash out the tracks. But he knew he could find the place known as Buffaloville. They were already some miles west of Simosa's, which had been seen in the cloud shadows in the distance.

"We'll get 'em yet," Lassiter said confidently to Cosgrove and Borford, who were riding single file through the fringe of a forest. The aroma of cedar hung heavy in the air. It was colder here in the gloom of trees. Lassiter shivered, but kept his eyes on the tracks.

"A far piece we're comin', ain't it?" Cosgrove called to him.

Lassiter stiffened. Was Cosgrove laying groundwork for an excuse to pull out? "Stick with me, boys," Lassiter urged.

"We aim to, Lassiter," Luke Borford said.

Hearing that, Lassiter relaxed. But only slightly. There were still five men to face.

After another mile, he decided to gamble and swing farther west, which would cut some distance from the main trail Manly was now following, and narrow the gap. If he could arrive ahead of Manly and have a reception party waiting for him, it might give him an edge. Anyway, it was worth the gamble.

Chapter 15

Regina lay on her right side in one of the bunks. In the strong morning light, Dolan and Ander looked even more disreputable than before. The big room seemed dustier and Ruby even fatter. She still sat in a chair, the ever-present shotgun across her lap.

Whenever Regina turned her head, she found the two men staring at her. It put goose bumps on her forearms and set her heart to pounding in a cold breast. Dolan sat with his feet on a scarred table, his hat over his eyes. The two men had come inside after their night outdoors in their blankets. Ruby had heated up the meat and beans for breakfast. But the shotgun was always either in her lap or under a plump arm as she stirred the pan of food on the stove.

Tex Ander complained, "It makes me nervous, Ruby. You with that shotgun so close to the stove. It might go off from the heat. You better set it down somewhere."

Ruby turned her plump face with the myriad lines and roseate cheeks and said, "You'd like me to set it down, wouldn't you?"

"Only thinkin' of the gal," Harve Dolan put in, lifting the hat from his eyes and smiling at Regina.

"Yeah, I know damn well you're thinkin' of her," Ruby said in her gravelly voice. "You lay a finger on her an' Manly'll have your guts."

"Canada ain't too damn far," Tex Ander said with a laugh. "An' there's always Mexico."

"He'd find you, no matter where. Maybe you don't know it, but me an' him is shirt-tail kin. My Leo, who died on me, poor man, was Manly's cousin."

"Only foolin' with you, Ruby."

After breakfast, Tex said he was going out to hitch up the team. "Ruby'll have to ride back in the wagon, anyhow," he said after giving Regina a speculative look. Regina shivered, taking the look to mean that he didn't quite know whether she was to remain alive to ride in the wagon or not. "I don't reckon there's a horse the Lord ever made that's big enough for Ruby to ride," he finished with a chuckle.

"Go ahead an' hitch up," Ruby snapped. "Things you say don't bother me none."

Soon Dolan began to emit faint snores at the table. Regina could hear Ander walking around in the yard, his boots crunching gravel. Occasionally one of the horses would snort and stomp the ground. The breakfast lay like lead in Regina's stomach.

There was only one mistake Manly had made that Regina could name, and that was to have tied her wrists in front instead of in back. He assumed, no doubt, that Ruby would always keep a close watch on her. Ruby was slumped in a chair across the table from Dolan. She was yawning and her eyelids drooping.

Carefully, so as not to make any disturbing sounds, Regina rolled over on the bunk so that her back was to both of them. Making sure they weren't watching her, she put the knot of the rope between her teeth and began to tug on it. In the early stages of her capture and last night, she had been too panicked to even try. But this morning her nerves had quieted and her mind was clear.

The rope in her mouth tasted awful, but she kept

trying to loosen the knot with her teeth. Her jaws began to ache from the strain. Always under her nose was the frayed mattress that smelled of dust and stale perspiration. To take her mind off the agonizing task she had set for herself, she allowed her eyes to wander to the front of the building where there were some broken chairs. A counter had been pulled from its anchor on the floor and lay on its side. A row of empty shelves was behind it. Everything was covered with layers of dust and cobwebs.

After what seemed like hours, a giant spider with furry legs came crawling up over the edge of the bunk. Regina's mouth opened instinctively to scream for Ruby, then she caught herself. She lay still as death as the spider slowly walked across her legs and down the far side of the bunk. She was trembling and her skin was moist under her clothing when she returned to the tedious attempt to free herself.

"What're you doin'?" came Ruby's sudden, harsh question.

Regina held her breath as she heard the woman padding across the rotted floor. Ruby threw a wide shadow as she stood above Regina.

"I'm trying to take a nap." Regina sounded cross.

Ruby stared a moment at the bound wrists, then plodded back to her chair. Its legs squealed as her weight settled once again.

After waiting a few minutes, Regina licked her dry lips, then again returned to her task. Anxiety made her heart thump in her ears like a drumbeat. Her jaws were growing tired from trying to undo the knot with her teeth. If only she could get her hands on the shotgun and run away from them in the wagon. She would be free. How glorious that would be. Then she would drive as fast as possible to a building that she had seen from a distance when they were coming out from town. She remembered a large sign across the front that she could barely make out: SIMOSA'S.

Surely someone there could help her. It would be much better than trying to find the town. At least she knew where Simosa's was located, but she might miss Villa Rosa by many miles.

The knot she was working on so desperately gave slightly. Her heart skipped a beat. Please let me be free of these ropes, she prayed. Feverishly she kept at it. After what seemed like hours, she felt the knot loosen even more, the small success spurring her on. It was almost in a frenzy that she attacked the knot, her nerves screaming, for at any moment Dolan could push back his hat and see her, or Ruby could look her way, or Tex Ander could rush back inside.

When the knot finally came apart, she breathed a sigh of thankfulness.

"What're you bobbin' your head for?" It was Ruby again. Regina froze and pressed her wrists under her body and lay with her heart thudding.

Ruby came to cast another wide shadow and peer down at her. "What're you up to, anyhow, gal?"

Regina turned her head and looked up at Ruby, a large body of flesh, the shotgun under a plump arm.

"I was crying," Regina said.

As Ruby reached down to inspect her wrists, Regina came suddenly to life. Twisting on the bunk, she seized Ruby by an arm and pulled her off balance. A grunt of surprise burst from the overweight woman. Impulsively, she put out both hands to break her fall against the bunk. The shotgun came loose from under her arm. Regina grabbed it and sprang up. The rope she had so laboriously untied with her teeth fell to the floor.

Harve Dolan came awake, pulled his feet off the table and slammed down the legs of his tipped-back chair. "What the hell!" he yelled.

At the same moment, Tex Ander burst inside, reaching for a belted gun.

A pale Regina straightened up, holding the shotgun. "Don't you move!" she screamed at Ander and Dolan.

Ruby had fallen to her knees, her weight shaking that end of the building. Dolan stood frozen in the center of the room, Ander rigid in the doorway.

Dolan was first to find his voice. "Hey, put that shotgun down. It might go off an' you'd sure mess things up." He gave a nervous smile.

"I intend to mess things up! If you come near me, I'll shoot. I swear I will!" Dark hair framed her tense face. Violet eyes held a wildness that seemed to impress both men.

Keeping the pair covered, she gestured for Ander to step away from the doorway. As she drew closer, he made a move as if to grab her. But she swung up the twin barrels of the murderous weapon so that they were at eye level.

"Chris'sake, lady, don't touch them triggers!" he screeched.

Carefully she backed out the door to the yard. From a corner of her eye, she saw that the team had been tied to the collapsed corral, as were the two saddle horses.

"Get back inside!" she yelled to the two men as they started to crowd out to the yard. "And shut the door!"

Dolan slammed the door, crying nervously, "The bitch!"

With the shotgun anchored under one arm, she untied the team, gathered in the lines and climbed to the seat, not once taking her eyes from the building. She was gambling that the wagon was safer for her. With a saddle horse she might have had difficulty mounting, what with long skirts and the awkward shotgun, and given them a chance to rush out and grab her.

Fear and anger congealed in her as she flicked the lines over the backs of the two horses. "Giddap!" she cried, remembering the command used by wagon drivers.

The wagon started to move.

"What'll we do, Harve?" she heard Ander wail. "Shoot her?"

"Hell, no. We'll go after her."

"But that goddamn shotgun . . ."

"We'll keep outa range an' trick her some way into shootin'. Then, when the gun's empty, we'll grab her."

"My poor knees," Ruby was moaning. She had come down hard and was now sitting on the floor. "Help me up." She put out a hand, which Dolan ignored.

"You was s'posed to keep an eye on her, damn it!" Dolan snarled.

"Manly'll have our heads if we don't get her back," Ander said angrily.

Regina was forced to make a wide turn because the way ahead was blocked by tree stumps, and parallel to the house were the remains of an old wagon, some barrels and crates. Just as she finished making the turn, her heart like a giant drum in her ears, Ander and Dolan loped out the door.

The shotgun roared. Buckshot lashed the front of the house. But the two men had seen her swing up the shotgun and flung themselves flat against the hard ground.

Holding the reins in one hand, the shotgun in the other, Regina had the team increasing speed.

"That was close," said Dolan shakily as he got to his knees.

Tex Ander was examining the brim of his hat, which had been perforated by the lowest edge of the circle of screaming buckshot. He got to his feet, staring at the wagon that was bounding over the flatlands, raising a great cloud of dust.

"She's got only one shell left!" Dolan yelled as he sprang for his horse.

"One's all it takes to blow off your head," Tex reminded angrily. "Another couple inches an' she'd have had my brains instead of my hat."

"Keep far enough back," Dolan shouted above the roar of their hoofbeats as they spurred after the careening wagon, "so she can't reach us with that damn Greener!"

Regina was looking back, her hair blowing. "Stay away!" she cried as she saw them gaining on her through the screen of yellow dust. But they kept on coming. "Keep back!" Hysteria laced her voice.

In the dust, Dolan saw a spark of gun flame. Whether she had discharged the weapon intentionally or the jolting of the wagon had set it off, Dolan didn't know. Buckshot screamed overhead, but none came near them.

When the tense moment was past, Dolan let out a whoop of delight. "We've got her, Tex. The damn Greener's plumb empty!"

They spurred up quickly on either side of the speeding wagon. She tried desperately to swing the butt of the shotgun at Dolan's face when he leaned toward her. But at that moment the wagon hit the edge of a buffalo wallow and began to skid. It threw her flat to the seat. In trying to keep from getting pitched out, she lost her grip on the shotgun. It made a great clatter as one of the iron wheel rims passed over the twin barrels.

Dolan managed to snatch the reins, and gradually the lathered team began to slow.

Regina straightened up on the seat, her fists clenched. Tears of rage and frustration rolled down her cheeks.

"Damn you both to hell!" she screamed at them.

"There's ways of tamin' a she-cat like you," Ander

snapped, leaning close from the saddle. She struck him in the face with her fists. His nose burst. He let out a yelp of pain, as blood ran down over his chin.

Dolan seized her around the waist. "Behave! You already got us in a peck of trouble."

A sudden wrenching of her body pulled Dolan halfway out of the saddle. He leaned back just in time to save himself.

Regina scooted across the seat to the far side as the wagon came slowly to a halt. She leaped out and struck the ground running. With skirts lifted high, she sprinted across the flatlands in a desperate attempt to get away.

Dolan flung himself out of the saddle and started after her. After only a few easy strides, he caught her. He threw her to the ground and stood over her, a menacing redhead with bared teeth.

"You're more damn trouble!" he cried.

Tex Ander, who had been holding a bandanna to his bleeding nose, suddenly screeched a warning: "*Lassiter!*"

He waved an arm wildly to the north where Lassiter's horse was coming across the prairie like a streak of black lightning. Some distance behind Lassiter, two other riders were just putting spurs to their mounts.

Chapter 16

inutes before, Lassiter had spotted the dust. Then, from the raised lip of a great buffalo wallow, he saw the long skirts of someone running. A woman. And he guessed at her identity, because he recognized Harve Dolan even at that distance. Dolan had lost his hat back by a halted wagon and there was no denying his flame-colored hair. In Lassiter's mind it added up; Dolan worked for Manly. And it seemed he had a wildcat Regina on his hands.

As Lassiter pounded closer, Dolan bent swiftly, got Regina by an arm and dragged her up in front of him. But instead of becoming the passive shield he undoubtedly intended, she violently clawed at his face and moved to the eyes.

Dolan ducked and screamed at Ander, "Shoot Lassiter, damn it!"

A crackle of gunfire erupted. Spouts of dust blossomed along the ground. Lassiter, coming at a hard run, also missed a shot because of the speed of his horse. A pressure of wind pushed up the brim of his flat-crowned hat. When he saw the girl, his heart dropped like cold iron. She had gotten away from Dolan and stumbled in her wild run, brushing loose hair away from her face. Ander, back at the wagon, was firing dangerously close to her.

"Get down, Regina!" Lassiter yelled above the drumming hoofbeats. *"Down!"*

His next shot, snapped off instinctively, caught Ander in the midsection just as the man fired a bullet into the sky. The force of Lassiter's gunshot twisted him out of the saddle. His body hung, legs and arms dangling, for a moment over a front wheel of the wagon, then spilled to the ground.

"Lassiter, look out!" It was a shouted warning from Cosgrove, who was coming up fast from the rear, followed by the heavyset Borford.

"Manly!" Dolan was yelling in a new direction. "Get that bastard Lassiter," he shouted as he tried to cope with an enraged Regina.

For some moments Lassiter had been aware of thundering hooves to his left. Turning his head, he saw Rex Manly and Lake Burne and three other men, less than a quarter of a mile away. In their zeal to gallop closer to Lassiter and finish him off, they had neglected their prisoner.

Rod Rucklor's hat blew off as he suddenly kicked his horse into a hard run. His long brown hair danced crazily in the wind as he spurred away from Manly.

It was a time for marksmanship, Lassiter well knew, instead of wild shooting from the back of a plunging horse. He flung himself from the saddle, hit the ground at a run and crouched beside a thick clump of chaparral. His black horse spun away, its reins dangling.

As Manly and the others charged nearer, Lassiter came to one knee. He took aim at Burne, but just before Lassiter squeezed the trigger, the speeding horse reared. Instead of the bullet catching the rider, it went straight into the breastbone of the animal. As the front legs collapsed, its hindquarters started to slip over in a somersault and Burne was flung like a large rag doll, straight at a clump of buck brush.

Another of Manly's men, black-bearded, his heavy legs pressing the barrel of a blue roan, was ahead of his companions, firing a rifle at every jump of his horse. One of the bullets clipped through the chaparral at Lassiter's side, just as he fired. The man dropped heavily, like a slab of granite.

A screech of male anger came suddenly from behind Lassiter. He whirled in time to see that Dolan had again caught up with Regina. But he was being pulled off balance by the raging tigress. She had him by the shirt and was hanging on with her full weight to bring him down. Dolan stumbled to his knees.

"Keep away from him!" Lassiter shouted at her and leaped aside to escape fire from Manly's remaining two men.

But as she spun away, leaving Dolan fully exposed to Lassiter, the man's arms shot into the air. He threw his gun away and screamed frantically, "Don't shoot!"

"Yellow bastard," Lassiter said through his teeth, then spun to face Manly and his two men. But Cosgrove and Borford had been directing an erratic but steady stream of gunfire at the trio.

Manly was reining in, still some distance away. With Lake Burne no longer in it, and Ander and another man down and Dolan on his knees as if badly wounded, Manly was in no mood to continue the battle. His horse made a sharp turn and started back. He neared the clump of brush where Burne was just emerging, bent over and staggering. Even at a distance, his face could be seen streaked with blood from contact with the brush. Manly slowed. Burne ran nimbly for so large a man and clambered up on the rump of Manly's horse. The animal took off as Manly spurred it viciously. Ahead of him were his two men, driven off by Cosgrove and Borford. One of them sagged in the saddle. Both of them disappeared over a hump of ground. Manly was soon out of sight, heading in the direction of distant Villa Rosa.

Knowing he had enough on his hands already, Lassiter let them go. The main thing was that Regina and Rucklor were safe—at least for the moment.

Regina was shaken and weeping when Lassiter went to her. A white-faced Dolan, his hands in the air, was still on his knees. His mouth was twisted in pain. And no wonder; his shirt was in tatters and spots of blood showed through his underwear where Regina's nails had ripped his chest.

"I oughta gun you down," Lassiter snarled at him, "you . . ." Lassiter bit off the epithet because of Regina's presence. "Likely you're the one who put a bullet in Rucklor that day."

"Not me," Dolan protested. "Tex did it!"

Lassiter glanced at Tex Ander on the ground beside the wagon. The man hadn't moved. "Looks like he's dead, so he can't say whether he did or not."

Regina sighed deeply and came over to Lassiter, looking up into his face. "Let Dolan go," she said, fighting for breath after her ordeal with the redhead. "There's been enough tragedy already today."

Lassiter thought about it, then got behind Dolan, jerked him to his feet and ran an expert hand over the man to make sure he wasn't carrying a gun. He found nothing. Gesturing with his gun, Lassiter said, "Go on, get out of here before I change my mind!"

Dolan was hunched, obviously in pain from the clawing Regina had given him. "Thanks, Lassiter. I'll just take Tex's horse an' be ridin' on—"

"Hell you will. Start *walking!*"

Dolan looked stricken, but read the danger in Lassiter's blue eyes. It took him only a couple of moments to retrieve his hat. Then he started at a stumbling run across the hoof-chewed ground, anxious to get away.

Lassiter, mopping his face with a bandanna, stared at the dilapidated building beyond the wagon and team. A dejected-looking Ruby filled the doorway.

"Ander and Dolan were the only ones with you?" Lassiter asked Regina. And when she nodded, he said, "Ruby was company for you, huh?" He wore a thin smile.

"Company I could have done without."

"I've got to go find Rod." But just then, Rucklor came riding up, his aristocratic features reflecting the rigors of the day.

"Hello, Regina," he said in a dead voice, but avoided her eyes. "There's something I must tell you . . ."

Regina interrupted with a cutting gesture. "Don't bother, I know all about it."

Lassiter had gone to look at Tex Ander's body. "We better clear out," he said. "Manly might come back. Although from the looks of it, I figure he's had enough." He called to Rucklor. "Rod, you drive the wagon. So you and Regina can be alone together."

He looked at each of them in turn. Neither one showed any outward appreciation for the idea. But he didn't care. It was time they straightened out the mess.

Rucklor's face was pale and drawn. "I didn't have a weapon," he said, his eyes apologizing to Lassiter for not having joined in the fight. Lassiter didn't even bother to reply. His nerves were raw with the responsibility of trying to protect Regina during the exchange of gunfire.

Then the Fork Creek heir turned his attention to Dolan, a dim figure by now, far out on the flats. "Why in the world did you let him go?" he complained.

"What in the hell would you suggest I do with him? Hang him?"

"No, but as a prisoner . . ."

"He'd take watching around the clock. We haven't got men enough." He pointed at Borford and Cosgrove. "Here's two of the four-man crew we've got left. Or did Manly take care of Quimby and Barnes?"

"I saw him run them off."

"I figured as much."

That reality sobered young Rucklor. "What in the world do we do now?"

They were walking toward the building. As Rucklor got a close look at Ander's body crumpled on the ground, his face lost even more color.

A frightened Ruby stood with her back to the doorway. Lassiter jerked his thumb at Ander's horse that Borford was leading. "Yours, Ruby. Better than walking."

"But the wagon," she wailed.

"After all she's been through, the young lady needs some comfort going back to the ranch. And the wagon's better than a saddle."

Ruby hung her head. "I guess I got no choice."

"That you haven't, Ruby. I'm a little surprised you'd let yourself get roped into Manly's vicious game."

"He's got a powerful way about him. I was scared not to."

"Or he pays well," Lassiter put in, giving her a hard look. She lowered her eyes.

Regina looked up into Lassiter's face. "I'd rather be riding in the wagon with you," she whispered.

"It's a chance for you and Rod to get to know each other again."

She gave him a hurt look, but climbed reluctantly into the wagon.

Ruby was out of sight by the time they had dug two shallow graves with a rusty shovel found in back of the building. Then they were heading north for Fork Creek, with fresh danger possible at every bend in the road.

Chapter 17

The long journey home would be no pleasure trip. Everyone was on edge because of the possibility that Manly might regroup and try to hit them again. Or he might be able to hire drifters who hung around Simosa's.

It wasn't long before Lassiter noticed that Regina sat stiffly on the wagon seat, as far from Rucklor as possible. Near as he could tell, they had exchanged few words and those only grudgingly.

After a few miles he caught sight of a slim figure approaching on a pinto. At first he told himself it was a boy from one of the isolated ranches. But as the distance between them narrowed, he saw it was not male, but very definitely female. Blanche, still wearing her range clothes, the pale hair down her back.

Upon drawing close enough to see that it was Rod Rucklor on the wagon seat, the frown of concern on her pretty face was exchanged for a broad smile of relief. Then, as she spurred up, her mood changed again as she seemed to realize who shared the seat with him. Until then, she had had eyes only for Rod.

"I was so worried about him," she apologized to the young woman. But Regina just gave her a stony look.

"Thank God you're all right!" It was Rod Rucklor coming to life after the awkward moment of meeting between the two women.

"I've been following your tracks," Blanche said to Lassiter in a strained voice. "I . . . I just wanted to be sure Rod was all right. And now that I know he is . . ."

She broke off and gave him a wan smile. Without looking at Rucklor again, she turned her horse and started at a trot toward the east.

Rucklor had halted the wagon team. "Lassiter, don't let her get away!" he cried.

Lassiter went after her and caught the pinto by a headstall. "Blanche, where do you think you're going?"

Her look was bitter. "Simosa's isn't so far. I'll see the horse is returned to you."

"Hell with that." Lassiter pulled the pinto around so that it faced the Fork Creek party. "You're riding with us."

When they reached the wagon, Regina was standing on the ground. "You ride with Rodney, or Rod, as you call him," Regina said firmly, looking up at the blonde with the windblown hair. "May I borrow your horse?"

Blanche looked at Rucklor, who was beckoning from the wagon. "It was Regina's idea. And I agree."

Blanche seemed uncertain. "Are you sure?"

"Very," Regina assured her.

When Blanche, looking embarrassed, walked woodenly to the wagon, Regina looked up at the pinto. "I've ridden nothing but sidesaddle. But there's always a first time."

Before Lassiter could dismount and give her a hand up, she was on the horse. "I wanted so much to ride at your side," Regina said in a voice husky with emotion, "and now I shall." She leaned over in the saddle and squeezed his arm. "You saved my life today. An act I'll never forget."

After a mile or so, Lassiter glanced back at the wagon. Both Rucklor and Blanche seemed animated, despite the harrowing experience of the day. Rucklor put the reins in one hand and touched her tenderly with the other.

Regina saw the direction of his glance but did not look around. She spoke again of Lassiter coming to her rescue, and how being with him now washed out the terrors of those terrible hours. Her obvious signs of affection made Lassiter uncomfortable. Whatever she felt for him, he told himself, would soon vanish in the strong light of reality. She had to face up to repairing the strong bridge that had once existed between herself and Rucklor. In spite of himself, he had begun to like Blanche and admired her spunk. But she was not cut out to be the mate of a man raised in Philadelphia luxury by a doting maiden aunt.

At the first opportunity, he'd have a long talk with Blanche. He'd convince her to take the two hundred dollars he had offered and make a new life for herself somewhere other than the Villa Rosa country.

The next time Lassiter looked back he saw that Blanche was handling the team, that Rucklor sat hunched a little, his lips locked against obvious pain. He was hugging his bad arm that had gradually given out on him.

It was with relief that Lassiter finally saw the Fork Creek buildings amidst the cottonwoods that looked healthy and green, not charred stumps. He wouldn't have been too surprised had Manly, in his rage, swung this way and burned everything to the ground.

When they had unsaddled, Lassiter got Rucklor aside and asked for details concerning his abduction. It was all Rucklor could do to hold himself in as he told how Manly hoped to use Regina as leverage to get him to sign over the ranch.

"And if I refused," he went on, his voice tightening,

"I suspect he'd have killed me. And quite possibly Regina as well. Thank God you came when you did."

"A lot of it was luck."

"Don't tell me it was Lassiter luck. It was you out-fighting them."

They were standing by one of the corrals. Cosgrove and Borford had gone to the bunkhouse. It had been a strange sight to see Blanche and Regina walk up to the house, talking together on the way, in view of their initial obvious dislike for each other.

"I want to thank you for saving Regina," Rucklor said sincerely. "She told me it was you being so heroic that pulled her through that ordeal. I . . . I certainly wouldn't have wanted anything to happen to her."

In the shadowy twilight, Lassiter studied the face of Ham Rucklor's heir. The eyes were reddened with smudges beneath. His nose and cheeks were peeling from sunburn. And the way he was hugging his bad arm indicated it was giving him some pain.

"Then you must still feel something for Regina," Lassiter said, having a breath of hope for the alliance after all.

But Rucklor's response dimmed that chance. "She's an old friend, a very dear friend. Of course I feel something for her."

"Then maybe you two can straighten everything out," Lassiter said, trying to push it.

"But I'm in love with Blanche."

"Damn it, you just think you are," Lassiter flared.

But Rucklor was hurrying up to the house. Lassiter didn't know whether he had heard him or not, or if he had, preferred not to comment.

The following day Lassiter intended to take his two men and head north to take care of the delayed business at

Devil's Canyon. Before leaving the ranch, he made sure Rucklor and the two girls had weapons. He gave each of them a loaded rifle. Blanche knew how to shoot, but Regina had to be shown.

He walked with her to some stumps beyond the last corral which they would use as targets. Here the big barn hid them from the house. He showed her how to load and cock the weapon. When firing, she stood close to him. She had pushed up the sleeves over her forearms, which were warm against the back of his hand as he adjusted her position. All she had to wear, until her trunk could be brought out from town, was the one dress that Ruby had pinned up after Manly had ripped it.

As he taught her to sight the rifle and squeeze the trigger, she turned suddenly. Coming to her toes, she kissed him on the mouth. Warm lips and a darting tongue were like being shocked by a miniature lightning bolt.

As every nerve in his body came alive, she said, "I've wanted to do that for ever so long."

He started to lean down so that he could see himself mirrored in her shining eyes. Then he suddenly straightened. She caught his hand, turned it over and kissed the palm. As she lingered over it, he found the experience to be almost as exciting as her lips on his mouth.

She then caught his hand in both of hers and drew it up between her breasts so that he could feel their softness against his forearm.

"I find that coming West has matured me greatly," she confided, leaning her weight against him. "It was throwing off the Philadelphia shackles that has done it."

He told her brusquely that he had a job to do and it was time he got at it. "We'll be back from Devil's Canyon by dark."

"Hurry," she said in a velvety voice.

It was still running through his mind as he and the two men headed toward the herd of cattle trapped in the canyon.

The way things were turning out, he'd have to stay around until the business with Manly was settled. His conscience refused to allow him to abandon young Rucklor. He couldn't let either of the Rucklors down, Rod alive or Ham in his grave.

For the midday meal, they munched cold bacon and biscuits as they rode. So far as Lassiter was concerned, he might as well have been eating sand. He worried about those left behind. He had thought about bringing them along. But Rod was still done in from his ordeal. And even though Regina seemed vibrant when around him, he felt it was only a pose.

When he got his first glimpse of the restless herd, he soundly cursed Lake Burne. To hold a herd this size boxed in a canyon and then abandoning them when his grand rustling plans were thwarted was heartless.

It took half an hour under a hot spring sun for Lassiter and Cosgrove to tear down the brush fence that had been erected at the narrow mouth of the canyon. Borford was kept busy shunting aside those animals who attempted to crash through the half-dismantled barrier to reach good grass on the flats.

At last the job was done. Cattle streamed through the opening, hooves clattering on stones, horns clicking.

All the grass on the canyon floor had been cropped to the ground. A thin stream had been muddied when weight of the frenzied animals had caved in the low banks. At the opposite end of the canyon was a very steep ribbon of hard cap littered with shale. Several of the animals had attempted to negotiate it in a search for grass, then tumbled back and expired from injuries.

One of them was barely alive. A bullet from Lassiter's rifle ended its suffering.

By the time they rode back through the canyon, every cow had fled what had been a prison for so long. In another day they would be well scattered on the Fork Creek range, no longer in a bunch for easy stealing. A weary Lassiter nodded in satisfaction at a job well done; at least he had accomplished that much for the young heir.

On the way back he rode between Cosgrove and Borford. "I appreciate you boys sticking with me," he told them sincerely. "When it's over with, I'll see to it that you get a bonus."

They had certainly earned it. Rod Rucklor would have to agree to that.

The following day Lassiter said he was going to town to try and hire men. He took Willie Cosgrove along to drive John Simosa's wagon. Lassiter drove the ranch wagon, his black horse tied on behind.

Mid-morning, when they reached Simosa's, there were only three customers in the tavern. Simosa stood at one end of his bar, the small eyes widening when he saw Lassiter. He dropped a hand below the bar.

"Careful, John," Lassiter warned softly, as he reached the bar. "Don't make any mistakes."

Simosa licked his lips as he eyed Lassiter's .44 snug in the oiled holster at his belt. "What do you want?" he asked tensely.

Lassiter said he had brought the wagon.

"Damn nice of you," Simosa said with a hard smile.

"I want to hire on some men. Any ideas?" Lassiter asked.

Simosa tilted his head toward the three bearded and rough-looking customers down the bar. "Buffalo hunters," he confided. "Poor pickin's this season, so they claim. They smell like they been sleepin' with bears. But maybe they can shoot. I hear you got a range war shapin' up out at Fork Creek."

"Where'd you hear that?"

"Ear to the ground." The porcine Simosa gave a wise smile. Something in Lassiter's blue eyes caused the smile to vanish. "Hope you win the fight out there."

"Rex Manly been in?"

"Yesterday."

"He have anything to say?"

"Claimed he heard two men got killed in a gunfight out at ol' Buffaloville."

"I'll be damned." Lassiter studied him, knowing that Simosa's attempt to be friendly was marginal. Lassiter knew he was afraid of him. It showed in the eyes that were a washed-out yellow brown. If Simosa wasn't awed by Lassiter's gun speed, he would blow him in two the minute his back was turned. But he'd heard too much about the Lassiter luck to risk it. Lassiter smiled to himself.

He moved down the bar to ask the three men if they were interested in working. But they shook their heads. They were moving on.

After leaving Simosa's, Cosgrove drove the ranch wagon and Lassiter rode alongside on his saddler.

In town, Lassiter had Cosgrove pull the wagon in an alley behind the hotel. It took Lassiter five minutes to convince the owner-clerk that he was authorized to pick up the trunk and carpetbag belonging to Regina Balmoral. There was a matter of additional room rent, which Lassiter paid.

When her things were loaded in the wagon, Lassiter thought of the Saber and facing Kiley Boyle once again. It had to be done someday, why not now? he reasoned.

There were only a few drinkers in the place. Those who lived in town had gone home for the midday meal.

Lassiter's greeting from Boyle was a deep scowl. After ordering whiskey for himself and Cosgrove, Lassiter repeated the story he had told Simosa. He was hiring men. Did Boyle know of any prospects?

Boyle shook his head. Sunlight through a side window danced on his shaved skull indented by the deep saber scar. "A lot of boys drifted to the Rockies," Boyle grunted.

Lassiter stood looking around, but saw no familiar faces. "Kiley, about that argument we had the other day. I hated like hell to turn you down, but . . ." Lassiter spread his hands away from his body and let his words hang there.

It took Boyle a moment or two to react. Then he laughed. "Hell, I plumb forgot about it, Lassiter."

Lassiter nodded. Boyle had the best leads for men to hire. Besides, Lassiter would rather have him as a speaking acquaintance than as an enemy.

"If you run into any good men, send 'em out, Kiley." He paid for the drinks.

As he pocketed his change, Boyle said, "I reckon you'll pay top dollar for gunhands, eh?"

"I want 'em to know guns . . . and cattle."

"I hear gunsmoke out at Fork Creek is gonna be thick enough to chop with an ax."

It was the second time today Lassiter had heard references to a range war. "It's why I need men."

"I'll do what I can for you, Lassiter. Have another drink. On me, this time."

"Later. I've got to keep a clear head today."

He and Cosgrove entered Ruby's. They got the table where he had sat with Regina. On a blackboard was the special of the day: beef stew.

When she had a minute, Ruby waddled over to take their order. At sight of Lassiter, her jaw dropped.

"I see you made it back all right, Ruby."

For a minute she was nonplussed, then she said, "But I'm so sore I still can't sit down right. I ain't been on a horse in twenty years."

"Two bowls of stew, Ruby. Have you seen Manly?"

Ruby flushed. "Ain't laid eyes on him. I hear he's been keepin' to his house."

That day Ruby had a gray-bearded man helping her in the kitchen. Some said that when he was sober enough, Ruby even took him home with her for the night.

When Lassiter was paying for the two meals, Ruby moved in close, a stricken look on the plump face. "I'm right sorry about how things turned out the other day," she whispered. "I didn't know what I was gettin' into."

Lassiter shrugged and told her the same story about hiring men. If she heard of any available men, to send them out to Fork Creek.

That day he had felt reckless. He had faced up to Simosa by returning the wagon. He had made a peace of sorts with Kiley Boyle. And he had met Ruby head-on. It was Regina who had triggered his mood of the day by her lips, the pressure of the scented body against his. As a result he found himself lusting after the betrothed of another man. It not only upset but angered him that he had allowed such a condition to exist.

He had even looked forward to possibly meeting Rex Manly. Or Lake Burne. He was in a mood to call either man—or both of them. But it wasn't to be.

At least, the word would be spread that he was hiring men. And the way rumors grew, like spring grass
in the sunlight, they would soon be saying that he had
a small army out at Fork Creek. . . .

Chapter 18

When Manly finally decided to ride into town with Lake Burne, he learned at the livery barn that Lassiter had been in that day. His mouth twisted. "The nerve of that son of a bitch! The colossal nerve!" Then he calmed down because Burne was giving him a strange sidelong look, as if Manly might be losing control. "The other day was only a minor setback," Manly said in a calmer voice.

They stood together at one end of the long bar at the Saber. Manly was upset, but determined to keep it in, so it wasn't apparent. It was Lassiter showing up at the wrong time that had brought everything to near disaster. He and Burne had survived. And there was always another day to stomp that gadfly Lassiter.

Kiley Boyle commented on the many scratches on Burne's broad face, a result of being hurled into the brush by a dying horse. "You been in bed with a she-cat?" Boyle laughed.

Burne only glared.

The four deep gouges on Manly's left cheek, Boyle decided to ignore. From the spacing, they looked as if made by fingernails. He wondered who the lady might be. Boyle walked heavily back down his bar. Sunlight through a window glistened off the top of his shaved skull.

"What do you mean, a *minor* setback?" Lake Burne

grumbled, getting back to the subject of Buffaloville. "That goddamned Lassiter . . ."

"Steps will be taken to put Lassiter down."

"I'll tell you one thing, Rex. You better forget about Fork Creek."

"I'd sooner forget my own name. It's become an obsession. And I won't be thwarted in my ambition."

"If you ask me, you've already been pretty well thwarted."

"Well, I didn't ask you, Lake." Manly's temper slipped. He poured another drink for them and got himself calmed down. "I guess we were lucky to come out of it with whole hide. You especially, Lake."

"Why me especially?"

"If I hadn't been on hand with a broad-rumped horse, there's no telling where you might be at this moment."

Burne shifted uneasily at the memory. "What's the next move?"

Manly thought about it. His two remaining extra men were out of it, one with a bad chest wound, the other shot through the arm. The only solution was to hire more men. It would mean making the long ride to Beeler. There were too many memories of the bloodletting around Villa Rosa some years back, when the XK Ranch and Fork Creek squared off. Those locals who had not joined the stampede to the Rockies would not be eager for a renewal of the carnage.

"With a show of force we can drive them out," Manly said.

"What about the females?"

"Just too bad. Those things happen when unknown attackers strike a ranch." Manly sipped his whiskey. "The sheriff may look around a bit, but he'll accept my story."

"I hope you're right," Burne said glumly.

"My money makes it right. The last two times he's been up for re-election, I've backed him."

"Looks like you've got all bets covered."

"Exactly." But Manly wasn't so sure, although he tried not to let any doubt show on his bland features. During his last visit to the county seat, he had made the mistake of talking about the late Ham Rucklor's will. And how he, Manly, was next in line should Ham's son not survive to take over the Fork Creek Cattle Company. He shouldn't have bragged about it; he realized now, but there was no undoing it.

When Sheriff Worden heard the story, he became politely cool, waiting, no doubt, to see which way the chips might fall. Fork Creek was by far the most lucrative and powerful cattle ranch in the southern half of the county. There was time enough to kiss feet when it was definitely known who the new owner might be—either Rodney Rucklor II or Rex Manly. Up at Beeler, Manly had been a little miffed by the sheriff's obvious reluctance to declare himself until knowing the outcome for sure.

Manly toyed with his drink as any number of plans filtered through his mind. In spite of his confident words to Lake Burne, Manly knew the future was mighty unclear. It was the same as tiptoeing on eggs. One misstep and he'd be up to his ankles in egg yokes, and quite possibly have to run for his life.

He pondered his prospects, which all came back to one name: Lassiter. "After the debacle at Buffalo-ville," Manly said in a low voice, "I have a passion to make Lassiter's exit from this world as unpleasant as possible."

Burne lifted his glass. "Tie him over an anthill, soaked in honey. That'd do for the bastard."

"I've got a better idea." Manly waited until Boyle finished serving some new customers, then got his eye. The saloon owner ambled up to Manly's end of the bar and stood wiping his large blunt fingers on a towel.

"Remember that hundred dollars I advanced you?" Manly asked quietly.

Boyle gave him a blank look.

"There's nine more to add to it," Manly said, faintly irritated that Boyle refused to admit receiving the money.

"Nine more what?" Boyle asked innocently.

"Nine more hundreds to add to the one you already have."

Small eyes brightened in his oval face. "A thousand dollars? Hmmmm." Boyle rubbed his heavy jaw and said, "What I got to do for it?"

"I want a certain party crippled. So I can laugh in his face every day of the short and miserable life he has left."

"Sheriff Worden might not like it."

Forcing a smile, Manly turned sideways to the bar and held open a back pocket of his trousers. "That's him in there, big as life."

"In your hind pocket," Boyle said with a short laugh.

"You want to see the color of that nine hundred dollars?"

"Show me."

"I'll have it for you in fifteen minutes."

Telling Burne to wait for him, Manly stepped from the Saber and looked carefully along both sides of the street to see that Lassiter wasn't lurking about. There were only a few pedestrians on the walks and some wagons entering town from the east.

After climbing the outside stairs to his office, Manly entered and locked the door. Then he pulled his desk from the wall. He knelt and lifted a fitted square of wood that matched the floor. The steel lid of a strongbox was revealed. Using a key, he unlocked it. He purposely had left Lake Burne in the Saber; he didn't want him to know he had a place for hiding money in addition to the office safe.

If Burne had come along, he might have started a conversation again about taking what he called his share of the Fork Creek money and quitting the country.

Manly was back in the saloon in ten minutes, instead of fifteen, breathing slightly hard from the exertion of moving the heavy desk back in place. Manly was finishing the drink he had poured earlier when Kiley Boyle sauntered up, an expectant look on his broad face.

Manly set down his glass, made small talk for a moment or so to whet Boyle's appetite, then shoved a money sack across the bartop. There was a faint clink of coins.

"Count it, Kiley," he said softly.

Boyle loosened the drawstrings and gave the contents a cursory inspection. Then he closed the sack and shoved it into his pants pocket. It made a bulge. "I'll take your word for it, Manly," he said. "I figure you know better'n to try an' cheat."

The way Boyle looked at him put a faint chill under Manly's breastbone, which made him shrug quickly. He needed men like Boyle—not lightweights such as Lake Burne and Dolan.

"Who am I s'posed to cripple up?" Boyle asked softly, still with that wintry look in his eyes.

"Lassiter. As if you didn't know."

"Funny thing, but me an' Lassiter sorta made our peace. I'm gettin' so I kinda like that hombre." Then Boyle's smile turned thin as the saber that had scarred his bald head. "But who can turn down good money?"

"Snap his backbone like a stick, like you did that private up at the fort."

"Yeah. I reckon I'm still in practice." His guffaw brought the heads of drinkers down the bar swinging around.

Manly leaned close, faintly annoyed that Boyle seemed to be taking it so lightly. "I want the job done as soon as possible."

Chapter 19

Twice Lassiter started for town, but each time something came up at the last minute to prevent him. He wanted to see if Rex Manly had done anything about getting the cattle money for Rucklor. Either from the buyers, who had purchased the herd and not paid for it yet—so Manly claimed—or from the bank at Beeler. Such a confrontation with the lawyer could end in gunfire, but at this point he didn't give a damn.

Fork Creek was putting him on edge. Although on the surface there seemed to be a truce between the two women, he sensed an undercurrent of tension. And Rod Rucklor, looking miserable, seemed unable to make up his mind about anything.

In the middle of the week, he heard something that tightened his nerves even more. He was out with Willie Cosgrove, hunting down an old bull that had gone berserk and was goring young calves. It had been injured in a fight with another bull and the pain from the wound, which had become infected, had driven it insane.

Lassiter had just tracked it down and shot it when he saw two riders nearby. They sat frozen in their saddles—a disreputable-looking pair, both bearded and wearing shabby clothing. They had a pack burro.

"Who're you?" Lassiter demanded, still holding the

rifle used to kill the bull. A wisp of smoke drifted from the muzzle.

"We heard the shot an' figured maybe you was shootin' at us," said the older of the pair, lean and tough-looking, probably in his late thirties.

Lassiter rode over to the pair, Cosgrove trailing.

"I asked who you are," Lassiter reminded them coldly. "And just what're you doing on Fork Creek range?"

Their names were Adams and Scorfield. They had been down in Indian country hunting buffalo but had been chased out by the army. Now they were on their way to Montana where Adams had relatives.

Lassiter let down a little and introduced himself. "I could use a couple of good men."

They exchanged glances, then Adams, the older one, shook his head. "I reckon not. We never knew we was on Fork Creek. All we want to do is keep on goin'. After all that's been said in town about things out here. . . ."

Scorfield gave his partner a hasty shake of the head. "You talk too damn much, Art."

But Lassiter wasn't going to let it go. He demanded to know what they had heard about Fork Creek in town. Scorfield tugged at his beard, then repeated what he'd overheard a man named Lake Burne say. "He said he was going to drive Lassiter off Fork Creek, free the boss who was being held prisoner, and get his old job back."

"You heard Burne say that?"

"Right in the Saber, it was," Adams agreed.

"That I was holding Rod Rucklor prisoner?"

Scorfield nodded. "He claimed you had him in chains."

"Rucklor's as free as you are. Come along and I'll

show you." Lassiter started to turn his horse, but the two men didn't move.

"I reckon not," Adams said. "We lost two sidekicks fightin' down on the Brazos. We had enough gunsmoke for one year."

"Besides," Scorfield put in, "we heard you'll be walkin' in blood around here once the Fork Creek war gets rollin'."

Although they weren't the type of men he'd ordinarily pick for a crew, they were better than nothing. He tried to argue, to convince them that Rucklor was the victim of a plot to steal his inheritance. But they stubbornly refused to listen.

"If I get mixed up in the Fork Creek mess that's comin', sure as there's a sun in the sky, I likely won't even get buried," Scorfield said. They moved on.

"Seems like you're havin' a hard time hirin' anybody, boss," Cosgrove commented with a shake of his head.

"So it seems, Willie," Lassiter said angrily as he stared at the two buffalo men hurrying away with their pack animal.

When he got back to ranch headquarters, Lassiter tried to tell Rucklor about the story being spread in town that he was being held prisoner. But the young man seemed uninterested. He was upset because Blanche and Regina had had words that afternoon.

Lassiter gave him a look. "What else did you expect, for Chris' sakes?"

Rucklor turned red and walked away. At that moment, Lassiter was on the point of saying the hell with it and riding on. But he didn't. If he left, Rucklor wouldn't last long enough to take a deep breath. As much as he was exasperated by the complication of the two females, he just couldn't go off and leave. Not without settling the mess beforehand so Rucklor would have at least a halfway decent chance of survival.

He was going to town, he told Cosgrove and Borford the next morning after breakfast. It was Saturday, the town should be busy and perhaps there would be men he could hire. He had a very strong hunch that a show-down was just over the hill.

But he didn't voice this suspicion to the only two ranch hands left on Fork Creek. He didn't want them to start adding up their chances and then desert him.

"If anybody tries to move in on you while I'm gone," Lassiter told them, "start shooting."

He was about to mount his black horse when Regina came up behind him and flung her arms around his neck. "Lassiter . . ."

Feeling her softness pressing against his back sent his pulses soaring. He twisted around to face her and said sternly, "Don't try to make Rod jealous. Hell, it isn't worth it."

A faint smile curved her red lips, her violet eyes bright and challenging. "You think I'm trying to make Rodney jealous? No. What I feel for you is here."

A shapely left breast, he noted, more than filled her cupped hand. The sight of her deliberate move put a barb of heat through him that only made him angry.

"Damn you, Regina," he said. They stood together beside a corral. Cottonwood branches, heavy with leaves, arched above them.

"Take me with you," she whispered.

"Too dangerous."

"If we should happen to be in danger, you'd save us both."

"What you've seen me do so far is mostly luck."

"All the same, I want to go along. I'm tired of being

cooped up in there . . ." She glared up at the house. "With *her!*"

"What'd you and Blanche argue about, anyhow?"

"She told me she was going away, leaving Rodney for me. I told her I didn't want him. That I knew the man I wanted."

Her words made him uncomfortable. He had warned himself not to be upset by anything she might say or do. But he couldn't help a rush of color to his face. To have a stunning young woman hint at her true feelings for him was more than enough to spark the emotions. He almost lifted his arms to enfold her, then checked himself. She had been raised in a wealthy family; their money, at least most of it, he understood, gone now. But the background remained, an indelible mark on her character. He was used to more earthy females.

"I'll likely be back by sundown," he said gruffly, vaulted into the saddle and rode away, scattering a flock of hens that had come clucking around a barn.

Lassiter had gone only a little more than a mile when he realized someone was following him. Tension tightened his back muscles but he didn't look around. Waiting till he reached a high point of brushy ground, he suddenly reined into the cover. Just as he drew his rifle, he saw Regina coming at a trot. Evidently she had helped herself to a saddled horse.

What a fetching sight she made, he had to admit, in a green dress so tight in the bodice that he wondered how she could draw breath. Her skirts had slid up her slim legs so that the stockings showed.

"Don't be angry," she said, recovering from her surprise when he emerged so suddenly from the brush.

"Will you go home? Or do I have to tie you over the back of that horse like a sack of meal?"

"I want to be with you." She urged her mount closer.

Leaning over in the saddle, she reached out and touched his hand. Contact of her warm fingers quickened his heartbeat.

It was difficult to ignore the incipient passion she aroused in him. In a hard voice, he said he'd ride her home. Without giving her a chance to protest, he snatched the reins out of her hand and rode away, leading the Fork Creek horse she had appropriated.

When he was once again in the ranch yard, he dismounted and made the mistake of helping her out of the saddle. With a glad little cry, she fell into his arms. This time her warm lips were against his throat.

"You're enough to drive a man out of his wits," he said roughly.

"It's what I intend doing." Her breath was hot against his neck.

He stepped back and looked severely at her lovely face. "Look, I'm trying to save this ranch for Rod . . . for the two of you."

"I want no part of it."

"You had something together once. So I figure you'd want him to come out of this mess with something. According to what you told me, about all he's got is this ranch."

"Of course I want him to have something."

"Then quit acting like a kid. Whether he shares this place with you or with Blanche is none of my business. But I knew his father. There were things to like about Ham Rucklor. In some ways I thought he was a cold-hearted bastard. But mostly he was my friend and I want his son to have a decent shake in life."

She bit her lip. "Always Rodney, it seems. You never think of yourself—or of me."

"Will you stay put this time while I go to town?"

"I can't promise," she said slyly.

"I'll fix you." He led the two horses over to a barn

where Cosgrove and Borford were greasing the big wagon.

"One of you let Miss Balmoral have a horse," he accused.

The corpulent Borford lowered his grease rag and looked up. "Her bein' a friend of the boss, I didn't figure to argue with her."

"Next time don't let her get a foot in a stirrup."

When Borford took over the horse, Lassiter rode back to where Regina still stood. When he told her what he had done, she seemed hurt that he'd do such a thing. Then she shrugged and her face brightened.

"I'll be waiting for you." She blew him a kiss, then started walking toward the house. He rode quickly away.

There was danger in going to town, he knew very well. But it couldn't be avoided. He needed men and the town was the best source. Come what may, he thought and crossed his fingers as he rode south toward Villa Rosa.

Chapter 20

Since it was Saturday, he had looked forward to seeing a crowd in town. But when he arrived, it was disappointing to see only a few more people on the walks than usual, and mostly families from two-bit outfits south of Villa Rosa. A few small boys ran whooping along an alley.

The Saber was slightly more crowded than usual. His practiced eye ran over those at the bar, looking for potential ranch hands, but most of them were older men. Boyle wasn't behind the bar that day. His barkeep, a bearded, older fat man, seemed harassed by all the customers. He kept wiping his large hands on a stained towel around his waist as an apron.

Lassiter asked for a bottle and glass, but at that moment Boyle stepped behind his bar. He waved the bartender off and brought the order himself.

"I'm glad you came in today, Lassiter. I was just leavin'." He was grinning faintly.

"I need men," Lassiter said, coming right to the point. "It doesn't look to me like there's a young one under thirty in the place."

"It's that silver boom in the Rockies. Cleaned out every footloose kid in these parts."

"Yeah." Lassiter poured himself a drink and listened to the buzz of voices. He noticed that most of the talk was of the new silver strike.

"Wish I could go," a man at Lassiter's elbow was saying to another. "But I got Martha an' the kids . . ."

"I can't be choosy, it seems," Lassiter said, turning his attention back to Kiley Boyle, who stood leaning against his bar, his round head on a heavy neck sunk between powerful shoulders. He seemed amused about something.

"Manly's put out the word," Boyle said softly. "Choosy or not, I don't figure anybody around here will hire out to you."

"Manly, eh?" Lassiter stifled a flash of raw anger. "You point out any likely prospects and I'll talk to 'em. Then we'll see."

"Won't do you no good."

Lassiter felt the warmth of whiskey spreading in his stomach. Tensions of the past days had put him so on edge that he was liable to miss something important said to him the first time around. Something in Boyle's beady eyes reminded him of his greeting today.

"I recollect you saying you were glad I came in, making quite a point of it. Mind telling me just why?"

"Sure I'll tell you. A fella gave me a hundred dollars. I figured to hell with him." Boyle seemed to be laughing at some secret joke. "But when he gave me nine hundred more, I felt honor-bound to earn it. Know what I mean?"

As they locked eyes, the fat bartender in serving a customer let an uncorked bottle of beer slip out of his nervous hands. It fell to the floor behind the bar, breaking the tension in the room.

Boyle, still wearing that half smile, didn't even look around. His eyes bored into Lassiter's face.

"Just what the hell are you getting at, Kiley?" Lassiter started to ask.

Boyle's huge body moved suddenly. In that moment, Lassiter was reminded of a bear stung into action by a firebrand laid against its hide. One moment Boyle lounged behind his bar, and the next he was using his hands to propel himself over the lip. Obviously, he intended to clear the bar. And it was possible because he was extremely agile for so large a man.

But Lassiter had detected the move a split second before Boyle left his feet. Boyle, coming right at him over the top of the bar, met Lassiter's two hands at his chest. So powerful was the thrust of Boyle's body that Lassiter thought his arms might snap at the elbows. But his arms held firm. And Boyle crashed to the top of the bar as glasses and bottles were scattered, and startled men jumped aside.

Straightening up, Lassiter started to withdraw his hands. That was when Boyle seized him by the wrists. It was like suddenly being locked in irons. Boyle fell behind the bar, his weight dragging Lassiter over the top and down with him.

In the foam of spilled beer they lay, limbs entwined, both momentarily stunned from the fall. Lassiter pulled free.

"You gone loco, Kiley?" Lassiter demanded.

Boyle tried to grab him by the hair. Lassiter hit him in the mouth.

"You fool!" Lassiter shouted. "What the hell you tryin' to do?"

Yells from patrons filled the air. Boots crunched over broken glass. Excited men were backing away from the bar.

In all the confusion, Boyle leaped to his feet, glowering at Lassiter. He wiped a forearm across his lips that Lassiter had bloodied. His shirt front was reddened. A roundhouse swing aimed at Lassiter's head barely missed. Lassiter pulled aside at the last moment to seize Boyle by the shirt front. He spun the big man with such force against the bar that there was a screech of nails being pulled from the planking. Boyle's weight almost dislodged the bar from its anchor to the floor.

"You won't earn your money today," Lassiter was yelling, "if that's what this is all about. 'Cause I'll be damned if I fistfight you."

He barely had his fingers closed on the butt of the .44 he started to draw when Boyle's shoulder slammed into his chest. With the tremendous heft of his body behind it, the shoulder knocked Lassiter back on his heels. Fighting desperately to retain his balance, Lassiter's arms moved like windmills. But his feet shot out from under him on the floor, which was made slippery by the spilled beer. As he went down, his grip on the .44 was jarred loose. It arced through the air to land with a dull thud on the bartop.

"I'll keep it for you, Lassiter." A man brandished the .44 overhead and stepped back into the roaring crowd.

There was such a ringing in his head from a blow to the cheekbone that Lassiter barely heard him.

Boyle started to straighten up from bending low to deliver the blow. In only a clock's tick of time, Lassiter felt the spilled beer on the floor seeping into his clothing and against his flesh. It helped to clear his head.

Above him was Boyle's wide grin. He saw the large hands outstretched. All that poundage was about to hurtle down on him, he suddenly realized, to grind him into the wet floor. But there was barely room enough behind the bar so that Lassiter could wrench himself over on his side to miss the full impact. Even with this maneuver, one of Boyle's heavy legs slammed into his rib cage with the force of a felled tree. His only prayer at the moment was that possibly shattered ribs wouldn't puncture a lung.

Lurching to his feet, he found he could breathe without pain. Boyle, still on the floor, grabbed for his legs. Lassiter kicked his hands away. He was backing away when Boyle sprang to his feet and came after him, his long arms swinging, trying to land a telling blow. Lassiter seemed to stay just out of reach.

By then the Saber was a roaring madhouse. Men backing to the door were met by others fighting to get in so as to witness the excitement.

Word spread quickly. "Boyle's after Lassiter!"

When Lassiter tried to step out from behind the bar, he backed up against a jam of men. Boyle had him trapped.

Above the bedlam were the meaty sounds of fists against flesh. Lassiter, forced to stand his ground, tasted blood. The inside of his mouth was driven against teeth by another hard blow to the face. With vicious lefts and rights, Lassiter stood off his towering opponent.

Then the jam of men broke suddenly and they jumped aside. Lassiter backed out into the center of the saloon, Boyle following doggedly. He saw the ranks of excited faces, men at the rear jumping up and down to get a glimpse of the battle over the heads of those in front.

"I want my gun!" Lassiter yelled, not taking his eyes from Boyle's sweated face. "I'll put an end to this stupidity."

He was interrupted by Boyle's harsh laughter and another roundhouse swing to the head. Had it landed squarely, the brawl would have ended. Even so, the fist grazed his scalp with enough power to cause white lights to burst momentarily in his head.

Boyle's powerful arms pulled him in close. Lassiter shook his head to clear it and fought free of Boyle's embrace. He hammered away at the midriff, finding it surprisingly soft. But as the fists sank deeper, he encountered an armor plate of hard muscle.

A mighty groan burst from Boyle's lips as Lassiter

shifted his aim slightly to the solar plexus. Heartened, Lassiter continued the barrage. It caused Boyle to start backing. His large feet shuffled on the floor. His right slammed into Lassiter's forehead. But it lacked the power of earlier blows.

Lassiter struck with his left, flush on the jaw with such force it turned Boyle's head. Beads of perspiration became almost a mist as they were jarred from the large damp face. One knee started to cave. With his remaining strength, Lassiter landed a tremendous right to the jaw. Force of the blow crossed Boyle's eyes. He wavered, then sank to his knees in the middle of his own saloon. He stayed there, head down, as everyone stared in silence. Then the cheers started.

"How'd you ever manage it, Lassiter?" a gray-bearded man demanded in a shocked voice.

Lassiter, gasping for breath, leaned a hand at the edge of a deal table to steady his legs.

A man yelled suddenly, "Looks like it ain't over yet!"

Lassiter swore and turned to see that Boyle was indeed struggling to his feet. Blood drained from numerous cuts, but there was a grin of sorts on his cut lips.

He waved his hands for silence, saying, "Lassiter beat me fair an' square!" His eyes were on a dapper Rex Manly, who stood in the jam of men by the double doors. "Manly, it's your money buyin' drinks for the house!" he shouted into the silence. Manly reddened. Boyle gave a blare of laughter barely heard in the shouts from the crowd at the prospect of free whiskey.

Boyle lurched over to where a scowling Lassiter was standing. "Drinks include you, Lassiter."

Men were kicking broken glass out of the way as they trooped to the bar. By then the fat barkeep had recovered from tensions of the past few minutes and started pouring whiskey.

In the jostling crowd, a man handed Lassiter the .44.

Lassiter did not look down, but could tell by the feel that the weapon was his. He was keeping his eyes on Boyle, halfway expecting a trick. But Boyle got two glasses and shoved one toward Lassiter. Then he grabbed a bottle and filled the glasses. Boyle drank his at a gulp; Lassiter wasn't quite as fast.

Then Boyle yelled something at his barkeep and two clean towels were tossed across the bar. Boyle handed one to Lassiter and used the other to wipe blood and sweat from his own face.

"It seems we banged each other up a mite." Boyle grinned.

Then Boyle tossed the bloodied towel aside and leaned close. "I did my best to earn the money Manly give me." He looked Lassiter in the eye and gave a soft laugh.

"You're trying to say you *let* me win?"

Boyle refilled their glasses and winked broadly. "Fact is, we're both pretty damn good."

Lassiter glanced over the crowd but saw no sign of the urbane lawyer. "So Manly paid you to jump me." He looked Boyle in the eye; the left was already slightly purplish.

"There was a time when I didn't like you much—for turnin' down my proposition about them cows." Boyle was speaking in a low voice, amusement in his eyes. "But I like Manly less. You see how it is?"

"No," Lassiter said with a hard smile. Whiskey was starting to ease some of his hurts and his legs no longer felt as if they might fold on him at any moment.

"You said you want men," Boyle whispered.

"Yeah, I do." Lassiter was all attention.

Boyle spoke of some friends, buffalo hunters. "Pickin's was puny this spring. An' I got word they're headin' this way. Ain't no more buffalo around here, but I won't tell 'em that, see? I'll bring 'em out to Fork Creek."

"Buffalo hunters, eh?"

"They ain't much for cow punchin', but they can blow hell out of a man with them Sharps rifles of theirs."

Lassiter nodded. "Fifty-caliber slugs can do a lot of damage."

"When Manly tries to jump you, he'll have a real surprise."

"Maybe he's given up trying to hit us at Fork Creek," Lassiter said, fishing for information.

"He's sent for some fellas. He's waitin' till they get here."

"Thanks for telling me. Just how many buffalo hunters do you reckon you'll bring out?"

"Around two dozen."

Lassiter let out a low whistle. In spite of his misgivings, he couldn't help but be impressed. "I can use every one." He turned and looked at the double doors where Manly had stood. "Or I could face up to Manly here in town today and end the damn business."

"Gun Manly down an' you got Mike Worden to reckon with. That damn sheriff might fix it so you'd end up with your neck in a rope."

"He might try." Lassiter still kept one eye on Boyle, just in case. All this talk about buffalo-hunter friends might be true; and the possibility of twenty-four tough men out at Fork Creek was comforting. On the other hand, it might be a ruse just to make him lower his guard.

"But if Manly got killed while you was protectin' your boss's property, it'd be different," Boyle said in guarded tones. "Which would be the case at Fork Creek."

Lassiter nodded. A persistent buzzing in his head had finally stopped, but his ribs still pained him. "To be on the safe side, I'll try and hire a few men while I'm here."

"I tell you, Manly's put out the word."

"Just the same, I'll give it a try."

"How about me ridin' out to Fork Creek with you? I reckon you can use an extra gun till my friends show up."

The sudden offer was surprising, especially in view of the fact that only minutes before Boyle had been trying to beat him into the floor. And he wondered about Boyle's eagerness. "We'll see," Lassiter said.

"Fred can run the Saber till we settle Manly's hash," Boyle went on. "The fact is, I'd like to get outa here for a spell. Been cooped up too long. I ain't seen no action for a long dry year."

"You saw some today," Lassiter reminded thinly.

Boyle gave a faint grin and rubbed at a swelling on his jaw. "Fred can send the boys out to Fork Creek the minute they get to town."

"I'll let you know, Kiley."

Lassiter started his attempt at hiring right in the Saber. Holding up his hands, he asked for quiet, then made his request for volunteers. There was much hemming and hawing.

Finally a few of them gave one lame excuse or another, but they were adamant when Lassiter tried to plead his cause. One stalwart man in his early forties said that signing on at Fork Creek would mean getting involved in a range war. Nobody in the Villa Rosa country was that big a fool, the man pointed out.

At the livery barn, he received the same reaction from the loafer usually hanging around the place.

Dave Simkins, the owner, got Lassiter aside. "You've got to face up to somethin'. Ham Rucklor was the big auger in these parts. With him dead, it's Rex Manly."

They wouldn't even budge when Lassiter pointed out that their hiring on would be helping Ham Rucklor's son.

It seemed that Manly had sowed his seed well—a damn two-bit lawyer who had been lucky in land deals up around Beeler, then had drifted south. It was no secret that he had bragged that one day he would own a big chunk of this end of the territory. If he got his hands on the Fork Creek Cattle Company, he would be well on the way.

Lassiter returned to the Saber. Boyle had exchanged his torn and bloodied shirt for a fresh one. It seemed that Lassiter's only chances for recruits were the buffalo hunters. If Boyle could be believed, that is. And if they were really his friends as he claimed.

He had no choice but to give it a chance. He told Boyle so.

Again Boyle asked if he didn't want that extra gun out at the ranch until the hunters arrived. Lassiter thought about it, weighing Boyle's possible treachery against the need for that added gun till the hunters arrived. He knew he couldn't depend on Rucklor. Borford and Cosgrove were still an unknown quantity, although they had done some sporadic firing the day of Regina's rescue.

He reluctantly agreed to Boyle's suggestion.

Boyle seemed in good spirits as they started the long ride. He brought with him a Sharps rifle that went back to his buffalo-hunting days. "I rode with the boys that'll be givin' you a hand," he said. "Hunting is a risky way of life, though, and I saw the end of it comin' fast. So I bought myself a saloon."

As they stopped to water their horses, another possibility buzzed again in Lassiter's head. What if Boyle still played Manly's game? And one day when Lassiter had his back turned . . .

He flashed a sidelong glance, almost wishing he hadn't accepted Boyle's offer to side him until the arrival of his friends. But he had been desperate for help, had made the choice and now would have to live with it.

However, he was always on his guard, careful to see that the burly saloonkeeper rode slightly ahead of him and never dropped back.

At the ranch Lassiter introduced him to Rucklor, who shook the meaty right hand. Then Rucklor stared curiously at their faces.

"What happened?" he asked worriedly.

"We went to put our heads out a window," said Boyle, his small eyes merry. "Thought it was open. It wasn't."

Lassiter gave a tight smile, then noticed that Regina and Blanche were hurrying across the yard. He wished they'd stayed in the house.

He introduced them to Boyle. Regina gave him a cool nod. She had been staring at Lassiter's bruises with concern, but didn't ask questions.

The way Boyle smiled slyly at Blanche made Lassiter wonder if there had been a past association. It might ease the Rod-Regina situation if they picked it up again, he thought.

Blanche said quite calmly, "How do you do, Mr. Boyle."

Lassiter walked Boyle away from them and down to the bunkhouse. The two cowhands already knew Boyle, having patronized the Saber. They were obviously relieved when Lassiter told them some buffalo hunters would soon be joining them.

"We saw fellas watchin' the place while you was gone," said Willie Cosgrove uneasily.

"How many were there?"

"Looked like two. But I couldn't rightly tell."

"When we started ridin' that way to look 'em over, they cut away," Luke Borford explained.

Lassiter looked grim. To be on the safe side, he decided, they had better stand watches. "I'll take first watch, you the second, Willie." He nodded at the heavyset Borford. "You take the last one, Luke."

As he had so many times before, Lassiter was damning his luck at being left with only two men out of the original crew of twenty-five. Most of the good hands had quit when Ham Rucklor was killed. More of them drifted after Len Crenshaw got sick and Lake Burne was in charge.

In the early evening, when he was walking up to the house to explain in detail about the buffalo hunters to Rucklor, he heard a footstep behind him. He whirled around, a hand clamped to his gun. Boyle stood a few feet away, his arms spread wide to show he had no intention of drawing the heavy revolver at his belt.

"I just wanted to know how come I don't get to stand watch," Boyle said.

"We'll manage like it is."

"Scared of me?"

"Nope."

"Well, don't be. There's somethin' I shoulda said before this, I reckon."

"Then say it."

"I hate lawyers. That goes for Manly. One of that tribe threw my poppa off our place in Arkansas. It was a poor folks farm like they called it back there, but it made him a livin'. So I've hated them courthouse dandies ever since."

Lassiter was about to say he had known some good lawyers and that it wasn't right to condemn a whole barrel of apples just because of a few rotten ones. But he thought that under the circumstances his words would not be appreciated.

"You can start watch tomorrow night," Lassiter said. He'd face up to that risk, if there were one, when the time came. . . .

Chapter 21

Sometimes I think this whole business is hopeless," said Rod Rucklor despondently.

Lassiter had been invited to the house for breakfast. It was a bright spring morning, the air was balmy with only a faint breeze to stir the leafing cottonwoods by the windows. A few clouds sprawled lazily across the deep blue of the sky. Through a window he could see the flock of hens, white and brown, industriously pecking at the ground for worms.

Blanche seemed startled by what Rucklor had said and impulsively reached for his hand. When she saw Regina watching her, she quickly withdrew her hand. "You shouldn't even think it's hopeless, Rod," she murmured, "let alone say it."

"She's right," Lassiter put in as he cut through a slice of bacon. But secretly he was beginning to wonder. A week had passed since Kiley Boyle had ridden out with him. Every day, Lassiter joined the three men in chores to keep the ranch operating even marginally. Without a full crew he felt like a man without a leg.

When the meal was finished, Lassiter studied Regina, who had hardly opened her mouth. That morning she seemed withdrawn. Sitting at the table in a funnel of sunlight through a kitchen window, she was truly beautiful. Dark hair caught the light and made her violet eyes luminous. With his coffee cup in hand, he shifted his attention to Blanche, noting the contrast. Strangely enough, there seemed to be little. Blanche wore her golden hair pinned atop her head. Seeing her sitting straight in the chair, chin lifted, clear-eyed, one could never guess at her rather lurid past. She spoke well and it was usually in a well-modulated voice. What remained of the brassy exterior of Simosa days seemed to have been rubbed clean. Yet he knew she could not have acquired this ladylike demeanor in just a few short days. She had been raised with it, he decided, and something had happened along the way to push it all in the background.

She got up, slim and attractive in a yellow dress, re-filled their coffee cups, put the pot back on a stove lid, then sat down again. She caught him watching her and a slight show of sadness appeared in her blue eyes.

Later that morning on the veranda, she reminded him of the incident. "You'll never think I'm good enough for Rod. You're always thinking of Simosa. . . ." Even mentioning the name of her former tormentor caused her chin to tremble.

Abruptly she whirled, the skirt of the yellow dress sailing out from her fine legs, and ran to the house.

As he walked across the yard on the bright morning, he kicked savagely at a stone and sent it crashing into the trunk of a cottonwood. But it did little to lessen his anger, aimed mainly at himself. Why had he ever listened to the dying Len Crenshaw? But on the other hand, how could he have possibly ignored the old Fork Creek foreman and his plea to give Ham Rucklor's son a hand?

Later in the week, Rucklor decided his arm had healed sufficiently to let him help with the work. "I need something to do, or I'll go mad in this place."

"Cattle ranching not quite what you expected?"

Rucklor only grunted something. Lassiter had taken breakfast with them again that morning. As he crossed the yard, Kiley Boyle and the two ranch hands were saddling up. Boyle seemed out of sorts.

"Damn that bunch, they should've been here by now," he complained.

"Maybe something happened to change their plans," Lassiter suggested, watching the scarred face to note any reaction.

"Si wrote me an' said they'd be here the first of the month. It's come an' gone, damn it."

"Looks like we'll have to stand off Manly ourselves," Lassiter commented, which caused worried looks to be exchanged between Cosgrove and Borford. It made Lassiter wonder just how dependable they might be in a showdown.

"My boys'll be here," Boyle asserted truculently. "I feel it in my bones."

"Let's hope your bones speak the truth," Lassiter said with a sour laugh.

That morning they spread out to see if they could spot any activity on Manly's part—especially to spot the dust of a large body of riders heading for Fork Creek—which Lassiter hoped wouldn't happen. Not until Boyle's friends finally arrived. Or was it all a pipe dream on Boyle's part? He was beginning to wonder.

When they rode in at noon, Blanche came running from the house. She had changed into a shirt and jeans, looking very young and pretty, her face flushed from the run. He thought it strange that she appeared from the back of the house.

She waited until the men had ridden on down to the corral, then blurted, "Regina's gone. And some of her clothes are missing."

"Are you sure?"

"I've looked everywhere."

"Has Rod got any ideas?"

"He doesn't know. I didn't want to upset him. He still isn't fully recovered, you know."

"He seems to think he is."

"Well, he isn't," she snapped.

Lassiter's face hardened. "Seems like she waited till we were gone to get herself a horse. Where's Rod now?"

"Shaving. She shouldn't be out there . . . alone."

Lassiter swallowed an oath at the truth of Blanche's statement. "You should've kept an eye on her, Blanche." His temper was slipping.

"It wasn't my place to watch her," she said defiantly.

"I thought you'd be back at Simosa's by this time," he said, as if being nasty would ease his anxiety.

"Not *that* place," she said positively.

"You said you were going back."

"Only talk. I got in that trap once. Never again."

Because she seemed close to tears, Lassiter's anger began to melt. He gave her a pat on a soft shoulder. "I'm sorry. So much has happened, I . . ." He gave a deep sigh. "And now Regina."

He rode across the ranch yard, in a parallel to the house until he picked up Regina's footprints. These he followed to a barn where she had evidently picked up a saddle.

Jerking the brim of his black hat low to cut the sun, he soon found the tracks of a single horse. These he followed for well over two miles. He knew the tracks had not been made by any of his men, who had fanned out and gone no more than a mile from headquarters. These tracks led due south in the direction of Villa Rosa.

The farther he rode, the more concerned he became. He eased his Henry rifle into its scabbard and made sure there was no bind of leather on the metal of his holstered .44.

Suddenly something broke from the brush ahead. He was just reaching for his rifle when he realized that it was only two coyotes loping across the flatlands.

From this slight rise of ground he scanned the terrain ahead. It was mostly flat, but there were patches of brush and many coulees. Her horse could easily go over the edge of one and break a leg. That possibility was sobering. All he needed now was for her to run into Manly. No doubt this time the lawyer would be smarter and make better use of his luck in drawing an ace like Regina out of the deck.

After half an hour of tracking her horse, he suddenly came upon bits of clothing scattered at wide intervals along the tracks. Recognizing her green dress, his heart turned cold. He spurred on, dreading the possibility that she might be in the hands of marauders.

Around a knob of sand and brush, he suddenly came upon her. She walked along bent over, retrieving the pieces of clothing. Upon hearing his horse in the soft sand, she looked up. Seeing that it was Lassiter, a glad cry burst from her lips. She dropped the clothing and rushed toward him, her black hair flying. She reached up, clasping his leg.

"Lassiter . . . it's you," she breathed.

"What the hell's going on?"

"I had my clothes in a bundle, but I didn't tie them very well. And the first thing I knew the bundle was coming undone and everything was falling bit by bit."

"Yeah. You left quite a trail of stuff."

"And I didn't have the girth tight enough and the saddle began to turn . . ." She broke off, pausing for breath, still clinging to his leg. "I was getting frightened . . . by the silence, the utter loneliness. My God, am I glad to see *you*."

"Why in hell did you run away?" he asked as he dismounted. The dress she wore that day was brown, with a lacy white collar. It was badly wrinkled. Around her neck was a gold necklace—a perfect target for thieves. He shook his head at her stupidity.

"You're not answering my question," he persisted. "Why did you run?"

"I felt I was in the way."

"I s'pose you were trying to reach town. Then what?"

"Take a stagecoach to Denver. . . ."

"You ran a hell of a risk of bumping into Manly and his boys again," he pointed out harshly.

She only made a vague gesture and began picking up her scattered pieces of clothing. Lassiter helped her. Then he led his horse to where she had tied her mount. It was a sorrel. At least she had a good eye for horse flesh, he reflected, for she had selected one of the better ones. Lifting his knee sharply into the sorrel's belly, he took advantage of the contracting stomach muscles and tightened the cinch for her.

To his left, through a screen of buck brush, Fork Creek could be seen tumbling and frothing through a narrow cut. Twenty yards or so downstream a bank had caved in. Over a passage of time, crevices between large, scattered boulders had been filled in with dirt and bits of driftwood to form a fair-sized pool of calm water.

"That looks so inviting," Regina said softly when she found him looking at it. "I haven't had a real bath since I've been here."

"There's a good tub hanging on a hook on the back porch."

"I'd need Blanche to help me. And I hated to ask."

"Too stubborn, you mean."

She was looking at him and he couldn't deny that her smile held a degree of wickedness. A pressure of heat began to build throughout his body. Had he heard her right? Did she really want to take a bath out here in the wilderness? Or was she just talking to see if he was impressed, and then might throw back her head and laugh at him?

"Probably some of it was stubbornness," she said. "But you'll have to agree it hasn't exactly been easy for me at the ranch."

"No, I suppose it hasn't. Rod . . ." He didn't finish it. But she knew what he meant; Rod turning from her to Blanche.

She was standing so close on the warm day that her perfume stirred him more than usual. Its scent substantially increased his pulse rate. Only a chatter of birds in nearby trees and a faint rattle of rocks on the bed of the swiftly flowing stream broke an almost complete stillness.

"And every night . . ," Regina had to pause for a deep breath. He saw her teeth touching her lower lip. He hadn't noticed before how even and white they were. And her red lips, so moist in the sunlight. "Every night," she tried again, "I hear him sneak into her bedroom. It's not that I'm jealous, you understand. Only that it's quite . . . quite disturbing."

"Yeah, I suppose," was all he could think to say in the presence of this goddess.

"I feel like going in. Would you be so good as to turn your back until I tell you it's all right to look?"

He didn't reply. If he'd opened his mouth, he probably would have said something caustic, such as saving her bath for the ranch-house kitchen. But he turned dutifully and stood staring at the two horses. A faint rustle of cloth was the only sound of her disrobing.

"It's all right now, Lassiter," she called to him in an excited voice.

Turning, he saw her, clad only in an ivory camisole, running away from dress and petticoat, her shoes and stockings heaped on the ground. He saw the long hair swinging against her back and noticed the softness of her shoulders. Her legs were long and supple, flashing white in the sunlight.

She waded into the water, finally to her waist, then hunched down, until only her face was showing. "It's cold at first," she called. "Are you game to join me?"

While he debated about going in, she stood up, dripping wet. Clinging like an outer skin, the white camisole exposed every delightful curve of her sensuous body.

He quickly tied his horse, then, with trembling hands, laid his gunbelt on a patch of grass within reach. All he could see of her now was her vibrant face, the shining eyes and laughing mouth.

Within seconds, his clothes were on the grass. "I'm not as modest as you," he sang out. "With me, it all comes off."

She laughed, crossing her arms across her breasts.

At first the shock of the water's chill locked his teeth. But it was forgotten when she came easily into his arms.

"How I've dreamt of this moment," she murmured against his wet throat.

After their lips locked together for an exhilarating moment, she stepped out of the camisole. It became a blob of ivory satin, floating in the pool of still water, no longer hiding her magnificent flesh from his eyes.

At last he carried her up to the grassy patch of ground on the creek bank. Then she seized one of her dresses and used it to quickly dry herself. All the while her eyes feasted on his muscled shoulders, the strong torso, his thighs, which she said were like those of a gladiator.

Time slowed to the pace of a lazy snail while he, with fingertips and lips, leisurely searched her skin. At last the sun burned into his naked back and she was in his shadow.

In the warming sun, they lay together, savoring the memory of their pleasure.

"We better be heading for home," he said at last. "So far, nobody's come around. But you never know."

"Tell me, Lassiter," she said as she was dressing, "did I surprise you?"

"I don't think of surprise. Only the fun we had together."

"I think you know what I mean." She seemed suddenly shy. But in her eyes and soft mouth was a reflection of contentment. "I sensed you were a man of the world and wouldn't care. Had I married Rodney, I would have had to pretend . . . or worse, to explain."

"It doesn't matter."

"But I want you to know that I'm not a wanton."

"I'd never think that."

"Back in Philadelphia there was a neighbor. He was a year older than I. One time both our parents and the servants were away . . . well, I thought I loved him madly. But in time it faded to nothing at all. However, I'm sure Rodney would have been hurt to know that he hadn't been the first."

"Maybe he wouldn't have cared."

"Now we'll never know, will we?" She smiled wistfully. "Poor Rodney. I hope he'll be happy with Blanche."

As they rode back to Fork Creek, leaning in the saddle so they could lock their fingers together, he knew that today's experience had hammered one more nail into the complications of his life.

Chapter 22

It didn't take a superior brain to figure out that Fred Carver, the man who Kiley Boyle had left in charge of his saloon, was watching for someone to approach the town. Manly first noticed it one day during the week Boyle had ridden off with Lassiter.

Twice more that morning he saw Carver step from the Saber and stare east, shading his eyes against the sun.

"Sure as hell, he expects somebody," Manly said to himself. "But who?" Then he fell to thinking about his own situation.

One thing was for sure, his moves from now on had to be made more cautiously. At one time he'd had everything lined up nicely. He'd put such a fear in young Rucklor that the heir had finally agreed to sign off the ranch in exchange for Regina's release. And then Lassiter had appeared on the scene, giving Rucklor a chance to make a break for freedom. After that, everything went to hell.

At first he had toyed with the idea of having Sheriff Worden arrest Lassiter for the murder of Tex Ander. But then he decided it might prove embarrassing if some smart lawyer from the county seat representing Lassiter insisted on testimony from Regina Balmoral.

Several more times Manly saw Fred Carver peer down the rutted street to the east. It was beginning to get on his nerves. Kiley Boyle was up to something, but what?

Wednesday proved to be a slow night at the Saber, so Carver decided to lock up at nine o'clock. He hooked the swing doors aside, then closed and locked the storm doors. Just as he was about to step out the rear door, Rex Manly, followed by a scowling Burne, shouldered his way inside.

"I . . . I was closin' up, Manly," Carver faltered, because from the looks of the pair he sensed trouble.

Burne locked the rear door and stood with his thick arms folded across his chest.

"I . . . I got to be goin'," Carver said in a weak voice. "The missus is waitin' for me an' . . ."

"You want to see her again?" Manly asked bluntly.

Something in Manly's eyes turned Carver cold as if drenched with ice water. "What . . . what do you mean?"

"Boyle left you here to watch for somebody. Who is it?"

"Jesus, Manly, he never said nothin' like that."

"You've had your eye on the east road more than once lately. Who do you expect to come riding in, Fred?"

"Honest to God, I don't know."

Manly turned to Lake Burne and said calmly, "Hold him."

Carver sensed disaster. One thing the overweight man couldn't tolerate was pain. With a yelp, he tried to run. But Burne was faster. He grabbed him by the arms and thrust a knee into his back, bending him like a bow. Their shadows danced on the wall from the single lamp turned low.

"Please . . . don't . . ." Carver begged as Manly drew back his fist.

Manly struck him in his fat stomach. Carver groaned and started to double up, but Burne held him rigidly by the arms. An open-handed blow to the face brought a whimper of pain.

"Who are you expecting?" Manly demanded. "Speak up or you'll get more of the same. Only worse."

"Please . . . I . . . I'll tell you."

"Turn him loose, Lake."

"Let me get my breath." Carver was hunched. Droplets of blood dripped from his nose to stain the front of his white shirt. "It . . . it's some buffalo hunters Kiley knows. They wrote they were on their way."

"How many?"

"Two dozen or more."

Manly looked at Burne, who shrugged his heavy shoulders and appeared skeptical. "Two dozen?" Manly said. "You're sure?"

"It's what the boss claimed," Carver gasped. "That's all I know. Now can I lock up an' go home?"

"What are you supposed to do when they arrive?" Manly demanded. "That's what I want to know."

"Send 'em out to Fork Creek. But don't ever let on to Kiley that I told you. He'd skin the hide off me."

"We'll do worse if you're lying." Manly eyed him. "Keep your mouth shut about this."

"Sure will, Mr. Manly."

"And remember. The minute those buffalo hunters show up, I want to know about it."

Carver quickly agreed. After Manly and Burne slipped out into the darkness, Carver closed the door and leaned against it. His legs trembled. Damn Rex Manly. Carver made up his mind to keep his eyes open for the hunters. If at all possible, he would warn them about Manly, and with any luck, see them on their way to Fork Creek without interference from the lawyer.

Again he cursed Manly under his breath. He dampened his shirt with water from the tank behind the bar and tried to scrub out the bloodstains. If possible, he didn't want his wife to worry.

Burne said, "We could hit Fork Creek now, before them buffalo hunters get here." They were riding through the darkness toward Manly's place at the eastern edge of town. A moon hung low over the Santa Marias.

"I think we better wait," Manly decided, after thinking it over.

"Hell, we got our own men comin'. It'll be enough to handle 'em out there."

Manly shook his head. "Let the hunters get here. Then we'll use the new men to defang the bastards."

"What if they ain't so easy to defang, as you put it?"

"We'll manage. If necessary, we'll ride them up to the county seat. Worden can be talked into locking them up on one charge or another." Or could he? Manly frowned. He had recurring doubts these days about the sheriff's loyalty. "One way or another I'll get them out of the way, and get my hands on Fork Creek once and for all."

The two dozen buffalo hunters certainly put a new dimension on the business, Manly had to admit. He wondered what kind of a deal Lassiter had made with Kiley Boyle to bring them into the picture.

Burne was grousing again about the lack of activity. "I still say we oughta make our move."

Manly bit back a curse. Lately, Burne was increasingly morose and several times had hinted about taking his share of the cattle money and getting out, which was something Manly was determined would never happen. But for the present he needed to rock no boats.

"Tell you what, Lake. As soon as our men get here I'll decide. If the buffalo hunters haven't arrived in another week, it probably means they're not coming. That's when we'll move. Does that suit you, Lake?"

"I reckon," Burne grunted.

Chapter 23

Lassiter still didn't quite trust Kiley Boyle. In spite of him going out of his way to be pleasant and jumping to do any job that was assigned, Lassiter couldn't forget the man had once attempted to involve him in a plan to strip the Fork Creek ranch of cattle and split the proceeds.

Day by day, Rod Rucklor was recovering from his wound. He had youth on his side and the faithful nursing of Blanche to stand him in good stead. Lassiter had to admit that Blanche had proved to be a good woman. Most of the time she was cheerful. Occasionally, though, he'd catch her staring at her hands or out a window, a troubled look on her face.

She knows it can't last, he thought to himself, this fantasy of hers to marry a handsome young rancher and be the mistress of his domain. She was building dream castles which all too soon would crumble at her feet.

After his experience that day at the creek bank with Regina, Lassiter was on edge even more than before. It wasn't a time for him to get wrapped up in anything romantic. Not when he was trying to save a ranch for Rod Rucklor, mostly in memory of his father. Although he had detested the son at first, he had to admit that in the passing days, Rod had improved in disposition and shed most of his former obnoxious mannerisms. In fact, he was becoming almost human. Perhaps the gunshot wound had made him realize how quickly life could be snuffed out.

No longer did Rod dress like an easterner. He had switched to the range clothes purchased for him in town. Some of Rucklor's change in attitude, Lassiter was forced to admit, was probably due to his feelings for Blanche. However, Lassiter was still convinced the feelings were only transitory. Blanche and Rod had come from two entirely different worlds, Lassiter kept telling himself. Rod and Regina were much more suited. But whatever they had had between them now seemed to have turned hard and cold as winter stone.

He started taking his meals at the cook shack. Kiley Boyle was a better cook than the lanky Willie Cosgrove, who had tried his hand at it after the regular cook asked for his time. Boyle seemed to enjoy his new role and was always trying to turn out something different. He could do much with beef, adding just the right amount of seasoning and dried onions. It was hard to realize the scarred hands of the bare-knuckle fighter and wrestler could fashion a delicious cobbler out of dried apples.

One evening Lassiter was in the yard, his hands in his pockets, staring absently at the moon. He was smoking a last cigarette of the day when he heard a rustle of skirts. Regina pressed her warm hand against his cheek.

"You've been avoiding me," she accused lightly.

"I'm like a trout fighting off a hook. It's already in partway. And that's plenty far enough."

She laughed so heartily that he couldn't help but be trapped into watching the way her breasts moved under blue satin. A tautness in his throat lasted but a few seconds. He exerted his willpower.

"I've got to scout around," he said, unwinding her long fingers from his forearm.

"Let me go with you," she coaxed.

"You're safer here."

"I wasn't so safe the other day at the pond," she said teasingly.

But he won out, at least temporarily. He came back after touring the big yard. The watches were all filled and it was his night off. He sank into Len Crenshaw's easy chair and picked up a month-old copy of the *Denver Journal*. He was barely halfway through the front page when someone rapped lightly on his door.

Putting the paper aside, he went over and unbarred the door.

A smiling Regina slipped into the room. He peered into the darkness to see if anyone lurked nearby, then closed the door. In the lamplight he could see that she wore a heavy coat. It was an old one that he recognized as having belonged to Ham Rucklor. She had rolled up the sleeves and it dragged on the ground.

"You took a hell of a chance coming here," he whispered.

"I thought that by wearing this coat, anyone seeing me in the shadows would think I was a man."

"Not much chance of that," he said with a tight smile. "And you might have got yourself shot. My two men are nervous. And Boyle is nobody to fool with."

She took off the coat that had covered her blue dress. "I don't know whether I like Boyle or not."

"Has he been bothering you?"

"He just looks. That's bother enough." She glanced at the paper he had been reading. "Denver," she said and wrinkled her nose.

"They say silver's about as thick around there as dust."

"Oh, drat Denver." She moved close to him, her warm arms slipping around his neck, her lips invitingly close. "We have better things to think about . . . and do . . . than to worry about Denver and its riches."

It was the time to send her back to the house. But he didn't. The moment was gone. He walked woodenly to the door.

"I better lock it," he said in a voice suddenly charged with emotion.

"I should hope so," she said with a laugh.

The next morning he was just saddling his black horse when Rod Rucklor came to lean on the corral fence. His gray eyes were steady. Lassiter felt a flush begin to spread across his cheeks. Had Rucklor seen Regina enter his quarters? If so, he decided to say, "She's lonely. So am I."

And Rucklor might say, "I deserve that. I'm the one who made her lonely." But he didn't say anything—neither of them did.

Most of the early petulance had left Rucklor's face and there were new lines between his eyes and at the corners.

Lassiter tightened the cinch, picked up his Henry rifle and shoved it into the boot. A slight wind raised puffs of dust in the yard and rustled the cottonwoods.

"I've been meaning to bring something up to you, Lassiter."

Lassiter turned and braced for it. "Yes."

"But I didn't know how to do it. You seem to have such faith in Boyle."

Lassiter breathed easier. "Tell me what's on your mind."

"I'm wondering if his two dozen buffalo hunters are *ever* going to get here."

"I know what you mean. It's sure crossed my mind a few times."

"And if they ever do arrive, do you think we can keep them under control?"

"Why'd you bring that up?"

"Boyle was telling me they're a wild lot."

"He shouldn't be worrying you like that." Lassiter went on to explain that in the past the hunters let off steam when the season was over. "But they've had some lean years lately. Maybe the hell's been burned outa them. We can hope, anyway."

"At times I feel uneasy in Boyle's presence. I find him watching me. And when I catch him at it, he just gives a broad grin and walks away."

"Look at it this way, Rod: He's one more gun, which we'll need if Manly shows up. And he will."

Rucklor looked worried. "I suppose it's inevitable."

"If things were different, I'd say you and Regina oughta go to Denver. Stay there till it cools off down here." He tried to catch Rucklor's eyes, but he kept looking away. "But things aren't different, are they, Rod?" Lassiter continued. "It's you and Blanche now."

"And you and Regina." Rucklor swung his aristocratic head to meet Lassiter's eyes. "I see how she looks at you."

"I told you to be grateful to Blanche for introducing you to the female world, then to send her away. But you wouldn't listen. You said it was love."

"It still is, Lassiter."

Lassiter rode out. Inactivity and uncertainty were stringing his nerves taut as steel wires. He followed Fork Creek all the way to the junction where it bent to the west and the other unnamed stream flowed eastward. The latter was a mere trickle of water compared to the main branch, which was nearly bank to bank during mountain run-offs of early spring.

It was a beautiful expanse of country, rimmed to the north by the Santa Marias. Some of the higher peaks still held traces of dazzling white. In a way, Lassiter was sorry to see the changes the years had brought. He remembered coming through here as a boy and seeing the miles of buffalo herds, the flatlands black with them. Most of them were gone now, due to man's greed and to what some claimed was the army's deliberate plan to eliminate the Indian's main food supply. Buffalo herds as well as the Indians were eliminated because of the incursion of the white man. Men such as Ham Rucklor had seized Indian land to create a cattle empire, throwing the gates open to buffalo hunters to diminish the herds and make way for cattle.

And then came one of the ironies of the age: Ham Rucklor, pushing sixty, suddenly deciding to contest the right of passage of a magnificent old bison.

Well, his son was here now to take over. Lassiter envied him his fine education. But Lassiter had done well enough, fortunate to have access to books during his formative years.

That evening in the bunkhouse after supper, Kiley Boyle regaled them with stories, as usual pertaining to exploits as a buffalo hunter. His voice seemed a little shrill tonight, but Lassiter didn't think too much about it. Cosgrove and Borford always howled with laughter after one of Boyle's humorous recitals. He was a good storyteller, Lassiter had to admit, and knew how to hold an audience, even a small one of three men.

When Lassiter started for his quarters, Boyle followed him out into the star-filled evening with its sounds of crickets and the occasional neigh of a horse. Moonlight was pale yellow through the trees. Lassiter halted and looked around at Boyle, who seemed immense in the shadows. Lassiter was wondering, as he had so often, how he had been lucky enough to beat him at his own game—fists.

"Manly's sure takin' his time about makin' a move,"

Boyle said in his gravelly voice. For the first time, Lassiter got a whiff of whiskey on his breath. Then he recalled the man's voice in the bunkhouse, more high-pitched than usual. It was said that when drunk, Boyle was as hard to handle as a raging grizzly. Lassiter was in no mood to test the theory.

"Manly won't move till he thinks he's got all the aces," Lassiter replied. He couldn't help but throw a barb at the truculent saloonman. "Looks like your buffalo friends have forgotten about you."

"They'll be along."

"Let's hope they don't get here too late for the war. They're liable to find Manly's boot on our chests."

"When Gutch sends word he's comin', you can believe it."

"We'll see."

"He don't lie. Neither do I." Boyle's voice had taken on a dangerous edge, and in his anger he was beginning to slur his words. Lassiter hadn't paid much attention to him at supper or while he was telling his usual stories, but Boyle had obviously had his nose in a jug more than once tonight. He could still walk without stumbling and his actions, so far, seemed normal. But whiskey had built a fire under his brain that at any moment could erupt.

"See you tomorrow, Kiley." Lassiter started walking toward his lean-to at the end of the main barn. But Boyle followed him; his pride had been lanced when Lassiter questioned the arrival of his friends.

"Seen you had company of a night." Boyle was now spacing his words in the manner of drunks. And a slyness had colored his voice. A distant wolf howl knifed through the evening air.

Lassiter decided to ignore Boyle's sly thrust. He needed Boyle's gun in the showdown that was long overdue.

"I don't blame you none," Boyle called softly after Lassiter, who was walking away. "She's a fine set-up young female."

Lassiter halted by a cottonwood. "Let it alone, Boyle." In the moonlight he could see that Boyle's smile was more of a sneer.

"When the boys do get here, they'll be glad we got a fine-lookin' filly like her in camp."

"Look is all they'll do. The man who lays a finger on her is d-e-a-d. That means dead, in case you're no good at spelling."

Boyle's laughter was a half growl. "That Blanche, she ain't so bad either. But the black-haired one, she's got what folks call class. The boys'll appreciate that."

"Put a cork in that whiskey jug. And go to bed!"

"Did I ever tell you about one year down on the Red . . . ?"

"I don't want to hear about it."

"We'd had a good hunt an' we came across these two young fillies. Their menfolks had been killed chasin' Kiowas. Well, these two were hungry for company an' by God we gave it to 'em." Lassiter had started walking again and Boyle was matching his stride.

"Forget it, Boyle," Lassiter said.

"There was over twenty of us. By the time we were ready to head out, them two fillies couldn't lift a teacup without straining. Haw, haw, haw. Come to think of it, maybe you better keep them two fillies you an' Rucklor got outa sight. Wouldn't want them two gals to end up so weak they couldn't lift a cold biscuit."

Laughing, Boyle turned his broad body and lurched away. Whiskey was showing on him now, the brief flare of anger pushing him over the edge. A slow rage was beginning to build in the man over the failure of his friends to arrive. He had evidently been holding it in until the remark was made that they might not show up at all. A remark he shouldn't have made, Lassiter reflected. Too late, he realized Boyle had been hitting a bottle he'd brought out with him from town.

Not knowing just where Boyle's present mood might carry him next, Lassiter took his rifle up to the house where he declared himself a resident. He didn't explain the reason, only saying he thought it wise to have his and Rucklor's guns at the ready in case of trouble.

Rucklor looked drawn. "Yes, you're right, Lassiter."

Blanche declared herself a defender. "I'm a good shot. My father taught me how to use a rifle."

"Let's hope we don't need you," Lassiter said with a stiff smile. It was the first time he could remember having heard her mention her father. She must have been at least old enough to handle a rifle, twelve, perhaps. Even with a father's influence to that extent, a few years later she ended up at Simosa's.

Regina heard their voices and came gliding from a bedroom on her long legs, her hair in braids down the back of a blue satin wrapper. Upon learning that Lassiter would spend the night on a parlor sofa, a secret smile crept across her lips.

At Lassiter's urging, she and Blanche went to their separate bedrooms. He detained Rucklor and said softly, "I think from now on we'd both better keep one eye on Boyle."

"But I thought he was your friend."

"Not exactly. I figured we needed his gun and needed his hunter friends. But I don't think they're going to show up. And it's made Boyle jumpy. He's drinking too much. Tomorrow I figure to find his jug and either hide it or smash it."

"Hide it," Rucklor said with a strained laugh. "It seems my father left very little whiskey behind. And I'm beginning to find it eases anxiety."

"Just be sure you can handle it," Lassiter warned.

Lassiter got spare blankets from a closet and started to make a bed. Rucklor stood watching him, twisting his hands nervously. "I feel something's happened, more than what you've let on to me. I'd like to know what it is."

Not wishing to come right out and tell him about Boyle's oblique threats to the two women, he skirted the edges, saying that Regina and Blanche were their responsibility. "We didn't ask for either one . . . at least I didn't. But we've got them and so be it."

"And?" Rucklor leaned forward, his gray eyes intent on Lassiter's face. Shadows lay deep in far corners of the long room not reached by lamplight.

"Boyle said some things tonight I didn't like," Lassiter continued. "I know he'd been drinking, but maybe deep down he feels the same. Drunk or sober. Only when he's sober it doesn't show."

"What doesn't show."

"Rape, my friend," Lassiter hissed. Building pressures caused the word to erupt.

A startled look touched Rucklor's face. He flashed a glance in the direction of the bedrooms. "That's what Boyle threatened?" he gasped, facing Lassiter again.

"In a round-about way. I didn't want to tell you, but now . . ." Lassiter made a cutting gesture. "Now it's out. Just don't let on to Boyle that we've talked about it."

"My God, what'll we *do?*" Rucklor asked in a hoarse whisper.

"I tell you what I'll do." Lassiter's blue eyes were savage in the lamp glow. "If he makes a wrong move, I'll kill him!"

Rucklor was aghast. "You spoke of killing a man in the same tone of voice you'd use to order a glass of beer."

"I trusted him against my better judgment. We'll see how he is tomorrow. If he even hints at what he told me tonight, he's through."

"But what will you do?"

"Get his gun somehow and kick him off the ranch."

"I'm afraid that won't be easy," Rucklor said nervously.

"What is? If that happens, I think the best thing to do is take the two girls and hit for the back country. You can pick up a stagecoach in Overland. Go to Denver. I don't know what you'll do with two females on your hands, but it's your problem, not mine."

"You'll come with us, of course."

Lassiter shook his head. "I'll head south. Something I should've done before this. But I couldn't leave you and the girls."

"Head south? For what reason, Lassiter?"

"I know the country down there. I can recruit men. I'll come back and give Manly the fight of his life for this ranch. I'll collect that cattle money he's been keeping from you. If he's dead, we'll get a lawyer and go to court."

"I want to do it with you, Lassiter. The girls can go to Denver."

"Use your head, Rod!" Lassiter raised his voice. "Your job is to stay alive. If you're killed, Manly gets the ranch without firing a shot."

Rucklor put a hand to his eyes, then his jaw hardened. "How could my father have done this to me? Will me the ranch—but if I fail to survive, then Manly gets it. My own *father*. I just don't understand."

"He had some strange ideas, but he was my friend. I knew him and Len Crenshaw a long time. When I was a kid, I thought Len was about the greatest man alive. I wish you could have known him."

"So do I." Rucklor set his teeth. "If it hadn't been for you, I wouldn't have had even this much time in my father's house."

"Who knows what would have happened?"

"You've had the worst of it, Lassiter." Rucklor mentioned the shooting in camp the night they had met, Rucklor's flight to Simosa's, and how Lassiter had freed him from an ugly situation.

"Then I was shot by one of those same men who had me trapped at Simosa's," Rucklor continued in a shaky voice. "I've hardly done one damned thing around here. You've done it all."

Lassiter tried to minimize his own contribution, but he had to admit it was more or less the truth. Without him, Rucklor would either have sold out to Manly and left the country with a few dollars, or been under the sod.

Chapter 24

T he buffalo hunters finally arrived in Villa Rosa. Probably the reason Manly failed to note their arrival was that there were only five instead of the two dozen or more. The scruffy-looking bearded men clomped into the Saber Saloon in their heavy boots and looked around. It was early morning. They had camped out of town the night before. Only one customer was in the place and he stood far down the bar, his head buried in his arms, recovering from last night's whiskey.

The largest of the five men asked for Kiley Boyle in a booming voice. "Tell him Si Gutch has arrived."

Fred Carver, who was using a feather duster on shelving behind the bar, looked up. He placed a forefinger across his lips, gave the lone customer a worried look, then hurried to where the five bearded men leaned against the bar.

"Kiley said you'd show up," Carver whispered. "Where's the rest?"

Gutch got a sour look on his broad face. "They sniffed a hot wind blowin' up from Injun country an' figured it smelled of buffalo. Where the hell's Kiley? Me an' him are shirt-tail kin."

Carver looked carefully around, then in a bare whisper told Gutch about Manly and how Kiley Boyle waited for them out at Fork Creek. Carver's nose was still swollen from Manly's backhand.

"Kiley'll be plenty disappointed there's only five of you," he finished.

"We'll make up for them other bastards. We've been fooled too many times when word comes there's buffalo an' it turns out there ain't. How do we find this here Fork Creek place?"

Carver told him, mentioning landmarks such as the creek. "You can't miss the place."

Gutch and the others wanted a drink, but Carver was in such a state worrying about the possibility of Manly running into them, that he talked them into taking along a bottle instead.

After they had departed, by the rear door to avoid Manly seeing them from his office window, Carver began to worry. If the lawyer found out he hadn't reported the arrival of the hunters as ordered, he was in for a beating. The prospect sent a tremor through his large body.

Determined to suffer no more, he removed a .38 from a drawer that had been left in payment for a whiskey bill. The feel of the weapon in his waistband gave him some confidence. At least now he might have a chance, he told himself.

But later in the day, when Lake Burne came in with three strangers, he had to face up to reality. Burne was not only big, but known for a vicious temper. Carver sensed he wouldn't have much of a chance, gun or not.

But when they crowded up to the bar, he served them with a straight face. The strangers were laughing at something Burne had said.

Then Carver overheard Burne mention, "You'll have full-time jobs at Fork Creek. When do you expect the rest of the boys?"

That was all Carver heard because down the bar some new arrivals were clamoring for service.

Kiley Boyle seemed back to normal, which was a relief to Lassiter. And he didn't mention the two women; in fact, he barely looked at them when they came out of the house. Boyle moved slower than usual and the sun seemed to hurt his eyes. Lassiter smiled grimly at the price Boyle was paying for his drunk.

When Lassiter made his usual swing a mile or so out from the headquarters buildings, to try and spot potential trouble, he wondered if Regina would follow him and want a repeat of their frolic in the pond. Last night he had been put out at her when she first sneaked into his blankets on the sofa. But the warmth of her body and the passionate pressure of her lips melted him. Later, he whispered as a warning that it would be better if she didn't come to his bed again. Not while he was staying at the house, he amended. She had crept away in the darkness without speaking.

Later in the day Boyle came up to him. "Are you mad?" the big man asked bluntly.

"Mad about what?" Lassiter asked with a straight face.

"Last night."

"Forget it, Kiley" Lassiter started away.

"I kinda backed you into a corner, didn't I?"

"I don't think so." Lassiter read the slyness in Boyle's small eyes and was on his guard.

"I just figured to see how far I could push you."

"Not too far."

Boyle laughed and spat on the ground. "We're still friends, ain't we?"

Lassiter felt like saying they wouldn't remain even halfway friends if Boyle didn't stop trying to be cute. He did allow himself a nod of the head to Boyle's question about friendship. It was as far as he wanted to go on the subject. Boyle was no friend, and the only reason he was at Fork Creek was because Lassiter needed a tough man. And in the cold light of day he had to face reality; he still needed Boyle's gun.

Late in the afternoon, Lassiter was washing up when Rucklor asked a blunt question that sent his mind reeling back to the business with Regina on the sofa last night. Had Rucklor seen her shadowy figure?

Raising his dripping face from the wash basin on a bench next to the cook shack, he pretended he hadn't heard the question. Rucklor, embarrassed, repeated it.

"Have you and Regina ever been . . . close?"

Lassiter straightened out his features. "I think I know what you mean. No, we're only friends."

Rucklor looked relieved. "Sometimes I look at her and . . . well, I remember how much I thought of her at one time."

A wedge of hope began to warm Lassiter: Was it possible that Blanche was fading out of the picture? "You and Blanche," Lassiter started to say, but Rucklor interrupted.

"I still love her. I really do."

Lassiter felt let down.

"But Regina," Rucklor went on, looking anguished, "sometimes I . . . Anyhow, I'm glad you and Regina have never been . . . more than friends, I guess is the polite way to put it."

Lassiter wiped his face, at the same time trying to control himself. Rucklor was pressing it. After the business with the drunken Boyle, plus the uncertainties of Manly's next move, Lassiter's temper was on short fuse.

"What difference would it have made, for Chris' sakes?" Lassiter exploded. "You've had Blanche practically under her nose."

"But that's entirely different. . . ."

Lassiter stared at the wide-eyed tenderfoot in disbelief. "Entirely different? That sounds like a joke. A bad one at that."

"No need to get nasty."

"Hell, you send all the way back east for a gal to come out here and marry you. At least, I guess marriage was what you figured."

"Of course it was, but . . ."

"And then because some kind female not only nurses you through a gunshot wound, but lets you sample the real world in her bed, you turn your back on the gal from Philadelphia. Then you worry that she might be having a little fun out of life with somebody else. What the hell are you *talking* about, anyway?"

"But I was only concerned with Regina's morals."

"Jesus! Too bad you didn't let Manly pay you a few thousand for this damned place and stay east of the Mississippi where you belong!"

Instead of the expected flare of anger, Rucklor hung his head. "I guess by rights I'm a plain son of a bitch."

"You probably think I'll say no, you're not. That people just don't understand you. That's mule shit!"

At that moment, Kiley Boyle put his shaved skull with its saber scar out the window of the cook shack. He grinned at a distraught Rucklor.

"You better watch it, sonny," he grinned, "or Lassiter'll chew you with his bare teeth an' spit you into the dust."

"Keep out of it, Boyle!" Lassiter warned.

Laughing, Boyle withdrew his head and slammed down the window.

Lassiter glared at the window while Rucklor walked quickly away.

There was a commotion in the yard. It was just after the breakfast Lassiter took at the main house. Regina was still in bed. Blanche seemed so pale and ill at ease that Lassiter had a feeling she and Rucklor had quarreled during the night.

Hearing horses and loud voices, Lassiter slammed down his cup and jumped up from the table. He saw out the window five of the most disreputable-looking men he'd laid eyes on in years. Five saddle horses and two pack animals were standing nearby. The men had dismounted and were shouting and pounding Kiley Boyle on his broad back.

Without a word, a grim Lassiter picked up his rifle and went to the yard.

Boyle was saying, "But what the hell happened to Herm an' the rest of 'em?"

"They got a whiff of buffalo turds all the way from Injun country," said a man only a shade smaller than Boyle. "They went down to get some of the last big herds."

"You can't hunt in Injun territory," Boyle pointed out.

"Try an' tell Herm that. Hell, they'll run into the army sure as hell."

"Sure they will," Boyle put in.

"We holed up last night at a place called Simosa's an' there's this redheaded gal . . ."

Boyle turned his head. "Si, I want you to meet Lassiter. Lassiter, Si Gutch."

Lassiter shifted the rifle to his left hand and shook with Gutch. The pressure of the man's fingers was almost like having the hand trapped under the wheel of a loaded wagon. But Lassiter gave in return and Gutch's yellow eyes glowed at the accepted challenge.

"These here are my friends," Boyle said to Lassiter. "Ain't as many as I figured on. But these fellas you can sure ride the river with."

Lassiter tried to hide his disappointment at five men

instead of twenty-four. He met the others. Dodey, Loogan, Blackmor, and Bramble.

Maybe it was better this way, Lassiter reflected. With two dozen men at his back, Boyle might feel more adventurous than with only five.

"Tell 'em how things stand out here, Lassiter," Boyle suggested.

Something in Boyle's smile made him wonder if it would make any difference what he told them. But he decided to go ahead with it and outlined the trouble with Manly. "You'll draw fighting pay till it's over. Then if any of you want to sign on full-time, it's up to the boss. But I figure he'll be glad of all the help he can get."

"Fightin' pay would be what?" Si Gutch had missing front teeth and a twisted smile that was mostly hidden by a heavy black beard.

Lassiter told him fifty dollars a month, then said, "And a hundred-dollar bonus for every man when it's over." Rucklor could well afford it once he got the cattle money from Manly. If he didn't, it wouldn't matter much anyway.

A belt at the waist of each man sagged from the weight of a revolver. And running an eye over their shaggy ponies, Lassiter noted a Sharps .50-caliber buffalo rifle in each saddle scabbard.

What was needed at the moment, Gutch said heavily, was food to counteract the effects of the Simosa rotgut they had consumed. They started for the cook shack just as the flock of clucking hens came streaming around a corner of the bunkhouse. Barely breaking stride, Gutch stooped and snatched a squawking hen in each hand. As he walked he wrung their necks, then tossed them to Del Dodey.

"I got a hankerin' for chicken meat this mornin'," Gutch said with a laugh and wiped his hands on dirty pants. He wore a battered hat and an old blanket coat.

It looked to Lassiter as if his shirt hadn't felt soap and water all year.

Soon there was an aroma of chickens frying in bacon fat. Gutch, however, wasn't satisfied with two hens, and went out to twist the necks of two more.

Lassiter, just coming from the barn, saw what Gutch had done. He had let him get away with it once, but twice was too much.

"The next time you want something around here," he said to Gutch, "ask first."

Gutch stiffened, two still-squirming hens in their death throes in his hands. "I'll remember, Mr. Lassiter, *suh.*" He strutted on to the cook shack where smoke was pouring from the tin chimney.

At the cook shack doorway, Lassiter watched the five men tear into the chickens with their teeth, like wolves after a kill. They tossed the bones onto the floor. Lassiter was disgusted.

At least there was some consolation, Lassiter was thinking as he walked away. Manly would get quite a reception from those .50-caliber slugs that could tear a hole in a man as big as a bear paw. If the buffalo hunters could be trusted, that is, he amended grimly.

As he walked toward the house, he thought of a story he had once read as a boy, concerning the battle of Troy and a wooden horse. He wondered if his own personal wooden horse might possibly be in the person of Kiley Boyle and his five friends. And he had done it himself, Lassiter was thinking, by allowing Boyle to get his foot in the door in the first place.

But he had been desperate for help and had gambled. And now it was up to him to do his damnedest to see that it worked out.

Lake Burne took the three new men to Devil's Canyon, swinging far to the west in order to avoid the Fork

Creek headquarters. It was his intention to drive the herd he had gathered and penned there north to a rendezvous with cattle buyers that had been arranged at Star, a small town west of the county seat. This time he intended keeping the cattle money for himself. Aside from the shares he would be forced to give the three men, the bulk of it would be his.

It would mean forgetting about his half of the money from the previous sale that Manly was supposed to be keeping for him. But he'd have a stake. To hell with Manly. There was too much pussyfooting in the takeover of Fork Creek to suit Burne. He wanted to be on his way to a new territory with money in his pocket.

But upon their arrival at the canyon, he was in for a surprise. Instead of a thousand head of cattle penned there, the canyon was empty.

As he stared at the remains of the brush barricade, he could tell it had been destroyed by human hands, not stampeding cattle. He was gripped by a hot wave of rage.

One name streamed through his pounding skull: Lassiter!

Chapter 25

At the house, Lassiter told Rucklor about the buffalo hunters, but spared him the details of the run-in with Gutch and his crew's eating habits.

Blanche and Regina were looking out a window at the hunters, who had finished their quick morning meal and were in the yard, picking their teeth and talking to Boyle.

Regina shuddered. "They give me cold chills." She turned from the window.

Blanche, however, seemed unmoved and Lassiter supposed that in her time she had encountered men equally as disreputable-looking as this bunch.

Down in the yard, Gutch had been, staring at the house, a pleased smile on his bearded face. "Looky what we got here, boys." He pointed to Regina in the window and at her side, Blanche, standing as if carved from stone.

Lassiter heard the scrape of heavy boots on the veranda and sensed what it meant. With a hand on his gun, he jerked open the front door. Gutch, who was just reaching for the doorknob, backed a step from Lassiter, who was framed in the doorway.

Behind Gutch loomed his four grinning companions.

"What is it, Gutch?" Lassiter demanded.

"I saw them females in the window. Are they somebody's wives?"

"No . . ."

"Then they ain't spoken for." Gutch stretched his lips so that the missing front teeth turned the grin ugly.

"You're to stay away from them," Lassiter snapped. "All of you!"

"I told you, Si," Bert Loogan said. He rubbed at a dirty patch worn over his left eye. He started back down the porch steps, with three of the others trailing along.

Only Si Gutch, with thick biceps and legs that looked as if carved from solid oak, remained at the door. "Wasn't no harm in me askin', now was there?" he said innocently. He gave Lassiter a wink, then tromped on down after the others. They crossed the yard, laughing together.

Rucklor had a worried look on his face when Lassiter shut the door. "You think they mean trouble?"

Lassiter pounded a fist into the palm of his hand. "If we were here alone, we could make a fight of it," Lassiter said without answering the question. "But we've got the women to think about."

"Maybe they'd be safer in town."

Lassiter looked at him. "Think, man. Remember what happened to Regina in town."

"Then what in the world can we do?"

"Sometime today I'm going to try and get my hands on those Sharps rifles," Lassiter said, more to himself than to Rucklor. "It'll cut down the odds a little. And when it's done, we'll clear out."

"And go where?"

"Overland. Where the two girls can grab a stage for Denver."

"I'm glad that this time you aren't suggesting I go to Denver with them."

"I've been thinking it over. This is your ranch, amigo. I figure you better stay here to fight for it."

"Yes, after all, it is my responsibility." Rucklor's jaw firmed. "Then do you plan as before? To head south and recruit sufficient help so as to allow this ranch to remain in our hands?"

Lassiter snapped his fingers and waved aside the rather long-winded question. He was thinking rapidly. "Why wait till dark? I'll round up Cosgrove and Borford. We'll watch our chance and get the drop on that bunch. And while we've got 'em covered, you get their guns. Think you can do it?"

"Of course I can." Rucklor licked his lips and swallowed. A corner of his mouth twitched.

But the plans had to be delayed. Kiley Boyle called up to the house, "I'm goin' to show the boys some of the country!" And before Lassiter could say anything, they rode out.

It was long past midnight before they returned. No doubt they had ridden all the way to Simosa's. Where else? Well, it was too late to make a move now. It would have to wait for morning.

Before breakfast, Lassiter went to the bunkhouse to get Borford and Cosgrove, but they had already left on a scouting expedition, so Kiley Boyle told him. Lassiter had forgotten that yesterday he had told them to take an early tour of the area this morning.

Only Boyle was awake; Gutch and the others were still in their bunks. The place smelled like a bear cave.

As he left the bunkhouse, he thought of going after the two cowhands so the business of getting started for Overland could be speeded up. But that would mean leaving Rucklor alone to guard the two women. He decided that was too much risk. As much as he hated to waste the time, he'd have to wait until Congrove and Borford returned.

During breakfast, he told Regina and Blanche to be ready to move out. They were to bring with them only one change of clothing because they would have to be traveling fast. Then he went down to the corral to saddle his horse so it would be ready to go.

Just as he tightened the cinch, he heard sudden sounds of hilarity coming from the bunkhouse. Something had produced a gale of laughter. From the sounds, it seemed the lot of them were together, including Kiley Boyle. If he could get the drop on them, then yell for Rucklor to come and get their weapons, the job could be done.

Deciding to take a chance, he started for the bunkhouse.

Laughter still continued, though dwindling, when he stepped inside. Boyle had been laughing so hard that tears rolled down his scarred cheeks. Seeing Lassiter in the doorway, he said, "You shoulda heard the story Gutch just told. About the whore an' the tame bear."

A sweep of Lassiter's eyes had settled on the Sharps rifles on the big table near the winter stove—weapons well out of the reach of their owners. All he had to contend with were holstered revolvers.

He'd be facing six men. And there was always the chance that one of them would get lucky and kill him. But Lassiter had been too long on the frontier, had run too many risks to give the possibility more than a passing thought.

Gradually the laughter diminished and all eyes turned to Lassiter, standing tall, the brim of his flat-crowned hat pulled low to his brows. His arms were loose at his sides. He forced a disarming smile and was about to draw when he was suddenly aware of a drum-beat of hooves in the distance. This was followed by a crackle of rifle fire and a man's scream of pain.

"Looks like it's started, boys!" Lassiter yelled as faint shouting added to hoofbeats and rifle fire.

There was no turning back now. As much as he hated to admit it, he needed every man. With a shout, the buffalo hunters snatched up rifles and followed him outside.

Just as he reached the yard and sped past the barn, he saw Willie Cosgrove in the saddle of a speeding gray with a twenty-yard lead over Luke Borford. The latter was bent over in the saddle, his right shirt sleeve the color of spilled wine. He was weaving.

"It's *Manly!*" Cosgrove shouted as he drew in his reins in a spurt of gravel and dust and jerked a thumb over his shoulder.

It looked to Lassiter like perhaps a dozen riders, but he couldn't be sure because of the dust. All of them were coming full tilt fifty yards away. Braving rifle fire, some of which was peppering the barn wall, Lassiter grabbed the reins of Borford's horse, dug in his heels, and was dragged for several feet before the animal came to a partial halt. But it was enough so that Lassiter could pull the half-conscious rider out of the saddle. He yelled at the squat Hank Blackmor to drag Borford behind the barn.

Blackmor put down his Sharps to grab the wounded man. Lassiter snatched up the heavy weapon and shouted to Kiley Boyle, "Let's get 'em!"

Yellow dust churned in the wake of the speeding attackers. Defiant yells were louder now, gunshots closer. One hit the edge of a water trough. A slug dug a groove in one of the corral posts near Lassiter's head. Another threw a geyser of sand against his boots.

Dropping to one knee, he took aim at Rex Manly,

but at that instant the lawyer, as if from instinct, pulled in behind one of his men.

With the roar of a cannonade, the line of Sharps rifles exploded almost simultaneously. Lassiter's bullet knocked a heavy, bearded man out of the saddle and under the hooves of following horses. One mount stumbled over the body, somersaulted and threw its rider high into the air. Arms and legs beat the air as the man's scream knifed into the crash of buffalo guns. Hoofbeats rumbled and seemed to shake the ground. Riderless horses charged across the ranch yard, their stirrups flapping.

After the barrage from the Sharps rifles, there was a rattle of revolver fire, and more screams. Men fought to control their frenzied mounts. When the dust began to clear, Lassiter saw four empty saddles. Three horses were victims of the fusillade. Three stunned riders struggled to rise after having been thrown to the ground.

When the trio realized their companions had not only ceased firing, but were galloping for open range, their hands shot into the air.

A quick inspection showed the man Lassiter had shot was dead, as were three others.

Lassiter put down the borrowed Sharps. He was breathing heavily. The battle had been short and vicious. In the distance, the dust of Manly's retreating force stained the air.

Kiley Boyle stood up from where he had taken refuge behind a water trough. A wisp of smoke curled from the large muzzle of his Sharps.

"Besides the dead ones, three or four of the bastards got hit," Boyle said.

Lassiter nodded. "Yeah, I know. How about your boys?"

"Not a scratch. Borford's the only one with blood on him. For now," Boyle added with a hard smile and stalked over to the three survivors who stood with their hands lifted.

"You remember me, Kiley," one of them whined, a short, bowlegged little man in his forties.

Boyle laughed. He got behind each of the trio, jerked free their belt guns and tossed them into the dirt. He beckoned to the lean Del Dodey.

"Get three ropes." He pointed up at a broad cottonwood limb.

"No!" screamed the man who had spoken to Kiley Boyle. He was obviously petrified because drops of moisture began to grow on his forehead. "Kiley, I played cards at your place. I drank your whiskey."

"Hang 'em!" Boyle snarled.

At which point, Lassiter shouldered through the buffalo hunters who remained; Blackmor and Loogan had gone to get ropes.

"There'll be no hanging," Lassiter announced coldly.

"I say yes," Boyle countered with flashing eyes. "It was me an' my boys that saved your neck, Lassiter. Yours an' Rucklor's. An' the white an' pretty necks of them two ladies you got penned up in the house. Those two are especially worth savin'." Spittle arced in the sunlight at each word.

"You heard me!" Lassiter aimed his hard gaze in the direction Manly had taken. The dust had dwindled but was still moving rapidly away. In the group of attackers, he had also glimpsed Lake Burne and Harve Dolan. There was a chance Manly would regroup and make another run for it. But on the other hand, Lassiter doubted he had men enough to try again.

It seemed, however, the more present danger was this battle for supremacy between Boyle and himself. Boyle was demanding to be top dog, and Lassiter was equally determined not to let him.

With a snarl, Boyle started to lift the barrel of his Sharps, but found himself staring into the muzzle of Lassiter's cocked .44. The move was so swift that the buffalo hunters stared in awe.

He ordered them to put their rifles at their feet. Si Gutch glared at Lassiter, then at a scowling Boyle, as if awaiting a cue. A spate of harsh words boiled between Lassiter and Boyle. But Lassiter's steady gun, aimed at Boyle's face, won the moment. Five rifles went down. Lassiter well knew the tricky part was to come.

"Your revolvers. On the ground. Every damn one of 'em! The man who tries any tricks is finished!"

Instead of obeying, Boyle gave a broad smile that thinned his lips over blunt teeth. "Look at it this way," Boyle drawled. "You got a six-shooter. You leave one chamber empty . . . so the hammer comes down on air instead of a shell in case it gets fouled up somehow. So that means you got five shots in that .44 of yours. There's *six* of us."

"I can count," Lassiter threw back at him.

"You can get five of us. But the sixth man will nail you dead, my friend."

"Which one of you is it gonna be?" Lassiter asked through his teeth as the men stared, their viciousness bottled for the moment by the threat of his gun.

"You want to figure it out, which one it's gonna be, Lassiter?" Boyle went on. "Or just start shootin'?"

At that moment a white-faced Willie Cosgrove came up in his loose-jointed walk. In a shaky voice, he said, "If you want, I'll get behind 'em, Lassiter, an' take their weapons."

Lassiter nodded. "You do that, Willie. And the first one who even twitches is stone dead."

Si Gutch took a threatening step, which caused

Lassiter to line his gun on the man's great slope of belly. "Gutch, you want to be first?"

Gutch eyed the eared-back hammer, then said, "Damn you," under his breath, but made no further move.

One by one, Cosgrove relieved the cursing hunters of their revolvers.

"You're makin' a mistake, Lassiter," Boyle said coldly.

"I thought I could trust you, Kiley. I found out different."

Boyle's small eyes burned into Lassiter's face. "All on account of the three I wanted to hang."

"I won't stand for cold-blooded murder," Lassiter snapped. "And that's what it would have been."

Cosgrove wanted to know what to do with the weapons he had collected. A large barrel stood at a corner of the barn. It was filled with water to be used in case of fire. Lassiter pointed at it.

When Gutch realized what Lassiter had in mind, he snarled, "You'll ruin them guns."

"Better that than our heads rolling in the dust."

Rucklor, holding a rifle in white-knuckled hands, came up. He looked to be in a state of shock. There were moist patches on the rifle stock and barrel from his sweaty hands.

"My God, the battle was over before I could even take a deep breath."

When the captured guns went gurgling into the depths of the water-filled barrel, Lassiter told Cosgrove to pat down each man in search of hideouts. None were found. Nor were there spare weapons in saddlebags or their gear in the bunkhouse.

Only then did Lassiter tell them to get out. "It goes without saying, don't come back!"

"We saved your bacon sure as hell," Boyle grumbled.
"An' this is how we get treated."

"I know what your next move would have been."
Lassiter meant Regina and Blanche, which Boyle well
knew.

When Boyle and the others were riding out, Lassiter
turned his attention to the trio of Manly men. Even
though they had overheard what Lassiter had said about
cold-blooded murder, there was still anxiety on their
faces. Cosgrove, who was well armed with rifle, revolver
and long-bladed knife carried in his boot, had them under guard. Lassiter had Rod get their saddle guns. When
this was done, Lassiter told them to clear out.

There was a chance they'd rejoin Manly, but it
couldn't be helped. He was not the type to gun down
prisoners, as Manly would probably have ordered had
the situation been reversed. Nor would the three men
fit in with his plans. They'd need constant guarding
and he didn't have the manpower for it.

He found Luke Borford in the bunkhouse.

Somehow the man had managed to peel out of his
shirt and was just doctoring his wound. A bullet had
ripped an ugly gash on the underside of his right arm,
then cut another one along his ribs. Lassiter bandaged
both wounds for him while the man told how he and
Cosgrove had spotted Manly making a leisurely approach to the ranch. Manly had spotted them, chased
them, but they'd gotten away.

"Those buffalo fellas really saved our hides," Borford finished.

"They helped, for sure." He and Borford were alone
in the big silent bunkhouse.

"I saw 'em ride out. Where're they headin'?"

"I kicked 'em off the place."

Luke Borford, overweight and slow-moving, took a

moment to react. Then his jaw dropped. "You kicked 'em off? Why?"

"They had their eyes on the two women. Couldn't have that."

Borford thought about it, then said, "No, I reckon not. You reckon we can stand off Manly if he makes another try?"

"We're getting the hell out."

"We are?" Burford stared at him in amazement.

Lassiter told him they would go over the mountains to Overland, put the two women aboard a stagecoach for Denver, then head south to recruit men for the showdown with Manly.

Regina stamped her foot when she heard about it, saying she had no intention of leaving Lassiter. But Lassiter's word finally prevailed.

"But after Denver, then what . . . for us?" she whispered, her large eyes fixed on his grim face.

That was when he winked and gave her arm a reassuring squeeze, but didn't commit himself. "We'll travel light, so bring only a change of clothes. Leave the rest here. I'll send them on to you."

"Bring them yourself. You've got to promise, Lassiter. Or I refuse to budge."

"All right," he reluctantly agreed. In these times of peril, he reasoned, a white lie could be overlooked.

Lassiter's final chore was to lock up the house. He saw Rucklor staring up at it, with such a tragic look on his face that it seemed he might burst into tears at any moment.

"Rod, don't look so glum," Lassiter advised.

"I was just thinking of the times my father walked out of that house. I never got to know him."

Lassiter handed over the house key. "It's yours. You'll need it to unlock, when we come back."

"You do expect to return, don't you?"

"Hell, yes." Laughing heartily, Lassiter slapped the younger man on the back. But he didn't feel quite so confident as he tried to sound. Unless he could get more men, the cause was doomed—either that or meet Manly face to face in a showdown. And if he killed the lawyer, there was the risk of a vengeful sheriff.

Chapter 26

To get the two women away from danger was the prime consideration. After that, he could act without the weight of those heavy chains of responsibility.

Borford, although in pain, swore he could make the long ride. Cosgrove had saddled a horse for him. Lassiter turned the rest of the horses into a pasture and could only hope they wouldn't be stolen before their return.

Wearing a checkered shirt and Levis, Blanche looked very young. The ends of her braided wheat-colored hair blew in a light breeze. They started out with Cosgrove leading a pack animal with blankets and cooking utensils. They carried beans, flour and bacon. With an antelope or a deer to fill out the food supply, they should be able to subsist and reach their destination with a minimum of discomfort for the two women.

It was a warm morning, and so much had happened already. After the attack by Manly, graves had been dug for the dead. The only identification on any of them was a letter addressed to Buck Pelley on the bearded one Lassiter had killed. It was in a woman's handwriting and signed "Mary." It had an address in Missouri. Lassiter had saved the letter. If he survived what was to come, he would write Mary to say that Buck Pelley was dead. It was the least he could do.

Cumulus clouds dotted the azure dome of the sky. A herd of antelope broke from the trees and went bounding across the prairie where thousands of buffalo had once roamed in such a spring as this.

When Ham Rucklor had started his ranch, he had set it down in the middle of buffalo country. His men had added to the slaughter of the herds in those early years, so Lassiter had been told. It was too bad that most of the bison were gone now. Thanks to certain politicians who wanted to starve the Indian into accepting bounty from the government.

During the early afternoon, Lassiter found himself riding beside Blanche. Regina had dropped back and was talking to Cosgrove. One thing about Regina, Lassiter had noted, despite her upbringing she was no snob. Her laughter rang bright and clear in the stillness of the day. Cosgrove had said something to make her laugh, and Lassiter thought it was good to get her mind off herself.

Blanche, he noticed, seemed to have eyes for no one but Rod Rucklor, who was riding next to Borford. He noticed that she kept biting her lips and giving an occasional deep sigh. Was she worrying that her tenuous hold on the Fork Creek heir was unraveling?

They were following wheel tracks that climbed through skimpy pines. Early tomorrow they would be going over a high pass—a cut through the mountains too narrow and steep for a stagecoach but not for saddle horses. In this back country they were crossing, chances of trouble were slim, Lassiter had estimated.

But no sooner had the thought crossed his mind than he felt a sudden chill along his spine. He directed a tight glance at Blanche on his left, riding with her head bowed and staring absently at the saddle horn. While he watched, in that flash of time, she lifted a hand and wiped at her eyes. Was she thinking that when she and Regina took the stage north, it would mean she'd never see Rucklor again?

It had taken no more than a few brief seconds for him to look to the left at Blanche. But the coldness along his backbone persisted. He jerked his head to the right. The sight of a toothless grin jolted the chill at his spine into his heart and throat. Not twenty-five feet away, his back to the bole of a pine tree, was the thick body of Si Gutch, standing in a wedge of sunlight that shone down through sparse branches. The light fell across the bearded face so that Lassiter could see a deep scar at the right eye—an eye that was at the moment sighting along the barrel of a rifle.

Acting on pure instinct, Lassiter rammed in his spurs, yelling at the same time. As the others in the party froze, a rifle cracked. Blanche cried out and uttered a sob. Lassiter wheeled his plunging horse and saw her sagging in the saddle. A second rifle shot tugged at the open collar of Lassiter's shirt.

Trying to draw fire away from the others, Lassiter jumped his horse over a deadfall and at the same time pulled his right foot from the stirrup. As he made a running dismount, a bullet whipped past the tip of his nose. He struck the ground at a dead run, his .44 snapping into position.

Gutch was lifting his rifle for another shot when Lassiter beat him to the draw. The impact of the bullet slammed Gutch's head back against the tree trunk. Breathing hard, Lassiter waited tensely while Gutch seemed to hang against the tree. But after a moment or so, the thick legs collapsed and Gutch fell on his face.

Regina's screams had halted so abruptly that Lassiter worried she might have been hit. But when he looked around, he saw her dismounted and running to help Rucklor lift Blanche from the saddle. The sight of blood on the left side of Blanche's jeans turned him cold. The whole pants leg was rapidly reddening from the waist down.

But first he had to make sure Gutch was no longer a threat and that more of the buffalo hunters weren't lurking nearby. Scanning the area, he saw no one but Gutch, who was lying on his face, making snorting noises. Angered at the damage done by the man, Lassiter snatched away the rifle and turned Gutch over on his back. Gutch had both hands tight against his belly. Blood escaped through his fingers. His face was turning gray.

"Where's the rest of 'em?" Lassiter demanded, his eyes searching the woods and the twisting road of sorts they had been following.

"Gone," Gutch said in a weak voice.

"Where'd you get your hands on a rifle?"

"Peddler . . ." Gutch was gasping, his grin with the missing teeth frozen on the sweated face. "Only one gun. I got it an' rode . . . rode to get you, Lassiter. Seen you leave the ranch . . ."

A shudder twisted the large body and the grin was wiped off, to be replaced by lips locked tight against pain.

"Why the hell did you turn against Kiley?" Gutch gasped, looking accusingly up into Lassiter's face. "All we wanted was them damn females . . ."

A gleam of anger was washed suddenly from his eyes. As Lassiter watched, the light vanished. Gutch's large head rolled to one side and he drooled a bloody froth into his beard.

Lassiter scrubbed a hand across his sweated forehead, then reloaded his revolver. With Gutch's rifle, he trotted over to where Blanche had been placed in the shade.

A white-faced Rucklor turned to Lassiter as he came

up. "It's a bad wound, Lassiter," he said in a dead voice.

"Let me have a look."

"What'll we *do*? My God, we can't just let her . . . let her die."

Putting the rifle on the ground, Lassiter knelt down. Blanche's face was almost as gray as Gutch's had been at the last. His heart sank like a stone. Gently he unfastened her belt and pulled down the jeans. Her white undergarment was stained red from the wound.

"I'm sorry, Blanche," he said in a low voice, not knowing whether she could hear him or not. He carefully lifted the edge of the garment to reveal an ugly wound in her thigh. Apparently, the bullet had struck bone, then cut a deep but erratic pathway along the thigh.

The next thing Lassiter knew, Regina was tearing strips from the petticoat she had surreptitiously removed.

"Let me have her," Regina said firmly, and knelt beside Blanche.

Lassiter got to his feet, picked up the rifle and walked away a few steps to give the pair some privacy. Borford, his arm in a sling, was all too conscious of pain. "Poor kid," he said in sympathy. "She must be hurting like hell."

"We've got to get her to town and a doctor," Lassiter said, making up his mind. "She'll never last trying to get over the pass."

Rucklor overheard him and gave a sigh of relief. "Thank God," he breathed. "If you hadn't suggested it, I was going to take her to Villa Rosa myself."

Lassiter was staring at Gutch's rifle, which he held in his two hands. "The bullet that did that to her came from this goddamn rifle!" he cried suddenly.

Angrily, he strode to a large rock projecting from the ground to one side of the wheel tracks. He deliberately smashed the stock and bent the rest out of shape by hitting it repeatedly against the rock. Then he threw it away. His hands trembled. What next? What in the holy hell could happen next in his efforts to try and save a ranch for the son of a punishing father? A father who hadn't the decency to give his only offspring clear title to the Fork Creek Cattle Company. Instead he practically condemned the son to an early grave.

An angered Lassiter shook his fist at the sky and yelled, "Goddamn you, Ham! If I had you here, I'd beat you bloody!"

They looked at him in surprise. Rucklor wore a pained expression. "I didn't know you hated my father."

"I didn't. Not when he was alive, anyway. I thought he did some stupid things, though, such as tying you and Manly up in the same gunny sack." Lassiter wiped his face on a bandanna and began to calm down. "But after all, he was my friend," he finished in a more reasonable voice.

"Can I borrow your knife, Willie?" Lassiter requested. Without a word, Cosgrove drew the long-bladed weapon from its sheath in his boot. With it, Lassiter cut a blanket into strips and made a padding for Blanche's saddle that might partially ease her wounded thigh. No matter what, it would still be a hellish ride for her. Her eyes were open but seemed feverish. Regina had used most of the petticoat as a bandage.

Blanche, her teeth locked, nodded that she was ready to ride. But upon learning the destination was to be Villa Rosa, she protested that it would be too dangerous for the rest of them. Lassiter waved aside her objections.

It was slow going because of her pain. At times she would cry out and her eyes would roll back in her head. Finally, after a few miles, she fainted.

"At least she's out of it for now," Lassiter said. He tied her to the saddle, then told Rucklor and Cosgrove to ride on either side to see that, despite the ropes, she didn't fall.

All those miles Lassiter rode ahead, with his Henry rifle across his thigh, squinting into the trees, every brush clump and possible site for an ambush. He was watching for any sign of the other buffalo hunters, who might have gotten their hands on weapons. Gutch had gotten his from a peddler. What had happened to the man Gutch had run across? Either dead or badly beaten, Lassiter surmised.

Even traveling at a steady pace, it was late afternoon by the time they reached Villa Rosa. Instead of entering town by the main street, which was closer, Lassiter cut to the residential area on the north side of town. Some small boys rolling a wheel rim stopped their play to stare at the bloodied blond lady roped to a saddle, her head bobbing at each step of the horse. Her eyes were closed and she was deathly pale.

"Where's Doc Straffer's place from here?" Lassiter called to a freckle-faced boy.

The boy, feeling important that he was the one singled out for directions, jerked a thumb to the left. "Two blocks over!"

Lassiter thanked him and the cavalcade turned down the next street.

Doc Straffer's home and office were two small structures pushed together and painted white. His sign was on a post driven into the hard soil of the yard: NED STRAFFER, M.D.

A knock on the door aroused the doctor, who pushed aside a window curtain to peer outside. Then he opened the door. A tall, thin man, he walked with rounded shoulders as if to diminish his height. A neatly trimmed Vandyke beard lent dignity to his appearance. He gave Lassiter a stern look.

"I've been wondering, thanks to your reputation, how long it would be before you filled someone full of holes and brought them."

"It's a young lady, Doc. And I didn't shoot her. I finished the hombre who did."

Blanche, on her horse, had been slightly behind Regina and Rucklor. At sight of her with the bloodied leg, the doctor rushed from the house and urgently began tugging at the knots.

Cosgrove drew his knife and quickly severed the ropes.

"I remember her," Doc Straffer said as Lassiter lifted Blanche from the saddle. "One of Simosa's . . ."

A sharp warning shake of the head on Lassiter's part and the doctor's bearded mouth tightened. "I'll get things ready inside," he shouted over his shoulder as he rushed back into the house. "Bring her in."

Harve Dolan had been strolling along alleyways after leaving Bessie's small house. It was always a risk, he well knew, showing up in broad daylight, but she never failed to welcome him with such enthusiasm that it pushed any hint of danger from his mind. Besides, she usually knew from letters just about when her teamster husband would be again swinging back through Villa Rosa.

He was vaguely aware of yelling kids and looked down the street he was crossing to see one of them rolling a wheel rim and being chased by three others. Dolan had just moved on down another alley so as to keep out of sight as much as possible, when he was aware that the yelling behind him had stopped abruptly. He halted as a man's voice asked directions to Doc Straffer's place.

Something about that voice . . . Dolan wheeled in time to see a horseman ride past the alley. *Lassiter!*

Chapter 27

An hour ago Rex Manly had seen Kiley Boyle ride into town. A furious Manly had confronted him at one end of the big bar in the Saber. Boyle was behind his bar, wiping his face on a damp towel and telling Carver, his bartender, to go home. Carver avoided Manly's eyes, but Manly's venom at the moment was directed at Boyle.

"You've got guts coming back here, Kiley. After the reception you gave us out at Fork Creek."

"Guts I've got," Boyle said defiantly. He looked the lawyer in the eye.

Manly drew a deep breath. "Tell me something. Were you trying to kill me along with the others?"

"If you got in my way."

Manly gave a short laugh and shook his head. Boyle was a puzzle. At one point he seemed to like Lassiter. But he had come storming back into town with his four hunter friends, damning Lassiter to the skies. The fifth hunter, Si Gutch, had gone off on his own, and good riddance, so Boyle told it in his saloon.

Manly had gone home and had the luxury of a bath and change of clothes. It was a relief to wash off the Fork Creek grime. He spent no time thinking of the men he had lost that day.

"What did you really figure to do out there with Lassiter, anyway?" Manly asked when a disgruntled

Boyle came back down the bar after waiting on some customers.

"Two things. I figured to talk him into strippin' the ranch of cows and splittin' the money three ways. Him an' me. An' Gutch an' the boys."

"What about young Rucklor? Is he out of it?"

"That greenhorn's so far out you can't even smell him."

"You don't mind speaking right out, do you, Kiley?"

"The main thing at Fork Creek was them two females. That's when Lassiter got his back bowed."

"You hate him now?"

"Worse'n hate." Boyle bared his teeth.

Manly was thinking rapidly. There still might be a way to salvage the day. It had come as one of the surprises of his life to expect Lassiter to have no more than three hands; instead, he came up against a rush of rifle fire. He hadn't even been aware that the buffalo hunters had arrived. Fred Carver hadn't said a damn word. Last time he had only gotten a bloody nose out of it, but now he was due for a real beating for not alerting him. Even though they were only five instead of the expected twenty-four, their marksmanship had been devastating.

"Why don't you get your boys together and we'll—" Manly started to say, but Boyle interrupted with a string of profanity that came close to rattling the windows.

And when Boyle cooled down sufficiently to speak, he said, "Lassiter took our guns, goddamn it. Every damn one. I told 'em to come into town with me an' we'd get more. But Gutch, he said no. He said he'd get a gun somewhere an' go after Lassiter. I couldn't talk sense into that bull-headed Dutchman. I ain't seen Gutch since."

"That Lassiter," Manly said grimly. "How much longer will his luck last?"

"Only till I get my hands on him."

"If you're as angry as you sound, I shouldn't wonder. How about us burying the hatchet? Then you round up your four hunter friends . . ."

"They left."

Manly looked across the bar at a fuming Boyle. "Left?"

"Couldn't wait to get away from this hell hole, so they said. They blame me for what Lassiter done. Can you figure that?"

Manly smiled coldly. "That means you're here alone. That proves you've got guts. To face up to me like this with nobody at your back. Not knowing how I'd react when we came face to face again."

"I'll tell you one thing, Manly," Boyle said evenly, "you better not make a wrong move. I guarantee that if I go, you go with me. Understand, amigo?"

"You speak plain, Kiley." Manly felt uncomfortable under the piercing impact of the small eyes. "I like that in a man."

At that moment, Lake Burne entered the saloon, wearing a black scowl and a bloodied bandage under his hat. A bullet had creased his temple during the short but furious gunfight out at Fork Creek.

He came over to where Manly was standing. "I just saw Harve Dolan."

"Doing what, as if I care?"

"Hammerin' on your office door."

"What's he want?"

"I didn't stop to find out. I wonder what it'd cost to get Doc Straffer to carve that yellow streak out of his backbone."

Manly gave him a thin smile. "Is Dolan the only yellow belly?"

"Those new men you hired weren't much better." Burne started to say more but at that moment a

breathless Harve Dolan, ropes of bright red hair sticking out from under his hat, burst into the Saber.

Boyle shouted at him. "What the hell you tryin' to
do, Dolan? Bust down the doors?"

The dozen or so customers turned to look.

"Manly!" Dolan yelled, spotting the lawyer at the far
end of the bar. He rushed over, unmindful of Boyle's
glare. "I've been tryin' to find you . . ." Dolan gasped,
out of breath from the wild run across town.

"What is it, Dolan?" Manly set his glass down on the
bartop, and he turned with interest to the redhead.
Today Manly wore a checked gray suit and boots with
inserts of red leather. Ends of a string tie lay neatly
over the front of a spotless white shirt. A revolver with
ivory grips in a custom holster hung from a wide belt.

"It's Lassiter," Dolan finally managed to get out
when he had caught his breath.

"Where the hell is the bastard?" Manly demanded,
flicking a glance at Boyle, whose broad face lighted
with interest.

"Here . . . in town," Dolan panted. "Doc Straffer's
place!"

Manly laughed and rubbed his hands together. He
looked across the bar at Boyle, who couldn't help but
have overheard Dolan's loud voice.

"It seems, Kiley, that our prayers have been answered." Manly grinned.

Boyle nodded his bald head and flashed a hard grin
of his own.

Manly got Dolan by an arm. "Who's Lassiter got
with him?"

"Rucklor . . ."

"About as tough as a bug in amber. Who else?"

"One fella with his arm in a sling. An' another one
that used to hang around town. Willie Cosgrove. I don't

reckon he's got brains enough to put on his hat in the rain."

Manly was keyed up. He could solve all of his problems before Sheriff Worden got too inquisitive. A recent letter written to the sheriff outlining the current situation with the Fork Creek Cattle Company had prompted a rather cool reply. The political winds, it seemed, were shifting. As for Manly's suggestion that Lake Burne be appointed a deputy sheriff, it was out of the question, the sheriff had responded. At first, Manly had felt let down, but then was determined to go ahead and finish what he had started. The disastrous attack on Fork Creek had been the result of that attempt.

Well, everything could fall into place if that gadfly Lassiter was finally out of the picture.

The many possibilities Dolan's message presented made Manly's mind spin. Come to think of it, he didn't necessarily want Lassiter dead—better to be crippled. To spend the rest of his days begging for mercy was the way Manly wanted it after all the trouble he'd caused.

A grinning Kiley Boyle had removed the stained apron borrowed from his barkeep and was swinging his immense arms in the air to warm up.

Manly's thoughts swung to Rod Rucklor. Couldn't there be a stray shot in all the excitement of a full-blown battle between Lassiter and Boyle that could accidentally cut down Ham Rucklor's son? It would mean that Manly automatically took control of the Fork Creek Cattle Company, the principle heir having been unfortunately eliminated. Perfect. Manly slapped the bartop and smiled at Burne who hulked at his elbow.

By now the Saber buzzed with excited voices as word spread that another brawl between Boyle and

Lassiter was shaping up. It would be something to see, everyone agreed. Lassiter's luck couldn't possibly hold for another blood-letting battle with Kiley Boyle.

As men started trooping toward the doors, Manly leaned toward Dolan's ear. "I don't think for a minute that Lassiter will get the upper hand this time. But in case he does have luck, see that Boyle gets his hands on your knife."

Dolan nodded that he understood, putting a hand on the hilt of the long-bladed weapon worn at his belt.

As the patrons of the Saber started to push through the swing doors, Manly gave Burne's sleeve a tug. "Watch your chance. When the crowd really gets wild and yelling their heads off, see if you can't put a bullet in Rucklor's skull—without anyone seeing you, of course. But wait until Lassiter is down."

Burne's eyes gleamed. "It'll be as easy as slidin' on iced bricks."

"Don't take it too lightly, Lake," Manly warned. "We've been stung before by Lassiter."

Chapter 28

Blanche had lost a lot of blood. Her face was drained white, her eyes bright with fever. With a look of agony on his face, Rucklor stood beside her bed in Doc Straffer's office.

Straffer was checking her pulse. It was fairly strong, he said, despite all she had gone through. He then ordered everyone out of the room but Regina, who had found fresh bandages. She had gone to put a pan of water to heat on a small stove. She added kindling and soon had a fire going. When she returned to the sickroom, Blanche was wrapped in a sheet. Her bloodied clothing was piled in a chair.

"I hope to God I can save her leg," the tall doctor said more to himself than to Regina.

"You've got to save it, Doctor."

Straffer turned to look at the aristocratic young woman, her dark hair loosening from its combs. A lock had straggled across a cheek, which she impatiently brushed back. A person of obvious good breeding about to act as nurse for a girl who at one time had worked for John Simosa. The incongruity made him shake his head. Many strange things he had witnessed in his years on the frontier, but this unlikely matching would be close to the top of the list.

It pleased him that Regina Balmoral seemed to have no superior attitude that some of her set would have shown toward anyone of Blanche's class. Yet Blanche herself was soft-spoken, intelligent and at some period in her young life must have enjoyed at least a smattering of education.

His daughter, had she lived, would be about the age of either one of the girls. As a young man fresh from medical college he brought his family West in a wagon train. Although the Missouri River seemed to be in flood, the wagon boss said it was safe to cross. It wasn't. Three wagons were lost before the crossing was called off, with them Straffer's bride of a year and their baby daughter. Afterward he tried to kill the wagon boss who had insisted the crossing was safe, but he was severely beaten by the man's friends. He had thought of turning the gun on himself, but after a year of wandering from one saloon to another, he found himself alive and in the West. Searching for the most miserable and isolated place on the map in which to establish a practice, he finally chose Villa Rosa.

While laying out his instruments, he instructed Regina in how to administer ether. After making sure all windows were wide open, he warned her not to breathe too deeply or she might go under along with the patient.

After the bullet was removed, he washed blood from his hands and went to where Lassiter and the others were waiting outside. Through a hall window, he noticed that quite a crowd was gathering in the street in front of his house. It crossed his mind that a considerable segment of the town's male population had come to await word of Blanche's condition. Then a second glance through the window made him think otherwise. There was too much excitement stamped on the faces. Then he saw Kiley Boyle, standing apart from the others, facing the house, his thick legs spread wide, reminding the doctor of a Roman gladiator on the floor of the Colosseum.

As the doctor stepped out the front door, he could see that Boyle was taunting Lassiter. But Lassiter turned his back and stood waiting for Straffer to speak.

"She's going to be all right, God willing," the doctor said solemnly. "All she needs now is rest, and lots of it."

Rod Rucklor choked up. "Thank God." A tear rolled down his cheek.

And as Doc Straffer was about to open his mouth again, he saw two men launch themselves from the crowd and slam into Lassiter from behind. Lake Burne hit Lassiter just below the knees, Harve Dolan the upper body. The three of them fell to the street in a tangle of arms and legs. Dolan plucked Lassiter's .44 from the leather holster and held it aloft as if it were a trophy of victory.

"I got it!" he screeched to Manly, then darted into the gathering crowd.

"Let's see 'em fight!" a fat man yelled drunkenly.

"It's about time!" another shouted and the crowd roared its approval.

Lake Burne spun around and snatched Rucklor's gun before the man even knew what had happened. Then he leveled the weapon at Cosgrove and the wounded Borford. "You two keep out of it!" he warned.

Through the buzzing in his head, Lassiter was aware that for one of the few times in his life he had been careless, turning his back on a tormentor in order to hear Straffer announce Blanche's condition.

When he dazedly started to pick himself up from the street, he was suddenly aware of a large shadow. Looking up, he saw Kiley Boyle towering over him, saying, "Manly, I'm gonna earn that one thousand dollars!"

Then to Lassiter, "I oughta jam you in a fire barrel like you did to our guns, an' nail down the lid."

Lassiter, on one knee, now shook his head to try and clear it. From a corner of his eye, he saw Boyle start to swing a foot, the obvious intention to send the toe of his boot crashing into Lassiter's face. But Lassiter jerked his head aside, dodging the kick. Then he tried to seize the swinging boot and twist the foot so sharply that an ankle would snap. But the boot slipped out of his grasp.

He jumped to his feet amidst the swelling noise of the crowd. Dimly he heard Regina scream, *"No!"*

She started to run toward Lassiter, but Doc Straffer grabbed her by an arm. "You'll only get yourself hurt," he cautioned.

Then Lassiter turned his cold blue eyes on Boyle, who was circling slowly, a grin pasted on his scarred lips. "Kiley, this won't work," Lassiter said, his voice as well as his brain still not functioning properly. "Somebody give me a gun. . . ."

Lassiter's words were like a spark to gunpowder. With a bull-like roar, Boyle abruptly rammed a shoulder into Lassiter with such force that again he was knocked down. However, this time Lassiter doubled up, rolled, and swiftly came to his feet. Strangely enough, being slammed into again seemed to help clear his head of the fuzziness that had persisted since he had been downed by Dolan and Burne.

After his wild rush, Boyle was turning, circling back now, with both fists swinging. Mostly the blows were wide of the mark, but Lassiter was jarred by a few. A missed roundhouse to the head threw Boyle slightly off balance. Remembering the softness above Boyle's belt buckle, Lassiter moved in. His right fist sank so deep that Boyle uttered a great whooshing sound and started to double up.

"Get him, Lassiter!" a man yelled.

"Tromp him!" somebody else cried in the great roar of voices as Boyle staggered.

Lassiter's knuckles slammed the heavy jaw, but it was like punching an anvil. Pain shot up his arm. In backing off, he took a solid blow to a cheekbone. The warmth of his own blood touched the skin. The stinging blow seemed to drive out the last of the haze from Lassiter's skull.

Lassiter relentlessly followed Boyle slowly down the street, swinging a fist at practically every step. Most of them landed on Kiley's broad and bloodied face. A slight tremor in his own legs made Lassiter wonder how many more years he could weather such a pounding. But he had no time to dwell on it for Boyle suddenly halted his plodding retreat and charged. Lassiter sidestepped and attacked at a new level of fury. It forced Boyle to give ground, much to the delight of a majority of the howling mob.

Suddenly there was a glitter of sunlight on steel. Lassiter's throat tightened as he glimpsed Boyle's large fingers closing around the hilt of a knife—six inches of cold steel in the blade.

"Now we'll see the color of your blood!" Boyle lunged like a swordsman, the blade parallel to the ground. Before Lassiter could duck, he felt a bite of the steel as it sliced the skin of his brown forearm. Bright globules of blood pumped from the surface cut.

"Willie!" Lassiter shouted without turning his head. "Willie Cosgrove!" Boyle was coming for him again, slashing the air as Lassiter backed away.

"Yeah, Lassiter!" Cosgrove responded above the shouting.

"Your knife! Your *knife!*"

It finally got through to the lanky Cosgrove, who bent suddenly. He withdrew shining steel from his boot top and elbowed his way through the screaming onlookers. Lassiter had eyes only for Boyle and his lethal knife.

Holding the weapon by its tip, Cosgrove slapped the hilt into the palm of Lassiter's open right hand.

"All right, Boyle," Lassiter said, his teeth locked against the pain of the superficial knife wound. "We're even up."

Now, instead of the meaty thump of fists against flesh, there was a clanging as blades came together. Lassiter parried, knifing Boyle under an armpit. A great howl of pain burst from Boyle and the small eyes glittered.

Lassiter's heart pounded. Sweat dripped off his face and pasted the back of his shirt to the skin. The last clouds had vanished from the sky and the sun was pouring spring heat over the two gladiators who were battling to the death. The end of the game would be death, they and the crowd seemed to realize. Only one finish was possible in this historic battle. On the one hand, the giant Kiley Boyle, matched against the slender, determined Lassiter. Boyle's shirt clung to his torso, damp with blood and sweat. Between lunges, Boyle would use his left hand to wipe blood from his nose.

They lunged again, sunlight glittering on naked steel. Blades scraped as they locked, each man striving for advantage, sweating, cursing. A gasp escaped the crowd as the combatants, their right hands locked in steel, pounded midriffs with their left fists.

A savage blow to a kidney was so numbing for a moment that Lassiter was barely able to avoid a thrust aimed at his right eye. He pulled aside and Boyle lumbered on past him. Lassiter's knife tip ripped along Boyle's rib cage.

"Damn you, Lassiter," Boyle gasped, seemingly

about to give up. Then with animal cunning, he suddenly slashed upward, intending to rip Lassiter from bellybutton to Adam's apple. Lassiter, sensing the move, flung himself back at the last moment. The tip of the blade, sharp as a razor, cut through the front of Lassiter's shirt. Buttons popped. At one point the blade cut through chest hair, barely breaking the skin. So great was Lassiter's rage at the flash of pain, he was barely aware his thrust was so savage that the knife was torn from Boyle's hand.

Pandemonium erupted in the street as Boyle's knife landed several feet away in the dust. Boyle, staggering, out of breath, looked around for it.

Lassiter stood poised, his knife extended, only inches from Boyle's heart.

"Back off, Kiley," Lassiter gasped. "I've had enough. Or so help me, you're dead."

One moment Boyle seemed a pitiful beaten hulk, his face misshapen from the pounding of Lassiter's fists, bleeding from knife cuts. But with a howl of rage he moved with the grace of a giant cat. Twisting away from Lassiter, he hurled himself into the street and snatched up the knife. Agile as an acrobat, he rolled to his knees and came up on his feet.

"Now, you son of a bitch!" Boyle's teeth gleamed. He started plodding forward, step by step.

Lassiter felt a moment of dismay. Was there no end to this madness? He should have finished Boyle when he had the chance instead of threatening him. How well he knew it now. It was almost too late now, for the big man was coming at a lumbering run with the crowd screeching in anticipation of the kill.

And above the hoarse cries came the sharp crack of a revolver shot. A woman screamed, "*Rodney!*"

It was Regina's voice.

Lassiter danced aside and turned his head. He saw

Rod Rucklor in front of the doctor's house beginning
to sag. Lassiter glimpsed a bloodied skull as the
younger man toppled into the street.

He saw something else in that flash of time. Lake
Burne held a gun. A wisp of smoke curled at the muzzle. He wore a broad and satisfied grin.

As Lassiter danced out of the reach of the sweeping
blade in Boyle's hand, all he could think of was the
pain and suffering so many had undergone, ending
now with the Fork Creek heir bleeding in a side street
of the frontier settlement known as Villa Rosa.

Chapter 29

A great roaring burst suddenly from Lassiter's lungs, a cry of rage and frustration. He bared his teeth, his legs steady with newfound strength. All he could think of was vengeance. And this bleeding giant who stalked him was in the way. When Boyle's knife hand whipped toward him again in a great sweep from left to right, he tensed all his muscles. As the center of the sweep was past, the great arm moving to the left, Lassiter stepped in, the knife an extension of his hand. It drove into the left side of Boyle's chest, between ribs and into the flesh.

Instantly, Lassiter turned the knife loose and lunged toward a gaunt and shouting spectator, his eyes riveted on the man's holstered .45. His right hand clawed it from the holster, giving the man a violent shove that knocked him out of the line of fire.

Lake Burne, still holding his weapon, heard the change of pitch in the crowd roar. There was more fright now as men fought to escape the probable path of bullets.

"*You killed him, Burne!*" Lassiter yelled through his teeth.

Then came Willie Cosgrove's cry of warning.

"Behind you, Lassiter. *Dolan!*"

Lassiter's backbone froze. Instinctively he dropped to one knee as a gun exploded behind him. He whipped around and saw Dolan in a cleared space in the panicked crowd, his legs braced, frantically drawing back the hammer for another try.

But Lassiter beat him by a hair. Dolan broke in the middle and fell down into the street.

Lassiter sprang up from his knee and into a zigzag run. Burne was firing. One bullet cut through a flapping section of Lassiter's shirt that had been cut by Boyle's knife. Burne whirled as some men almost sobbed in their desperation to escape the lethal scene. They were falling over each other, stumbling, getting in Burne's way. Dust from their flailing boots became a yellow haze.

With a look of desperation, Burne fired again and missed. But Lassiter was closing at a weaving run. As Burne swung to cover him, Lassiter snapped the hammer. Thank God, the gun he had ripped from a stranger's holster was in working order. Burne's jaw sagged. He stared down incredulously at a redness bubbling from the breastbone.

As he collapsed, Lassiter said, "I hope to hell you live so I can see you on the gallows!" Then he yelled at Cosgrove. "Get his gun, Willie. I'm going after the main fish!"

"I assume you refer to me!"

Lassiter spun around and saw Rex Manly thirty feet away in the center of the street. Manly's chin was up, his fawn-colored hat set at a jaunty angle.

In the sudden stillness, Manly said, "That madman Lake Burne is the one who downed young Rucklor. I had nothing to do with it!"

"The hell . . ." Lassiter's grin was ugly.

By now a deeper hush had fallen over the tense crowd. Men with strained faces had formed two ranks on either side of the street, with a wide aisle between Lassiter and the lawyer. Their eyes swung from the immaculate, debonair Manly to Lassiter, who had lost his hat, the black hair tousled. His shirt was bloodied and halfway off his shoulders. His face was covered with lumps and cuts.

"Obviously, I am now the owner of the Fork Creek Cattle Company," Manly said in ringing tones. "So I have the law on my side and I hereby give you notice to vacate that property."

"Rod isn't dead."

The voice was a woman's, shaking from tension. Lassiter flicked a glance at a white-faced Regina just rising from where she had been kneeling beside Rucklor. Doc Straffer's tall figure was bent over him. He was using a clean white cloth, soon reddened, on a head wound.

"Only grazed him," the doctor said. "It seems that he is still the Fork Creek heir." And he looked directly at Manly in the center of the street.

"It can't be," Manly said, but there was a shred of doubt in his voice. Suddenly, he drew himself up and began removing his coat. It was gray with small checks and showed the mark of a fine tailor. As if it might have been a rag, he dropped it into the street dust.

His gun rig, Lassiter noticed, was slanted forward at a slight angle. The tip of the revolver barrel protruded from the bottom of the holster. A professional. All this time Manly had let others do his fighting, staying back himself.

"We'll settle this, Lassiter." Manly used the ringing tones of an executioner. "If you have the guts, that is." His teeth flashed. "I'm ready anytime you are."

"Oh, no!" Regina cried. "Lassiter, you're in no condition . . ."

Manly laughed. "I see you have a pretty skirt to beg for your life."

Steady, Lassiter warned himself. He's trying to

throw you off and make you do something stupid. While keeping his gaze locked with Manly's, he took several deep breaths. The sight of the bold hazel eyes and the arrogant smile deadened his own pain to the point where it blended into his raw hatred of the man he faced.

Deliberately, he relaxed his right hand. He was about to draw another deep breath, then saw a faint widening of the hazel eyes. Len Crenshaw had taught him when he was just a kid: "Always the eyes, Lassiter. When a man's about to draw, they'll give him away."

And in that thin slice of time Lassiter observed, his hand flashed down. Even as Manly moved with blinding speed toward his holster. Am I too late? was Lassiter's numbing thought.

As his gun cleared leather, he saw that Manly did not intend to draw, but was simply tilting the holster. A shaved second in time. That was the advantage— usually. Both guns thundered. Manly with his swiveled holster could do no better than put a bullet into the street five feet from the toes of his polished boots. A pulsating redness, which he never saw, spoiled the snowy bosom of his shirt. His knees caved and he came down in an attitude of prayer, the gun slipping from his fingers. Then he fell forward on his face. His hat rolled and the ends of silky brown hair were in the dust.

Lassiter stood woodenly, staring at Manly stretched out in the street. Shouting men were crowding around. What they had hoped to witness was a bare-knuckle brawl between two stalwarts. It had turned into the bloodiest episode in the history of Villa Rosa. Three men dead—Boyle, Dolan and Manly. And one Lake Burne badly wounded.

And Rod Rucklor had a long gash just above the right ear that Doc Straffer said would probably leave a scar.

Rucklor, sitting on the steps of the doctor's house, gave Lassiter a funny smile, even though he was undoubtedly suffering. "A scar will always remind me of this day, Lassiter. And what you did for me. When Blanche and I have kids, they'll know the story and pass it on to their kids."

When the affairs of the Fork Creek Cattle Company were finally settled and a new crew hired with a good foreman, Lassiter and Regina left for Denver. She had received a letter from her friend Ellen. "If for some reason you and Rodney should decide not to wed, there are scads of eligible young bachelors here in Denver. . . ."

Regina showed Lassiter that part of Ellen's letter, then said mischievously, "See, if you don't treat me right, there are others I can turn to."

It was Regina's idea to go to Denver on horseback with a tent and a pack animal, instead of taking a stagecoach.

"We'll be together that much longer," she whispered, because Lassiter had already told her that once in Denver he would leave her in good hands, then be on his way.

Although Regina was confident she could change his mind, she didn't know Lassiter. It was in his blood to move on and to test his luck on new horizons.

LOUIS L'AMOUR
Grub Line Rider

Louis L'Amour is one of the most popular and honored authors of the past hundred years. Millions of readers have thrilled to his tales of courage and adventure, tales that have transported them to the Old West and brought to life that exciting era of American history. Here, collected together in paperback for the first time, are seven of L'Amour's finest stories, all carefully restored to their original magazine publication versions.

Whether he's writing about a cattle town in Montana ("Black Rock Coffin Makers"), a posse pursuit across the desert ("Desert Death Song"), a young gunfighter ("Ride, You Tonto Riders"), or a violent battle to defend a homestead ("Grub Line Rider"), L'Amour's powerful presentation of the American West is always vibrant and compelling. This volume represents a golden opportunity to experience these stories as Louis L'Amour originally intended them to be read.

ISBN 13: 978-0-8439-6065-5

The Bloody Texans

Kent Conwell

Trapper and scout Nathan Cooper returned home to his cabin in East Texas, only to find a sight he would never forget—his wife, his young niece and his niece's intended, all slaughtered. With his heart broken and blood in his eyes, Nathan buried his family in the cold ground. Then he made an oath. He swore that the men who did this would pay. Nathan would use all of his skills to hunt the murdering scum, and he would see them suffer. One by one, he will track them and kill them, even if he has to break down the gates of Hell to do it!

ISBN 13: 978-0-8439-6066-2

Max Brand®

Luck

Pierre Ryder is not your average Jesuit missionary. He's able to ride the meanest horse, run for miles without tiring, and put a bullet in just about any target. But now he's on a mission of vengeance to find the man who killed his father. The journey will test his endurance to its utmost—and so will the extraordinary woman he meets along the way. Jacqueline "Jack" Boone has all the curves of a lady but can shoot better than most men. In the epic tradition of *Riders of the Purple Sage*, their story is one for the ages.

ISBN 13: 978-0-8439-5875-1